She didn't
resisting…

When their mouths met, the whole idea of conducting research on her own to avoid him flew from her mind, even as she pulled him even closer.

His hardness against her was irresistible. "Owen," she whispered against his mouth.

"Good thing we're in your bedroom," he said hoarsely. "Or was this why you came in here?"

Despite herself, she laughed a little without pulling back very far. "Believe me, I came in here to avoid this."

"Nope, I don't believe you." He softened his words by deepening the kiss.

Selena moaned against him, even as her most sensitive body parts warmed and tingled in anticipation.

But though she still reveled in her memories of the last time despite recognizing what a bad idea it had been, having sex with Owen again would be an even worse idea…and it was absolutely foolish to even contemplate it here.

CANADIAN WOLF

LINDA O. JOHNSTON

MILLS
BOON

Published in Great Britain 2015
by Mills & Boon, an imprint of Harlequin (UK) Limited,
Eton House, 18-24 Paradise Road, Richmond, Surrey, TW9 1SR

© 2015 Linda O. Johnston

ISBN: 978-0-263-91749-9

89-0915

Harlequin (UK) Limited's policy is to use papers that are natural, renewable and recyclable products and made from wood grown in sustainable forests. The logging and manufacturing processes conform to the legal environmental regulations of the country of origin.

Printed and bound in Spain
by CPI, Barcelona

Linda O. Johnston loves to write. While honing her writing skills, she worked in advertising and public relations, then became a lawyer...and enjoyed writing contracts. Linda's first published fiction appeared in *Ellery Queen's Mystery Magazine* and won a Robert L. Fish Memorial Award for Best First Mystery Short Story of the Year. Linda now spends most of her time creating memorable tales of paranormal romance, romantic suspense and mystery. Visit www.lindaojohnston.com.

My special thanks to my wonderful agent Paige Wheeler of Creative Media Agency, and to my delightful Harlequin editor, Allison Lyons, who have been so fantastic in helping to keep the stories of Alpha Force an ongoing miniseries.

Thanks, too, to writers Leslie Knowles and Ann Finnin, who read my manuscript and gave me some great revision ideas.

And as always, thanks to my amazing husband, Fred, whom I always acknowledge in each of my books because he inspires me.

Like my other Alpha Force Nocturne™ books, *Canadian Wolf* is dedicated to shape-shifters and the readers who love them.

Chapter 1

"I'm still so jazzed!" said Lieutenant Rainey Jessop, clasping her hands under her chin. "Working with Mounties. This'll be so much fun!"

Lieutenant Selena Jennay sent a wry smile toward her aide. Rainey had been excited from the moment the two of them had first been given this assignment—yesterday. As for herself, she was skeptical. She'd reserve judgment until she better understood the players in this new mission.

She took a seat across from her aide at the table in the small meeting room with gray wallpapered walls, the secluded area to which they'd been shown after arriving at the Royal Canadian Mounted Police's northwest Vancouver facility. Her cover dog, Lupe, a canine who resembled a mix between a wolf and a husky, lay beside her.

She glanced at Rainey. "Do you think it's more fun than working with shapeshifters?"

Rainey looked momentarily shocked, a rare occurrence for the outgoing and chatty young woman. "Hardly. But I'm going to get to work with both Mounties *and* shapeshifters. Amazing!" She paused, and her smile morphed into a frown as two men in white shirts and blue pants walked into the room. "Although I'd hoped that we'd get to work with Mounties in their gorgeous dress uniforms and tall hats," she added under her breath.

Selena and Rainey rose to meet the men, smoothing down the camo uniforms of Alpha Force, the highly covert US military unit to which they belonged. Selena's light brown hair and Rainey's darker brunette locks were both pulled back tightly into clips.

"Good morning," said the first man to enter. He appeared middle-aged and had short white hair. Walking around the oval wooden table to where Selena and Rainey now stood, he held out a veined, long-fingered hand. "I'm Anthony Creay, deputy commissioner of the RCMP's general policing services."

Then he was the head of the group who'd contacted Alpha Force, Selena reasoned. "Hello, sir," she said, shaking his hand. She introduced both Rainey and herself. Then she let her gaze drift to the other man.

"Sergeant Major Owen Dewirter," he said, proffering his hand for a shake, too. "Also with general policing services."

And most likely the man with whom they'd be working over the next few weeks, Selena figured. The other guy was his superior officer and probably just wanted to make sure things got started well.

"Which one of you is the shapeshifter?" Owen asked. The sergeant major had a distinctively handsome face, with brilliant blue eyes beneath strong brows that matched his short, wavy black hair. His nose was aquiline, his chin broad with just a hint of a beard shadow.

Yet judging by his unreadable expression, Selena had the impression that he wasn't overly fond of shifters. Did he even believe in them? That wasn't clear, at least not yet.

"That would be me," she said in as mild a tone as she could muster, considering her initial bout of irritation. She could be wrong. She didn't know the guy, let alone how RCMP members thought or acted. He might be attempting to impress his superior officer by remaining emotionless.

"How fascinating!" Anthony did indeed appear fascinated. He stood behind a chair at the opposite side of the table, his eyes wide, his mouth slightly open. "I'm pleased that you're here to give us a close-up demonstration."

"Yes. About that." Rainey drew their attention as she sat down again. Her movement caused Lupe, who'd stood up as the humans did, to sit as well. "We've discussed that and are not sure about the best way to handle it. You see, we need a bit of privacy. Actually, Lieutenant Jennay needs a bit of privacy," she amended. "I'm her aide, and I'll be with her, but a shift requires that someone, er—"

"I'll be nude," Selena interjected. She remained standing for now, her arms crossed. "That's why I have a female aide. We use a special proprietary elixir, and we will make some available to the shifters you have recruited into the new RCMP team that we're to train. When the rest of our Alpha Force team arrives tomorrow or the next day, they'll include a male shifter or two. They may be more amenable to being observed by men when they change. But although you can definitely see me once I've shifted, you unfortunately can't watch me shift." She found herself looking straight into Owen Dewirter's still-unreadable gaze. "Too uncomfortable for me. And I don't like to feel uncomfortable."

"I see." The words were drawn out slowly by Anthony Creay as he sank down into a chair across from the two women. And clearly, to Selena, the point was that he could *not* see. Not everything. "Nude? I didn't consider that—but I believe that observing a shift was part of our understanding. So we would be sure of the genuineness of the help we're getting." As he scowled, his fleshy lower lip protruded.

Owen took a seat beside him, then exchanged glances with his superior officer. When he turned back to Selena, he had a decided frown on his face, too. "We need to work something out here," he said. "We have to watch the process to be sure you're a real shifter and not just trying to put something over on us."

His pronunciation of the word *out*—with an almost long *O* sound—emphasized that he was Canadian. But his accent wasn't the only difference between them. He wanted her to get nude in front of him for her demo shift? Not gonna happen. Even though he was one great-looking guy. The thought of him observing her body as she stripped sent waves of heat through Selena that made her feel as if this meeting was on the hottest summer day in the US South instead of a cool evening in the Canadian West.

Was this whole thing primed to be a fiasco? Selena hoped not. She and Rainey were here representing

Alpha Force and, since they had been in the western United States and were therefore the closest of those in their unit who had been selected to help the RCMP form their own similar unit, they'd been ordered to Vancouver to give a small and limited demonstration.

Limited being the key word.

Even Lupe must have sensed the tension in the room since she stood beside Selena and whined. Selena reached out and hugged the wolf-dog closer to her.

"Here's the thing," she said to the men in as reasonable a tone as she could muster. "Let me introduce you first to my cover dog. Lupe, this is Deputy Commissioner Creay and Sergeant Major Dewirter." She scratched Lupe behind the ears in a manner that caused the dog to turn her head toward the two men, not that Lupe, a genuine canine, could understand her words. "Gentlemen, this is the canine who looks a whole lot like me when I'm shifted. The way I figured we'd do this demonstration is for Rainey and me to go into another room. You can keep Lupe with you and lock the door to the room. With Rainey's help, I'll shift. Then when you unlock the door there'll be Rainey inside with a canine who looks a whole lot like Lupe. Voilà! That'll be me, shifted. There'll be no other person in the room. With doors locked and all, there's no way we'd be able to do this without it being the real thing." The very suggestion that they'd try to pull a scam on representatives of a national police department that had requested their help really peeved Selena.

"But we understood we could see the actual shift take place." Creay's tone was icy.

Selena glanced toward Rainey, who looked uneasy

and bewildered. Well, she needn't be. Selena was in charge here, at least for now.

"I understand your wish to see the process, gentlemen," she said. "Maybe you'd have been able to if you hadn't requested Alpha Force's presence so urgently. You said you needed at least our initial representation within one day. We were the closest team members available. So here we are."

"I recognize that," Creay retorted. "But we don't have any extra time, either, to wait—or to deal with a situation where things aren't as represented to us."

"Are you accusing us of lying?" Selena hated to be confrontational, but their attitude was forcing her into it.

"We're not accusing you of anything." Owen's voice sounded placating, but his expression remained unreadable. "We just want to ensure we've got what we were promised by the US military."

Selena wanted to make good on that promise, too, for the sake of Alpha Force. She took a deep breath, then said, "Look, we want to cooperate with you—but certain things are nonnegotiable. If you don't feel you can trust us, if you think we'll play some kind of hoodwinking, magical game even when you can watch to make sure the room stays locked—well, maybe we'd better just leave right now."

Selena saw Owen glance once more into the angry face of his commanding officer. Then Owen looked directly toward Selena. "Okay," he said. "We understand your concern, and I hope you understand ours. Our mission is highly important. And…well, it's probably no surprise to you that not all people believe in shapeshifters. We just need—"

"Do you believe in them?" Selena glared as if daring him to say that who she was, what she did, wasn't real.

"Yes," Owen said quietly, planting his arms on the table in front of him and leaning toward her. "I do. But this is all new to Deputy Commissioner Creay and he has his doubts."

Interesting, Selena thought. Creay's position was that of the majority of regular people. But the sergeant major was a believer. How did he know the reality?

Well, if he was the one who'd be working with them, maybe she would find out. Or not, if things continued to deteriorate.

He leaned in closer toward Selena, and his confrontational posture made Lupe tense up and growl. Glancing at the dog, he backed up slightly. "We seem to be at a stalemate. I'll be with you at the headquarters of the new team we're forming. But Deputy Commissioner Creay won't be with us. He's going back to our headquarters in Ottawa when we're done here. I may be able to watch some of the male shifters change then, but he needs to see you shift now." His expression changed then from demanding to something Selena couldn't interpret at first. Challenging?

Could be, considering his next words.

"I'll tell you what, Lieutenant Jennay. If you strip and show us your change, I'll strip right along with you. That way we can both feel uncomfortable, not just you. Although I have to admit that I'm just a normal human being."

Selena blinked in surprise at his outrageous offer.

Normal? She doubted that. The idea set her body on fire, and it was all she could do to prevent herself from letting her gaze slide down his fully clothed body toward the area she really would like to see nude.

But was he serious? Or was this some kind of additional challenge? "That's not—" she began.

"Not necessary," Deputy Commissioner Creay interjected. Selena drew her gaze away from Owen and focused on Creay. His expression had calmed a bit. "I trust the people I spoke with at Alpha Force, and I'll trust them more after one of us gets to observe a shift. But that's apparently not going to happen now, so why don't you do your shift, as you suggested, inside a locked room. We'll check out the room before you enter and then monitor the shift from the outside. For now, that should be fine."

Selena gave a sigh of relief that the face-off had now been averted, even as she continued to watch Owen Dewirter. Now his eyes, too, were unreadable.

What would he do if she told him that she accepted his offer to strip bare?

No matter how much she liked the idea on some level—like, deep inside her now-blazing body—she wouldn't agree. Handling her shift the way she had already described was the best way to go. It should satisfy them. This was an RCMP facility. Where would Alpha Force find another dog that looked like Lupe and be able to sneak it in?

Besides, she was aware that others in Alpha Force sometimes used this method of shifting in a secured room to prove to nonshifters who—and what—they were, and she hadn't heard of any problems resulting.

But all she said was "Fine. So…shall we get started?"

Owen Dewirter observed Selena from across the table—for the moment, at least—as she stood.

Maybe he'd been way out of line with his suggestion. It had been impulsive. But it had also been born out of irritation and a need to end their impasse.

Owen hadn't wanted to strip here—although the idea of seeing Selena Jennay nude definitely stiffened a certain part of his body. But he also knew Anthony Creay well enough to be certain that his superior officer didn't like to be denied anything he believed he was entitled to.

This way, Anthony wound up making the decision— a good thing, and probably the only way to make the superior officer stand down. And now what Lieutenant Selena Jennay had proposed had become acceptable. She would shift without a male audience.

She would shift, though. He didn't actually doubt that she was a shapeshifter.

Although he believed—no, knew—they existed, he had major concerns about shapeshifters.

But this one was also a gorgeous, sexy woman— even dressed in the sexless camouflage uniform of US soldiers.

She was slender, moderately tall, with full lips and high cheekbones. Her light brown hair seemed most unusual, with highlights that shimmered in even the low artificial lights in this conference room. Her amber eyes flashed with emotion as she spoke—like now, as she conversed softly with the other woman, glancing occasionally toward the two men.

Owen rose, too, as did Anthony. "Do you know of any suitable room?" his superior asked in a low voice.

"Why not in here?" Owen asked. "We can leave." As he spoke, he scanned the small chamber, furnished only with the table and chairs. They were two stories up, so their visitors couldn't slip Selena out and a dog in—especially since the window overlooked the parking lot and the station's inside guard post. Whoever was on duty would no doubt see any shenanigans.

"I suppose that would work," Anthony said, also looking around.

As they spoke, Lieutenant Jennay speared them both with a sharp gaze that gave no quarter. Owen had no doubt that if her demeanor was typical of the US military's Alpha Force, that explained how the covert group accomplished its sometimes impossible missions.

He looked forward to this assignment.

He'd been one of the very few members of his division within the RCMP's general policing services who hadn't immediately scoffed when Anthony asked in his interview whether he believed in shapeshifters. Owen knew they were real.

He just didn't happen to like them. Experience had taught him to mistrust them.

And yet, it was in his country's best interests for a group of shifters from the States to help the RCMP to form its own covert unit, similar to Alpha Force, but a police unit instead of a military one.

Owen was all about helping his country. He would head the team. The fact that he'd previously worked with canines at the RCMP's police-dog service training center wouldn't hurt, either.

"So what do you think?" Selena eventually asked, her hands on her hips and confrontation in her expression.

"We'll lock you right in here," Owen said with no inflection, as if he had no interest in continuing the confrontation. "This is as good as any place. Maybe not the most comfortable location to get naked, but you won't be aware of it for long anyway."

"Not true," Selena snapped back. She clearly hadn't lost her attitude. "You may believe in shapeshifters, but you don't know anything about Alpha Force and our elixir if you think we lose awareness. For your information, the elixir developed by members of Alpha Force allows us to shift without a full moon and to keep our human awareness when the moon isn't full, and neither is the case with other shifters."

"Sounds like a useful concoction." Owen had understood there was something that made Alpha Force members different from other shapeshifters, but hadn't known what it was.

She seemed to relax a little after that. "But that's okay for now. You'll learn more as we help to train your RCMP shapeshifters." She drew out those words as if to rub the concept back in his face.

He realized that he was smiling—wryly perhaps, but genuinely. She wasn't only lovely. She amused him.

Even though she was a shapeshifter. Or so she said.

She was right. He knew little about Alpha Force, its elixir or anything else related to the unit. But if she could genuinely shapeshift now, when the next full moon wasn't due for a couple of weeks, it would tell him a lot.

"There aren't any security cameras in here, are there?" Selena asked. He watched as she scanned the walls.

"No," said Anthony Creay. "This room is usually used for secure and private meetings."

"Okay, then we're on." Selena looked around a little more as if she didn't trust what he said, but there were no places that Owen saw, either, where equipment could be hidden.

"Fine," he said. "Now, what would you like us to do?"

It was her turn to grin. "If you'd like, you can go ahead and get naked anyway." She let her eyes scan Owen's body up and down, and he felt himself start to respond. Not a good idea. Not here, and not ever.

But since they were going to be working together, should he call her bluff after all? He gave it a second's thought before he knew the answer. No sense in angering his commanding officer. "Nope," he said. "I think this is your cue, not mine."

She shrugged one shoulder, as if she had no interest in whether he kept his clothes on or not. Too bad, he thought. But it was better that way.

"So what would you like us to do?" he asked her.

"Leave." She began walking around the table, holding out the leash attached to her dog's collar. "Just watch out for Lupe. She's a great dog—but like me, she's got quite a bite if you rile her."

He assumed she was still just teasing. Even so, he gingerly grabbed hold of the leash's looped handle. It was his responsibility, not his superior officer's. The furry wolf-dog looked up at him with eyes that did indeed appear a similar amber shade to Selena's. Her cover dog. The way she would appear while shifted, she'd indicated.

A fine representative of the wolf species, albeit with some traces of other canine stock, like, perhaps, Siberian husky.

"I bite, too, Lupe," he said, although the way he petted her furry head belied his words—justifiably. He liked dogs. A lot.

It was their shapeshifting counterparts that he didn't trust.

Was Selena different? He'd see, as time went on.

"Well, don't bite my dog," Selena said.

She turned around, waving her hand. "Right now is a good time for you gentlemen to leave." She glanced over her shoulder. "After you lock the door you can stand in the hall to make sure we don't slip out and play the games that you apparently expect. Rainey will knock for you to open the door when my shift is complete."

"Fine." Owen waited until Anthony had cleared the doorway, then followed.

He turned back for an instant, just long enough to notice that Selena was already preparing for what would occur after he locked the door. Her head was bent as she started unbuttoning her shirt.

Too bad he really couldn't stay and watch. Maybe some other time.

The other woman, Rainey, had crossed the room and picked up the large backpack she'd carried inside before. She studied its insides, and before Owen left, he saw her extract some kind of bottle. Was that the elixir Selena had mentioned?

He figured he would find out, if not today, then in the days to come, when he was with the Alpha Force members who had promised to help instruct the new RCMP members he had assisted in recruiting.

Those new members were also shapeshifters—or so they'd claimed—and had their claims confirmed by reputable friends and family, including others within the

RCMP. He hadn't yet had a chance to watch them shift, either, since they did so only under a full moon—so far.

"Hey, haven't you left yet?" That was Rainey, who'd looked toward the door after handing the bottle to Selena.

Selena had stopped moving and was also watching him suspiciously.

"On my way." He gave a small yank on Lupe's leash. The dog obeyed and preceded him out the door.

Owen shut the door behind him and took the key from Anthony's hand. He turned it in the lock.

"So," he said, "I guess now we just wait."

Moving her erect ears, inhaling deeply to further stimulate her sense of smell, Selena stared at the door.

Her shifting had finally ended. As always, there had been discomfort.

Also as always, she had finished taking off her human clothes before imbibing the elixir and waited while Rainey shone the special battery-operated light on her that resembled the glow of a full moon. But this time she had also turned to stare at that closed door.

Maybe the distraction had helped, since the discomfort hadn't seemed as bad as usual. Even now, shifted, she couldn't help wondering what it would have been like if Owen Dewirter had actually removed his clothes, too.

"You okay?" Rainey asked as she always did.

In her wolfen form Selena couldn't shrug and say, "Of course." Instead, she just gave a soft growl and lowered her head.

"So, you ready to show off to those doubting Thomases?" Rainey asked next. "Why would they even in-

vite Alpha Force to help save their Mountie butts if they didn't believe that our abilities—your abilities—were real?"

That wasn't something Selena could respond to, either. Not now, in any event. And in fact she had no answer.

But she'd definitely gotten the sense that the smart-alecky Owen Dewirter believed in, but did not appreciate, shifters.

She would find out why. Eventually.

For now, she padded over to the door and listened. Even as a human, her hearing surpassed that of normal people, but it was particularly enhanced after her shift, as were her senses of smell and taste.

She sensed that Lupe was still outside. The men were talking, perhaps joking a little.

The older man clearly did not know what to expect.

She lifted her paw and touched the door frame, which cued Rainey, who knocked to summon the two Mounties.

Selena heard footsteps on the hallway floor. In seconds, she heard the sound of the key in the lock. The door was pulled open, and Owen stood there, looking in.

On one side of him was Anthony Creay. On the other was Lupe, who pulled on her leash.

Selena walked forward and traded nose sniffs with her cover dog.

"Care to come in and look around, gentlemen?" Rainey sounded smug.

"Yes," said Anthony, and he strode through the open entry.

Owen just stood there, looking into the room and

down at her. She could not read his expression. It wasn't admiring, but neither was it full of scorn.

"It is real," she finally heard the older man say. "No Selena here, just the dog. The wolf. Whatever."

"Yeah," Owen agreed. "It's real. And that's a good thing, since our guys have a lot to learn to accomplish our underlying mission."

She might help to teach them a lot—but she needed to know exactly what that mission was. And soon.

Chapter 2

It was morning, the day after the three Alpha Force members, including the dog, had arrived in northwest Vancouver.

Now Owen was ready to drive them up to their new headquarters, where he—and they—could get to work.

For the moment, he had parked his SUV in front of the hotel where both he and the visitors had spent the night. He settled back in the driver's seat, waiting for them.

Last night, when their sort-of demonstration had ended, it had been too late to head out. Besides, Selena had looked tired after what she had been through. Once Anthony acknowledged that she must indeed be a shifter—Owen hadn't doubted it by then—she, her aide and her dog had remained in that conference room while Anthony and he went back into the hall.

Owen hadn't locked the door that time. He'd figured Selena, changing back from a wolf-dog into a human—a naked human—might have wanted that option, but she hadn't asked for it before shifting back, and neither had her aide.

Of course neither he nor Anthony had attempted to peek. Even so, Owen, who never considered himself to have much of an imagination, had still somehow visualized what her slim but curvaceous body might have looked like without any clothes on…

Well, he could imagine anything he wanted, including sexual attraction to a female shapeshifter in human form. That fantasy would remain far from reality, for a whole lot of reasons, not the least of which was that she was a professional colleague…and—oh, yes—she was a shifter.

The good thing was that Anthony now believed—which meant their operation could move forward.

Plus, Owen hadn't had to strip to get the dispute resolved. It had been a dumb offer on his part. He knew that. He'd recognized it even as he'd suggested it, Anthony's attitude notwithstanding. Worst thing now was that it might negatively affect his professional relationship with Selena. He'd have to be careful and treat her with total respect from now on.

And keep his clothes on.

Before they'd adjourned last night he'd called this hotel and made reservations for them and himself for the night. His current home was in Ottawa, since he'd been most recently stationed at the RCMP main headquarters there—until now. But he would become a resident of West Columbia as soon as they got there.

He scanned the front of the hotel and saw the trio emerge. He got out of the car to open the doors for them.

The women rolled suitcases behind them and carried bags over their shoulders. Rainey seemed in charge of the dog.

As they got closer, Selena blatantly looked him up and down. Interesting. Did she approve of what she saw?

"You're not wearing your Mounties uniform," she said. "Not even the casual kind you had on last night—although someday soon we're going to insist on seeing you in one of those classic and formal red jackets and rounded hats."

She had a smile on her face. She looked well rested and seemed clearly in teasing mode. Good. Maybe things weren't as bad as he thought.

"Only if you earn the right to see me that way," he said, keeping his face expressionless. "I have to admit that I like you in the civilian clothes you're wearing today a lot better than the camo uniform." The jeans and T-shirt she wore hugged her curves.

Why was he noticing such things? Especially after cautioning himself to resist any sexual attraction to her.

He quickly opened the rear hatch and helped them load their suitcases and backpacks, then watched as Rainey ushered Lupe into the backseat and followed the dog inside. Lupe was obviously a well-trained dog, one he'd enjoy working with, given the opportunity.

He doubted that the humans, while shifted, would be as well behaved.

By the time he closed the door after the woman and dog, Selena was already buckled in the front seat. He hurried to the driver's side and got in.

"So where, exactly, is our destination?" Selena said as he turned the key in the ignition.

"West Columbia."

"How far is it?"

Owen maneuvered the car away from the curb. It was his own vehicle. Even though this was an official mission, the whole operation was to be done undercover. Plus, he was moving to this area to be in charge of the new covert team. He would not drive his prior on-the-job vehicle, an RCMP sedan, around here.

"About an hour from here," he finally answered as he pulled into traffic. "It's a somewhat remote, moderate-sized town where tourists come and go, so we won't stick out as being intruders. It abuts some forested mountains and seems like a good location for our new detachment, but we'll see. The location is also part of our experiment. The new RCMP members who are part of my team are already located there, and to everyone they talk to they're on vacation but considering moving there. That's what all of us are to say, if anyone asks."

Owen drove north toward Highways 1 and 99, the Trans-Canada Highway nearest to where they started out, although it would turn into the Upper Levels Highway and Sea-to-Sky Highway before they reached their destination.

"Sounds good," Selena said. "Since you're national police and not military, you shouldn't need something like Ft. Lukman, which is Alpha Force's headquarters. It's an actual military facility in Maryland and has units stationed there besides ours. We'll tell you more about it, if you'd like, as we undertake our training sessions. By the way, what's your new team to be called?"

"It's the Covert Special Services Group. Our nickname for the group, at least for now, is the Canada Alphas, or CAs."

"That works," Selena said. "At least it's somewhat compatible with Alpha Force."

He glanced at her yet again and saw that she was smiling, and that lovely expression was aimed toward him.

"Now all we need to do is to get your shapeshifting team whipped into shape," she said.

Staring out the window at the lovely, forested Canadian countryside with vast mountains in the background, Selena couldn't help wondering how hard their assignment would be. From the little she'd learned when ordered to hurry to this area, the shifters Alpha Force was going to assist in training had only just been recruited into the RCMP. They probably had no experience in law enforcement or the military. Their shapeshifting backgrounds probably hadn't even allowed them to consider the possibility of shifting outside of full moons, let alone keeping human cognition while in shifted form.

Bless you, Alpha Force elixir, she thought.

Yet she had a sense that this man, who'd be in charge of the RCMP contingent, could make her job even harder.

She needed to figure him out.

What did he really think about shapeshifters?

And the idea of his offering to get naked...? *Stop thinking about that, Jennay*, she ordered herself silently.

She glanced into the backseat. Lupe lay down with her ears up but her eyes closed, and Rainey watched the view out the window, as Selena had been doing.

Yesterday, they'd been in a car most of the day—a rental vehicle they'd picked up hurriedly in Seattle and dropped off in Vancouver.

Good thing they'd had adequate ID with them to get into Canada—their passports and military identification. But Alpha Force members were always prepared for anything. It was part of the job.

She hoped she was prepared for the man beside her.

Turning to Owen, she asked, "I gathered that you believed in shapeshifters even before you got the assignment of working with them, right?"

"That's right."

Along with his bland acknowledgment, she watched Owen's physical reaction. There was none. At least none that she could see. He didn't look at her, and his handsome blue eyes didn't blink as they stared at the road ahead of him. His strong chin remained at the same level as before. He continued to drive at a speed compatible with the flow of traffic, watch the road and not say or do anything that would indicate his attitude toward shifters.

But she was curious. She wasn't sure why it mattered, but she hoped he not only believed in shifters, but also liked them, at least a little. Might even be interested in them as more than strange aberrations in the world of human beings. Maybe one of them in particular.

Not that she would encourage anything between them but a good professional working relationship. He might be attractive and hunky, and her human hormones might be tweaked just by looking at Owen Dewirter, but she knew far better than to get involved with a nonshifter. She had learned her lesson, and learned it well.

Besides, this nonshifter seemed to have an opinion, one she couldn't interpret.

But with him, or despite him, she intended to do all she could to make sure that the Alpha Force mission here was a complete success for both the US military and the Canadian Mounties.

Of course, she'd have help when the rest of the Alpha Force contingent arrived.

When Owen didn't follow up his acknowledgment with anything else, Selena decided to push him for more. "Most people don't believe in shapeshifters. Why do you? Have you met any? Seen any shifts?"

"Some members of my family knew a shapeshifter." He didn't look at her, but his icy expression as he regarded the road suggested he didn't want to say anything more about it.

Not that that would deter her.

"Knew? They don't now?"

"No," he said shortly.

"I gather that the experience wasn't a good one. But even if they told you about it, if you didn't see it yourself, why did you believe?"

"Let's just say I saw and heard enough to convince me. So how about you? What made you join Alpha Force?"

She must have hit a nerve. But surely the man must have realized that if he was about to work with a bunch of shapeshifters, they'd want to know his experiences with others of their kind.

For now, though, she'd go along with him.

"I grew up in Wisconsin, in the same area as the commanding officer who first developed the elixir. He helped to form Alpha Force, and his cousin's a member, too." That was Major Drew Connell and recently promoted Lieutenant Jason Connell. "I heard they were looking for new recruits, so of course I had to jump in."

Not to mention how the timing had worked. She'd needed something then to help her get over a bad romantic relationship.

The divorced guy she'd been dating then, and cared for a lot, hadn't known she was a shifter. His cute but sneaky young son had unfortunately seen her ending a shift once before her aide moved her away. The kid gleefully told his father that Selena was a werewolf. Her boyfriend had responded to his son that shapeshifters existed only in stupid stories and he wanted his kid to be realistic and smart. He had told Selena about it. Laughed about it.

So she'd left him and her teaching job and hurried home—only to find this position where shapeshifters were revered and treated well.

But she didn't want to talk about it. Not now and not ever. Like she'd done with her questions to Owen, he'd pushed buttons with his that really bothered her. It was time for a change in subject.

"I've always heard such wonderful things about the RCMP," she said. "How long have you been a member? And do you like it?"

He glanced over at her. Now those gorgeous blue eyes of his actually had an expression in them—pride, if she read it right. "Ten years, and I love it."

She asked more questions, and Rainey leaned forward to join in the conversation. For the rest of the ride they were regaled with tales of undercover adventure in trapping bad guys, enjoyable training sessions with those horses that the Mounties rode and antics of the

K-9s Owen had worked with. He apparently liked canines, even if his feelings about people who shifted into wolves weren't quite so warm.

Selena realized that, if she wasn't careful, she might actually come to like sexy Owen Dewirter. And that could really be bad news.

By the time they reached West Columbia, Owen could almost believe this was a pleasure ride instead of an official diplomatic mission of sorts: the Canadians requesting US assistance for a particularly touchy situation.

One he hadn't yet discussed with his new best friends.

Friends? Heck. Under other circumstances, he'd have seduced Selena, or at least attempted to, with more than an irreverent yet necessary offer to take his clothes off. She definitely attracted him that way...at least as she was right now, all sexy human female.

The glances they sometimes shared, brief as they were, suggested she might be attracted to him, too. That was fine here, in the car, when neither could act on any inappropriate appeal.

Later, he'd pretend those glances had never happened.

He drove through the residential area and onto a driveway that rose a short distance through a forest and into the hills.

Up that driveway was the small enclave of two homes that had been acquired to become the CAs' hidden headquarters—assuming everything worked out.

Owen parked on the paved area between the homes and was met by the four new recruits for the CAs who had rushed out of the smaller of the two houses. The one-story white wood-frame building would be used as the meeting place for the US and Canadian teams as the CAs learned how to use their shifting skills for the good of their country.

The group had clearly been watching for their arrival.

"Hi, Owen." That was Constable Sal Emarra, the youngest of the new recruits, only nineteen years old. Like the others, he didn't wear an RCMP uniform; instead he was dressed in casual civilian clothes of a tourist. He held out his hand for a shake, even as he peered past Owen into the vehicle.

It was too late for him to see the passengers since they had exited at the other side. In fact, they were already being greeted by the other recruits even as Owen hurried to open the hatch and extract the luggage.

"Where should we put our things?" Selena asked, joining him.

"I can handle them all."

"But—"

Before she could grab any, Owen hefted the backpacks over his shoulders, then took hold of the suitcase handles.

Selena shrugged and said, "Just be careful with the backpacks."

"Of course."

He put the luggage in the larger of the two homes, a two-story that would be used as the Alpha Force barracks. Then he joined the group for pizza in the other house.

Before eating, though, he stood and looked at each

and every member of the group. "Let's go around the room and introduce ourselves."

"Better yet," said Selena, also standing now, "don't just give your names but tell us whether you're a shifter and if so, what you shift to."

She gave him a small, smug smile, as if she'd somehow shown him who was boss.

He didn't contradict her, though. That information did need to be shared.

Selena went first and then Rainey introduced herself as another lieutenant and Selena's nonshifting aide.

The others went next: Constables Sal Emarra, Tim Franzer, Craig Neverts and Andrea Willburn. The men informed everyone that they all shifted into wolves, too.

However, Andrea, a pert young woman with short black hair and a long nose, said, "I shift into a falcon—and that's really fun. But tell us, Selena. How do aides work—and what's a cover dog?"

"Oh, you're all going to have fun learning what Alpha Force is going to teach you," she said, grinning.

Owen didn't miss the way her smile lit up her face or the way her amber eyes sparkled like twin topaz gemstones.

Oh, yeah, this was going to be fun, indeed.

Chapter 3

Selena couldn't start teaching anything until her fellow Alpha Force members arrived. She might have the teaching credentials and some experience with the unit, but Captain Patrick Worley was the commanding officer on the American side of this operation.

That was why she decided to excuse herself, leaving Rainey with the others who were peppering her with questions about how someone who wasn't a shifter worked with Alpha Force. There were things, of course, that Rainey could not reveal about their covert military unit, but Selena trusted her not to mention them. Right now, she needed a little time to herself.

"Where are you going?" Owen called to her from the porch as she walked across the lawn with Lupe beside her.

From there, Owen appeared even taller. Even sexier.

She caught her errant thoughts. "Nowhere in particular."

"Well, then, why don't I show you where your sleeping quarters will be?" He pointed toward the other house as he walked down the steps. "You can choose which room you want."

Selena liked that idea. In fact, as much as she loved being part of a large, close-knit outfit like Alpha Force, she hoped to find a room that would give her some privacy.

In fact, maybe she could just pick out a room and chill out there for a little while.

Although it would be hard to chill at all with a hot guy like Owen around. And if she didn't stop thinking about him that way, she was going to have one really tough time working with him on their training assignment.

She started toward the larger house and Owen walked beside her. "Ever been to Canada before?" he asked.

"No, this is my first time. Have you ever been to the States?"

"A few times." His tone suggested he might not have been impressed with her country, but when she glanced at him his face had gone to that neutral, unreadable expression she couldn't interpret.

She had to keep a lot of secrets as a shifter and member of Alpha Force, but she had a sense that Owen Dewirter might have an even greater number of his own.

The front of the other house was similar to the one they'd just left. They climbed stairs onto the broad wooden porch, Lupe following. It was empty, but Selena imagined sitting out there with the entire group one of these days, holding one of the lessons she intended to provide.

After he unlocked the door, she walked through the five upstairs bedrooms, but it was the one downstairs that called to her. It was an understated room with a narrow white dresser with a mirror on top, a small chair and a single bed that was not much larger than a cot. The bare essentials. There was even a private bathroom—small but convenient.

Feeling a presence behind her, she turned and realized Owen was in the room with her. She was in a bedroom, all alone with Owen. Why had she noticed that? And why did it make her feel so warm inside? In fact, the lower part of her body seemed to ignite.

She chilled it immediately. "I'll take this one."

"Somehow I thought you would." He looked at her with an expression that seemed heated—as if he also recognized they were alone in this house in a bedroom.

Then, clearing his throat, he said abruptly, "I'll leave you to unpack. See you back at the other house." And with that, he left.

That was a good thing, Selena told herself, though she felt suddenly bereft.

Instead of unpacking, though, Selena called Captain Worley. When she got his voice mail, she left a message, asking him to call with his expected arrival time.

Then she quickly opened her suitcase and pulled out a few items that she hung in her closet. Almost everything was civilian casual, to maintain their cover.

She next went to the entry and got both of the backpacks. She unpacked the remaining bottle of elixir stored in an insulated container and secured it at the back of the refrigerator.

Then she said to Lupe, "Ready for a walk, girl? When you're done we'll go back to the others."

But as eager as Selena was to get started, she had a feeling it would be a long afternoon.

Owen had returned to where the constables who now reported to him still surrounded Rainey in the small and crowded living room. They were asking her questions about Alpha Force.

Too bad he hadn't stayed around to listen to her answers. The more he knew about the group that would be helping to train these raw new candidates, the better.

Instead, he had gone off to spend time with Selena. Not that he regretted it.

He felt more than saw her enter the room a short while later. His nerve endings tingling, he looked up as she and her dog joined the group. But then he noticed that Tim Franzer seemed to sit up straighter. He even moved over on the sofa and waved at the empty spot for Selena to sit down.

The guy wasn't especially tall or muscular, and he didn't appear particularly good-looking to Owen, not with his round face and prominent nose.

Even so, Selena gave him a big smile as she joined him.

Which irritated Owen.

If she ever smiled at him that way... She wouldn't. But it was definitely hot. *She* was definitely hot—no matter what else she was.

"So, Selena," said Craig Neverts, getting her attention. He was a nicer-looking guy than Tim, with dark hair, a wide mouth and prominent chin. "I'm finding all the stuff that Rainey's told us to be amazing. She said you guys shift when the moon isn't full and you're going to teach us how."

"Soon," Selena said. "When our other Alpha Force members arrive. But maybe tomorrow we can give a brief demonstration of what I'm like while shifted even if they're not here yet."

She glanced toward Owen, her expression challenging as if she expected him to say something about how she had done the same for him and his commanding officer— shifting remotely. Not demonstrating the actual shift.

He remembered the demonstration and his lame offer of getting naked with her. Feeling those stirrings again, he banished the images that the mere thought brought to mind.

"Well, I, for one, don't appreciate just hanging around here like this," said Andrea Willburn. But she must have sensed that Owen, her new commanding officer, was glaring at her. "Sorry." She appeared somewhat chastised. "But if it's okay, can we maybe...well, go into town now rather than waiting till later? Party a little, as part of our cover? I mean if we're not accomplishing anything useful today?"

To Owen, she somewhat resembled a falcon, the kind of animal she apparently shifted into, with her cap of dark hair and large, beak-like nose.

He thought about her suggestion. It might be the best thing to give everyone the afternoon in town. He'd stay behind, alone, and get some much-needed distance from the woman who was getting under his skin. He looked at Selena as he said, "Why not? Go ahead."

That was fine with Selena.

As everyone left the room, she sat there. She had no

particular interest in shopping or partying. Besides, she needed time away from Owen. Time to get her mind away from X-rated fantasies and back on the assignment. She took Lupe out on the porch, where she planned to sit and rest.

"You're still here."

At the sound of his voice, she turned to see Owen. Why was *he* still here? "Why didn't you go with your troops?" Selena challenged him.

"Why didn't you?" he countered.

"I—I need to take Lupe for a walk." Not that she hadn't, just a little while ago.

"I'll go with you."

He wasn't her commanding officer, and she could have responded in the negative. But what the heck? Nothing would happen on a little walk in the woods.

There were worse things than hanging out a little more with Owen, her inner voice said.

Yeah, like not getting to be with him at all...

Now, where did that come from? She liked the guy, sure. But only as a temporary colleague. And if he truly didn't like shifters despite believing in them, as he'd hinted before, that was even more reason not to spend much time with him.

So was the fact that she was sexually attracted to him.

Without looking at Owen, she grabbed Lupe's leash and started out. The woods behind the houses smelled rather like citrus from the fir trees that formed a tight canopy, which nearly blocked out the sun. A carpet of downed needles crackled beneath their feet.

"Good area for shifters," Selena told Owen, wanting to hear his reaction to her touch of goading.

"Glad to hear it." She looked up to find him grinning down at her. Grinning? He now accepted the idea of her being a shifter?

Heck, that was what she was and why she was here.

Lupe didn't have much to do except explore, sniffing the ground and air. They nevertheless stayed in the woods for twenty minutes or so.

"Ready to go to town, too?" Owen asked as they headed back.

"Sure," Selena said, glad she'd survived the walk unscathed. Then she tripped over a branch and Owen grabbed her arm to steady her.

She found herself smiling in thanks up into his handsome, rugged face and saw that there was more than concern in his eyes. Not just casual heat, either.

More like lust.

She opened her mouth just a little as she attempted to thank him…and Owen's lips came down on hers.

The kiss seemed to ignite the cool forest, especially when his arms went around her and pulled her close. She held him tightly, too, tasting him with her tongue as his teased hers.

Her eyes closed, and for a moment she was aware only of Owen. And herself. Here. Together, in the wilds, where anything could happen.

Before she could conjure any steamy scenarios, he pulled away. His breathing was hard and irregular, as was hers, and his expression was still full of heat, but his words were just normal and friendly, as if nothing had happened.

"Let's drive into town, shall we?"

"Right. Sure. That sounds fine."

* * *

Selena put Lupe in the kitchen of the house where they'd be staying, then joined Owen at his car.

Neither of them mentioned that kiss or where it had come from—let alone how inappropriate, yet suggestive, it had been.

Maybe it was just an act of closure after their initial discussions of nudity. Something they just had to get out of their systems. Now it was over. At least she hoped so.

Why, then, did it leave her aching for more?

Owen drove them carefully down the hill, then parked along the main commercial street and led her into the Yukon Bar. It was crowded, but even so, there were a couple of available tables. At his urging, Selena chose one—the one closest to the door and therefore the farthest from the noisy bar.

"Is this all right?" she asked.

"Definitely."

She ordered a glass of red wine; he ordered a beer. When their server left, he asked, "Is it okay— I mean, you're all right drinking alcohol?"

She laughed. "You mean…people like me? Yes, when we're like this, all usual activity is fine."

He smiled at her. She liked his smile and the way it raised his hint of dark beard ever so slightly. "I think I have a lot to learn about people like you."

"And I have a lot to learn about the Mounties. You've told me a bit about your background, but how did you wind up here, in this kind of assignment?" One he didn't seem to relish. "And when are you going to tell me the main reason for the formation of the CAs unit? I gather it's something important."

"It is." He moved a little closer and spoke softly. "It's

actually a bunch of serial kidnappings that have justifiably gotten our senior officers' attention, but it would be easier to explain more about it when your folks get here and I can do it all at once."

The server brought their drinks, and since neither was especially hungry after that pizza, they ordered only a small appetizer to share.

When the server left, Owen looked at Selena with his gorgeous blue eyes and said nothing for a long moment. She felt her insides heat as if those eyes were igniting her nearly as much as his lips had. Before she lost herself in their depths she said, "Okay, tell me why you're here."

Shrugging, he took a drink of his beer. He still kept his voice low as he responded. "Not much to say that you don't already know. As a kid, I always loved to see Mounties in their formal red uniforms riding horses and all. I told you about some of my assignments, but most recently I was assigned to the task force investigating those kidnappings I mentioned. That's partly why I was chosen to help form the Canada Alphas— so I could use a different direction to catch the kidnappers."

"Your career sounds amazing," Selena said.

They started speaking again of Canada and what Selena might see here. The rest of their outing was pleasant. More than pleasant. Selena found herself looking into Owen's face constantly, sharing smiles and laughs and banter, almost as if they were flirting.

Which, of course, they couldn't be. Despite that onetime, unforgettable kiss. They were professional colleagues—that was all. Her role was to teach him and his fellow RCMP members what they needed to know and then leave.

Developing any other kind of relationship just couldn't happen.

Sitting across the table from the lovely Selena, Owen now wished they'd found the rest of their crowd and hung out with them.

As much as he was enjoying Selena's company, he was…well, he was liking it too much. Liking her too much.

Trying too much to remind himself what she was. Why she was here.

How touching her, kissing her, had been way out of line.

But he'd absolutely enjoyed their kiss. He also enjoyed the memory of it now, as he watched those full, sexy lips of hers while she talked and smiled and drank her wine and nibbled their appetizer.

This was unlike him. In all his assignments, he was totally professional. He got along fine with colleagues, sure. Even attractive female ones. But he had always behaved with absolute professionalism.

He had already blown that once with Selena. It couldn't happen again.

She was talking softly now, about her recent assignment, although just loudly enough that he could hear her over the roar of the crowd around them. "Rainey, Lupe and I were in the Seattle area on more of a recon kind of thing. There were some reputed AWOL soldiers hanging out there, around a secluded campground, and the regular army hadn't been able to confirm it. The idea was that the soldiers might be acting the roles of hunters or naturalists or whatever. They might be easier for a wolf to spot." She paused and smiled, raising the ends of those sexy lips slowly. "They were. The assignment was pretty well over when I got a call from my superior officer. So here we are."

"Yes, and I think your presence here will be a particularly good thing. We'd already been planning to form the CAs, but it had to come together even faster than originally thought because of those kidnappings. We—"

He heard a cell phone chime. "Mine," Selena said. She pulled it from her pocketbook and looked at it. "It's my captain. Excuse me." She rose and walked away.

At the same time, Owen's phone rang. He pulled it from his pocket and looked at it. Anthony Creay, his boss.

"Yes, sir?" he answered.

"I hope you're getting your CAs trained well and fast, Owen. There's been another kidnapping."

"But the last one was only last week. There's always been a good month or more before the next one." Owen realized his protest was inane. If there'd been another kidnapping, the criminals' prior MO on the four previous cases was no longer relevant.

"True. They've been so successful that they must be ramping it up. Which is all the more reason that your group is so critical."

Selena returned and sat across from him again, no longer holding her phone. He mouthed *Creay* when she raised her eyebrows in question.

"We're still waiting for some of the Alpha Force members," he said, this time keeping his voice low in case anyone was eavesdropping.

"I heard what you said," she told him in a soft voice. "Tell your boss they'll be here tomorrow."

Across the table his eyes met hers. The mission was about to get under way. And things were about to get interesting.

Chapter 4

They left immediately, at Owen's suggestion, which was fine with Selena. She didn't telephone Rainey, nor did Owen call his CAs. "I'd rather tell them in person to get their tails back to the hotel where they're staying for now so they'll get up early for a briefing, even if your Alpha Force guys haven't arrived yet," he told Selena, and she agreed.

Owen led Selena out the door, but instead of going to the parking lot, they turned left outside and began hurrying down the sidewalk.

"I'd thought the gang would end up at the Yukon, too," he said, "and we could have just talked to them here. But I'm aware of the other bars in town that my group also seems to like. I haven't been downtown much with them, but they took care to introduce me to their favorites."

Several cars drove by under the streetlights, but Selena and Owen were the only ones on the sidewalk outside the bar. The air was cool. Selena was glad she had grabbed a sweater to bring along after partially unpacking her suitcase earlier. She had removed the black wrap when they'd sat down, but now she pulled it on again over her T-shirt.

She was surprised, after sticking an arm through one sleeve, that the other sleeve was lined up so she could easily finish shrugging it on. Owen had grabbed it and held it up for her. Apparently, on top of being a member of the RCMP, he was a gentleman.

"Thanks," she told him, turning enough to glance at him. He nodded in acknowledgment and kept walking.

Evidently more used to the crisp air than she was, he didn't don a sweater or jacket over his gray plaid shirt. It fit well over his black jeans, hugging his chest in a way that suggested his training as a Mountie kept his physique in perfect shape.

West Columbia reminded Selena of countless small towns she'd visited back in the States. The street they traversed, Columbia Avenue, was lined with shops of various types.

There were also a number of restaurants, all with lights on and apparently still open. Selena didn't recognize their names, but they seemed to be an assortment of family-style and gourmet eateries. Some of the aromas wafting out of them, especially the gourmet establishments, filled Selena's senses and made her smile, even though she was far from hungry. Maybe she'd have an opportunity to sample some of the food here before her assignment was complete.

"This seems like a very pleasant town," Selena said to make conversation. She was very aware of Owen at her side. She had the sense he wanted to pick up the pace but had reined himself in somewhat to accommodate her.

He didn't need to. She was quite comfortable walking fast and did so often at home as part of a daily fitness regimen. She ran, too, when she felt like it—in both her forms.

Partly to accommodate him instead, and partly to challenge him, she began walking faster.

He kept up with her with apparently no effort. "I like your speed," he said, sounding not at all out of breath, which didn't surprise her.

"I thought you might." She glanced up at him at her side and caught a glance that appeared somewhat amused—and a whole lot sexy.

She looked away quickly and stepped it up a notch or two more.

The first bar they came to, in the middle of a retail block, was Myrtell's. Selena heard the loud hum of conversation even before Owen opened the glass door, and as they stepped inside, the sound level rose to near deafening, despite her being in human form.

Myrtell's was crowded and smelled of liquor and popcorn and people scents that probably were only somewhat discernible to the patrons here, but were strong and not all pleasant to Selena.

She wasn't about to mention that to Owen, let alone complain. But after they'd both looked around for several minutes and failed to see either Rainey or any of the CAs, Selena was glad when they left.

Once again, Owen allowed her to choose their speed. And once again, she walked fast, though she didn't settle into a run.

The next place—the Wonderbar—was on a side street about three blocks farther than Myrtell's. Its entry was covered by a sign that resembled a theater marquee, and Selena heard the crowd noises emanating from the place nearly as soon as they turned the corner from Columbia Avenue.

As they reached the door, Selena inhaled the aromas emanating from the Wonderbar. If she had to guess, the patrons here preferred beer over the other kinds of alcohol she had smelled at both of the other bars.

She first heard, then saw, Rainey when she looked inside the door. Her aide was sitting with the four recruits around a moderate-sized round table that held glasses of many sizes, indicating their differences in drinks. Wineglasses sat before Andrea and Tim. Sal had a tall glass in front of him with an amber liquid and ice inside, suggesting a drink with hard liquor—or perhaps it was just a soft drink. Craig and Rainey seemed to fit in better with more of the crowd here since beer steins were on the table in front of them.

Interesting choices, but Selena had no time to do more than give that a passing thought. Owen and she hurried through the door and up to that table.

"Hey, welcome." Sal stood to pull his chair aside to make room for the newcomers. Knowing the young, skinny guy was only nineteen years old, Selena glanced at his amber drink, but she knew that was the legal drinking age in British Columbia. If he had hard liquor in front of him it would be acceptable here, and the scent Selena detected told her it was alcohol.

"Yeah. Where've you been?" Andrea asked. Across the table from Sal, she, too, stood and looked around as if seeking another seat for them, her wide but smallish eyes peering over her prominent nose as she checked out the place.

"Looking for you," Owen said, not entirely truthfully, Selena thought, since they hadn't sought out the rest of the crowd when they first got to the Yukon Bar. "We needed to let you know we're going to hold an update session very early tomorrow morning."

"Then there's been some news?" Rainey was on her feet, too. Selena couldn't help grinning at her aide. Rainey was always eager to jump into whatever assignment they had, and being here with these other shifters seemed to only increase her enthusiasm. She'd pulled a Minnesota Timberwolves sweatshirt on, probably her attempt at a silent joke with regard to the wolf shifters here, including her commanding officer—Selena.

"Yes," Owen said. "We'll tell you about it first thing tomorrow."

"And discuss how we're going to handle things a little later," Selena added, "when the rest of our Alpha Force team arrives."

"Right," Owen agreed. "But right now I'd suggest you head back to your hotel rooms so you can get a reasonably good night's sleep. You have fixings for breakfast at our…site?"

Selena figured he'd avoided saying "headquarters" in case anyone around was eavesdropping. All the crowd she saw seemed caught up in their own conversations—and imbibing. But she appreciated his discretion.

"Yes, we do," Craig said.

"Great. Then get on back to where you're staying now."

"Soon as we finish our drinks," Craig agreed, and the others nodded. Selena suspected they had only recently ordered refills since none of their glasses appeared especially empty. But that was okay. The alcohol might help them sleep better.

"We'll see you in the kitchen of the main house, then, at o-seven...er, seven a.m.," Selena said, quickly getting herself out of military speak.

"Yes, ma'am," Rainey whispered with a sly grin.

Selena wasn't sure whether the RCMP knew US military protocol, speaking or otherwise, let alone followed it. But when she glanced around the table, all the CAs were grinning.

Especially Sergeant Major Owen Dewirter.

"You're staying downtown somewhere, aren't you?" Selena asked as Owen pulled her chair out so she could stand.

Despite being an officer of the law, he didn't always follow traditional etiquette with women. Even so, something about Selena made him want to revert to the old ways he'd learned as a child here in Canada—actions that had supposedly been imported from the mother country of the UK years, even centuries, ago. Odd, he knew. And he didn't want to overthink it now.

But on some level he realized he was hoping to make himself think of his obligatory partner in this program as a lady, not an officer in the United States Army whose rank might be in some ways equivalent to his own in the nonmilitary RCMP, or perhaps even higher. And certainly not as a shapeshifter from whom he had a lot to learn to fulfill his current assignment.

Plus, he got closer to her this way than he otherwise might. Could smell her fresh, almost floral scent—

nothing like the scent of dogs or wolves that he might otherwise have anticipated.

In addition, while being polite, he could imagine touching her for other reasons than assisting her in and out of cars or pulling her chair out for her.

Which most likely meant he should start being rude from this moment on.

"That's right," he responded. They left the others behind at the table and wended their way through the bar crowd to the exit door. Once they were out on the sidewalk he continued, "My team and I will move into the house you and your other Alpha Force members will be occupying now once you've trained us and moved on."

"So where are you all living now?"

"Hotels. I'm in one, and the rest of the CAs are in a different one." He'd thought that would help his subordinates bond without worrying too much about being part of a regimented system. That would come in time. And he didn't worry about his command. As soon as the training and the mission started, they'd know who was in charge.

She turned sideways to look up at him. "It would be more convenient for you to stay downtown right now rather than driving me back to the house. I could wait until Rainey is ready to go, then ride with whoever drove her here, or she and I could even walk back to the HQ if she doesn't have a ride. It's not that far."

"In the dark and in tonight's chilly air? No way."

He couldn't help but appreciate her offer, though. She didn't automatically consider him and the CAs her inferiors, who were required to take good care of her in exchange for teaching them.

"All right." She sounded relieved. He liked that, too.

He figured she had made the offer because she believed it to be convenient for him, even though she'd hoped he'd refuse it.

They walked back to his SUV in the Yukon Bar's gravel parking lot, and without thinking, he took Selena's arm and helped her into the passenger seat.

Despite the sweater she wore that kept him from touching her skin, he was highly conscious of her warmth. She, too, appeared to notice the contact, since her head turned quickly and her amber eyes captured his for just an instant. "Thank you," she said. He shut the door, then went around to the driver's seat and started off.

He had anticipated struggling to find a neutral topic of conversation on the short drive back to the enclave when he realized he wanted to know everything about this woman—including more of what she really thought about being a shapeshifter. But he didn't really want to bring that up. Not now.

He was relieved when she started the conversation. She sat in shadows in the seat beside him, but the lights outside the vehicle illuminated her enough that he could see her lovely face—and the fact that she was smiling as she watched the scenery while he drove.

First, she commented on the bars they'd visited. "I liked the Yukon best, but I can see why our gang likes the Wonderbar. There's more action there, for one thing."

"True. But I was with them once at the Yukon and they really got into talking about…what they were. Quietly, and using euphemisms, in case anyone was listening."

"Euphemisms like what? Although I might have heard them all. Used them all at different times."

He told her Andrea's description of what they all had in common as being windows through which illumination fell—like the full moon that changed them, he assumed. Did Selena still identify with that? He knew that shifters in her Alpha Force didn't need to wait for the right phase of the moon. He had even seen it, sort of.

His new unit members were also students, ready to learn all they could about the universe. They were animal lovers. And more. And with each description, Owen heard Selena draw in her breath and giggle.

He liked that he could please her like that.

"You enjoyed that conversation, too, didn't you?" she asked, facing him as he waited at a traffic light.

"I liked her ingenuity," he admitted.

"Did you ever think, when you decided to join the RCMP, that you'd find yourself in such an unusual situation?"

He hadn't. Not really. But he had previously become aware that shapeshifters existed, and the experience he'd had suggested that illegal, even violent, situations could result from contact with them.

"No," he said curtly as the light changed and he stepped too quickly on the gas.

He glimpsed Selena's movement beside him, as she was jolted back into her seat.

"Sorry," he added, but didn't explain his discomfort.

"You had a bad experience with shapeshifters, didn't you?" she asked quietly.

Damn, but the woman was perceptive. He would have to watch himself around her.

"No," he said only somewhat truthfully. He realized then that this might be a good time to tell her—and vent a little. "Not me personally. But a short while after I joined the RCMP I had a couple of family members killed in the States—in Minnesota—and others there asked me to come and talk to the local authorities and try to make sense of what had happened. I traveled there, and that's when I learned that one of those killed had been a distant family member by marriage who'd been a wolf shifter. He was shot with a silver bullet while shifted, after he'd killed my blood relative, a third cousin. Despite attempting to dredge out the details and help, I didn't get a lot of information on motive or anything else, other than that it was a family tragedy, and I never did make any sense of it. The cousin who was killed was apparently a prominent business owner in the area, and the details were hushed up so the shop he owned would survive. His wife and kids still own it and we stay in touch at the holidays."

It was something he almost never talked about, and neither did anyone else in the family, except maybe those in Minnesota. But letting Selena know that he genuinely believed in shapeshifters—and why—had seemed appropriate.

"Look, Owen, I understand that it's a difficult topic to discuss, but—"

"Glad you recognize that." He realized he sounded curt, but she apparently got the message and didn't push. In fact, they didn't say much as he continued onward until he reached the houses. She might not be satisfied with his silence, but that was the way he wanted it.

He pulled his car in front of the larger house, where she and Rainey would spend this night and should be joined by the rest of her Alpha Force team tomorrow.

They had left the lights on, and the two homes were illuminated.

He saw a half-moon off to the east. Not a full moon. It nevertheless seemed symbolic of what was to occur here.

As he parked, Selena opened her own door. He quickly exited the SUV and hurried around to hold it for her and to reach out for her hand as if to steady her.

"I'm really okay," she said, not touching him and giving him a stubborn look. Her full bottom lip stuck out obstinately. Sexily. "But—"

"You definitely are okay," he said. And then, as if he had planned it—maybe to keep her quiet—he bent down, put his arms around her curvaceous, struggling body and put his lips on hers.

Struggling? No. Maybe for a moment, but then she reacted. Positively. Hotly. She leaned in and placed her hands on his chest, and he relished the feel of her so close, her warmth.

The kiss went on for hours, or was it only seconds?

Didn't matter. Didn't matter that it was inappropriate, or that his body was reacting in a way that made him both uncomfortable and eager all at the same time.

She wasn't the one to pull away. He was, and he regretted it.

"Rainey could get back here anytime," he said breathlessly, looking down into Selena's face.

She looked bemused. And hot. And even inviting.

He declined the invitation. "Let me walk you up to the door," he said, taking her arm once more.

She seemed to realize who and where she was at that instant. Her expression hardened; her cheeks reddened in the pale light.

"No need," she said, pulling away, and he watched as she ran up the porch steps and used her key to enter the house.

Chapter 5

Lupe greeted her enthusiastically, whining as Selena walked into the house and jumping up and down in the kitchen behind the chair Selena had set up as a gate.

The wolflike dog had been alone for a while and needed to go outside for a walk.

Selena needed to go outside, too, to cool off in the Canadian breeze after that kiss. That hot, suggestive, sexy kiss that made her insides so aware that Owen felt like a lot more than a professional contact.

She also wanted to ponder some more, on her own, Owen's brief tale of how he had learned of shapeshifters—and his reason for not thinking much of them. Could she get him to discuss it further with her? He hadn't seemed inclined to do so. And she certainly couldn't fix the situation.

After Selena released Lupe from the kitchen, she

cautiously opened the front door and looked outside to make sure Owen was gone.

But his vehicle was still there, parked on the pavement linking the two houses.

Lupe whined—she didn't want to wait. So Selena figured she had better take her dog outside now.

She fastened the woven yellow nylon leash to Lupe's matching collar and picked up a recyclable bag for anything Lupe might leave. "Let's go," she said, smiling at her eager dog.

On the front porch, Selena looked around before closing the door behind her. No sign of Owen. Good. But she'd have to try to hurry since she'd no idea when he might reappear, most likely from the other house.

Lupe seemed interested in going to the area between the two buildings, which was mostly grass edged in neatly trimmed bushes. Needles from the nearby fir trees decorated the lawn.

Lupe pulled gently, her nose to the ground, and Selena followed. Since it was dark outside and the illumination from the lights around the driveway wasn't very bright, this area remained shrouded in shadows. That was fine. Selena stayed alert, all of her enhanced senses attuned to ensure that nothing perilous was around.

Selena detected the scent of some kind of small feral animal, although it was light enough to suggest that whatever it was had come and gone. But that explained why Lupe seemed extremely interested in smelling the grass and its light needle covering. The dog soon produced what she needed to, and Selena scooped it with the bag she'd brought.

That was when she heard a sound other than the

branches of the nearby trees blowing in the light breeze and the very distant sound of an occasional automobile.

No, this was soft footsteps on pavement. Lupe heard them, too, since she raised her head, and her pointed, erect ears moved like antennae toward the direction of the sound.

Had Rainey returned? Selena hadn't heard any car noises.

No, it was probably Owen heading toward his car. Selena remained still, listening. There was no reason to believe that whoever it was constituted a threat to Lupe or her.

Lupe pulled her lead and dashed toward the sound. "Wait!" Selena commanded, keeping her voice low. She didn't want the person to hear her, especially if it was Owen.

But Lupe didn't wait. Her leash taut, she kept pulling Selena in the direction of the driveway. She was usually quite obedient. Not now. Did she sense a danger from which she wanted to protect Selena? Or a friend she wanted to greet?

Selena found out in moments as the back-lit figure of a tall, well-built male appeared in the gap between the buildings. Lupe headed toward him, and Selena released her leash.

It was clearly Owen.

Selena followed her dog, knowing she needed to work to get Lupe even better trained here. Yes, she was mostly obedient, emphasis on *mostly*. Alpha Force cover dogs did get a significant amount of training, but they weren't necessarily expected to act as official K-9s who sniffed out explosives or cadavers or anything like that. Their function was to be there for their shapeshifter counterparts so that if anyone saw an animal in wolfen form, they wouldn't be surprised—even if that particular wolf happened to be a shifted human.

Same went for other types of cover animals, such as those for felines or birds or whatever.

Selena knew that the Canadians would soon need to find cover animals for all of their CAs, including a falcon counterpart for Andrea. But that was far from being her current concern.

"What are you doing out here?" Owen demanded as she got closer.

"Since Lupe's all over you, I'd imagine that's pretty clear. She needed to go out." Selena purposely made her tone sarcastic. That would certainly reduce any further possibility that he'd want to kiss her again, wouldn't it?

"Sure. But…well, even up here, you need to be careful. One reason we chose this area is that we don't know of any problems, but there are no guarantees."

As she got nearer, he wasn't silhouetted now and Selena could make out his features. Handsome features—with his brow knitted in apparent concern.

And that made him look all the more appealing.

She suddenly had an urge to rush toward him and be the one to instigate the next kiss.

Fortunately a noise sounded behind him. An automobile was heading up the driveway. Rainey was probably returning.

That sound also gave Selena an instant to calm herself—and her very human hormones. "I appreciate that," she said. Then, to remind him—and herself—of who and what she was, she added, "You may not be aware of it, or even if you are you might not be thinking about it. But shifters' senses are very much like the animals' they shift into. I heard you come outside the other house probably a lot sooner than another person would, for example. I'll stay wary, but you don't need to worry about me."

"Right." He didn't sound entirely convinced.

Rainey parked the car she had driven—a rental, Selena figured, although she wasn't sure whose—and came running up. "Hey, you two. Three, I mean." She bent to pat Lupe. "I'm ready to go off to bed so I can get up early tomorrow. How about you?"

Selena glanced toward Owen before answering. His gaze was on her, and it was probably a good thing that Rainey remained somewhat in the shadows behind him.

She hopefully couldn't see the very hot, very suggestive gaze that Owen leveled on Selena. But she caught it. And quite possibly she thought the same thing he did.

Yes, she was ready to go off to bed. Alone.

But the idea of sharing it with Owen?

After their earlier kiss, it definitely crossed her mind.

Off to bed. Oh, yeah, Owen had heard that. Thought about it as he regarded Selena. Sexy Selena. Hot Selena, whom he'd definitely enjoyed kissing.

Werewolf Selena.

She and her dog walked with him to his SUV as if she hadn't sensed the gist of his thoughts about bed when Rainey had mentioned it. Maybe she hadn't—although her expression seemed to say otherwise.

No matter. He could always act now as if Rainey's words hadn't triggered his imagination—not to mention a reaction from his most private body parts. Selena had, after all, reminded him earlier of why he wasn't fond of shapeshifters.

"I'll be back here first thing with the rest of the group," he said, slipping into the driver's seat of his SUV. He'd decided to stop in at their hotel to speak with them briefly before heading to his own room that night. "I'll make sure we get here early for them to get breakfast ready for all of us. As Canada Alphas, they've already begun to learn that their duties are diverse, and preparing meals can be among them."

He liked how Selena smiled under the faint lights. He was also amused when she shifted her dog's leash to free up one hand so she could grab hold of the car door.

"My turn," she said, starting to close it.

"Hey, you're a gentleman, too," he teased as he settled into the seat.

"You got it." She slammed the door shut.

But as he turned the key in the ignition, his mind rebelled against what he had said.

Selena was anything but a man, gentle or not.

And her very womanly characteristics just might drive him nuts as he continued to work with her on this assignment.

Once they were all inside the house, Selena went upstairs with Rainey and helped her choose the room she would stay in while they were here. Rainey opted for the one overlooking the front of the house. Selena then left Rainey upstairs and returned to the room that was now hers.

She had already changed into her long-sleeved navy pajamas, washed her face and settled herself beneath her bedcovers when Rainey knocked on her door. "Come in," she called.

Rainey, too, had put her on pj's, a frilly pink outfit

that contrasted pleasantly with her dark, curly hair. She grinned as she sat at the foot of Selena's bed.

Selena leaned back on both pillows that were resting against the plain black headboard. "Well, we're here," she said.

"Yep, and I gather that we're really supposed to start our assignment tomorrow." Rainey paused. "Are you ready to show these Canadian folks what real Alpha Force shapeshifters are all about?"

"That's what we're here for." Now it was Selena's turn to smile. "We'll teach them what being a US shifter—and an aide—is all about."

"And a cover dog, too." Rainey slipped her backside from the bed so she could kneel to pat Lupe, who lay on the floor nearby.

"Exactly." Selena didn't want to kick out her aide, but she did want to try to get some sleep. "So…" she began.

At the same time, Rainey asked, "So did you have fun tonight?"

It was all Selena could do to hide her startled reaction. Surely nothing on her face, in her demeanor, revealed that she'd shared a kiss with the man who was in charge of the Canadian group that Alpha Force was here to help.

No. Rainey must just be making conversation. Wasn't she?

Nevertheless, Selena made herself respond as if Owen was just some ordinary guy whom she didn't find attractive at all—maybe married and twice her age. Or at least that was what she attempted.

"Sure," she said nonchalantly. "I had a drink with Owen at one of the other bars in town before we found you guys. He wanted to know more about what Alpha

Force was about, but I doubt he got it from our limited conversation there in public. He, of course, knows that shapeshifters exist and that I'm one of them, but I still have the impression he finds them—us—weird." She wasn't about to reveal to Rainey how Owen had formed his opinion of shapeshifters. "I hope he gets over that enough to work well with his own CAs." That was the truth, at least. "He got a phone call that apparently suggested they'll be needed sooner than anticipated, and he'd better be ready for it."

"Well," Rainey said, "we'll see how he is at breakfast tomorrow. The rest of them, too. I had the impression that they're way different from our Alpha Force members, even though they're shifters. They were fun to be with, sure, but they struck me as being kind of wild kids. Good kids, though. Tim even let me use his rental car overnight. I just hope that giving them more control of their ability to shift will help tame them down."

"Guess we'll have to make sure of it," Selena said. But she was glad she wouldn't be the only shifter there as things progressed. She wouldn't be the most senior, either.

And surely having other Alpha Force members here, like Captain Patrick Worley and Lieutenant Marshall Vincenzo, as well as their aide, Captain Jonas Truro, would also make it easier for her to remember who she was and why she really was here.

And to remember to stay far away from Owen Dewirter except to teach him what she could as an Alpha Force member.

To ignore any attraction she felt for him and, definitely, to make sure she never touched him again, let alone kissed him.

When Rainey left a short while later, and after Selena gave Lupe a good-night hug and settled herself back into bed, she couldn't help rehashing those intentions and told herself she needed to focus on her assignment.

She just hoped she could.

In the meantime, she lay in bed conscious of the quiet here in the Canadian countryside, except for occasional hoots from local owls.

She mulled over all that had happened over the past couple of days, including Owen's tale of his family and shapeshifters.

She was concerned about what would happen tomorrow, and if Alpha Force—no, if *she*—would be able to do all that was expected to help the CAs start their team and deal with the kidnappings that Owen had mentioned.

Not to mention her concern about her absurd attraction to Owen Dewirter that she needed to find a way to turn off. Permanently.

Owen saw Selena almost as soon as he reached the CAs compound early the next morning.

She was outside again, with her dog, in the crisp early air. He knew that had to be a frequent ritual. Dogs had needs that had to be fulfilled often, especially last thing at night and first thing in the morning, no matter what the weather, no matter what the temperature.

No matter what the dog's responsibilities, such as acting as a cover for her owner.

Under the brightening morning sky, it was easier for Owen to remain less concerned about Selena's safety in daylight. Besides, he wasn't alone. All four of the CAs who needed to be trained and sent into the field were exiting the vehicles behind him.

They weren't trained at all, let alone as his special team—yet—but he figured they'd do something if he needed help.

He waved to Selena as he hurried up the front steps of the house. It was dumb, but he felt glad to see her wave back.

"Hey, sir, er, Owen," Andrea called from behind him. "What are we going to do today?" She, like the rest of them, had dressed in casual clothes—jeans and a sweatshirt.

Before coming here, the CAs had been given a brief amount of preliminary training as Canadian police officers and instructed in some of the formalities. Owen had nevertheless told them that, although he was in charge, informality was fine here.

When he had visited them at their hotel last night, he had briefly described to them part of what they'd be up to today, but it wouldn't hurt to repeat it, drum it into their heads, so they would be ready once the rest of the Alpha Force team arrived to teach them their methods of shapeshifting.

"First thing, I'm going to brief you about our assignment and the update I received last night that I didn't mention to you before. Then the rest of the day will depend on when the other Alpha Force members arrive."

"Got it." She was surrounded by the other CAs on the porch, their gazes all trained on him. Each watched him with concentration, a couple of them nodding.

They all looked interested and eager.

But that didn't mean they'd be able to do the job—especially with all the tweaks that needed to be added to normal, rational, predictable RCMP constable duties. Not that they were the usual RCMP constables.

Turning his back on them, he hurried into the house. Maybe he was just being naive, but he believed that Selena would be the ideal trainer—and not just because she was a shapeshifter. They'd studied her background, and since she'd been a teacher before joining Alpha Force, she should be able to take these young shifters and instruct them on exactly what was needed to fulfill the RCMP's needs here.

That was why she was here—not to create impossible sex fantasies in Owen's mind each time he saw her.

And at night when he tried to sleep…like last night.

He shook off the thought. Heading into the kitchen with the gang behind him, Owen began asking questions before giving orders for breakfast preparation. "Who's good about cooking eggs? Sal? Great. There are some in the fridge along with butter, and the frying pan is in the drawer beneath the stove. Who's our go-to toast guy?" Tim Franzer raised his hand, which left Craig Neverts, Andrea and him. Owen decided to brew the coffee, so he told Craig and Andrea where the items were to set the large dining area table.

"Now, let's get to work," Owen said.

"Need any help?" Selena, along with Rainey and Lupe the dog, had just come through the kitchen door.

"I think we're good," Owen said. But he watched as Selena immediately approached Sal and started helping to cook the eggs.

Was there anything that woman couldn't do? She was a US soldier, a teacher, a cook…and a shapeshifter.

And sexier than any other woman Owen had met.

With all that in her favor, he'd no doubt that she'd be one hot partner in the bedroom.

But that was one scenario he'd never see realized.

He walked over to the large coffeemaker, glad he had something entirely neutral to accomplish.

Something that allowed him to keep his back toward the rest of his cohorts—so no one would be able to notice the bulge at the front of his jeans.

Chapter 6

Selena was glad to keep busy, even though it was a challenge for all the CAs and her to stay out of each other's ways while whipping up their breakfast together.

Finally they had the meal prepared, and all of them found seats around the sizable dining table. She didn't plan it, but Selena found herself sitting beside Owen near the doorway to the kitchen. Not a bad place to be. In fact, the two of them were more or less in charge, so why not join forces for what needed to be said here?

Not surprisingly, Owen said he had a lot to tell them, including information he'd just learned yesterday that they needed to know. But he directed them to start eating first.

Selena wanted to hear Owen speak a lot more than she wanted to eat.

Nevertheless, Owen handed her a bowl so she could

scoop out her own helping of eggs. "These look great," he said.

"They *are* great," said Craig, who sat across from them. He had already dished himself a substantial helping and had his fork up to his mouth.

Sal and Andrea were on one side of Craig, and Tim had a seat next to him. Rainey was beside Selena. It was almost as though the two groups were opponents—except that Owen sat close enough to her to appear to be on her side.

That wouldn't be entirely accurate, though. They weren't enemies, of course, but the differences between them seemed as weighty as the matters they needed to work on together.

Then there was the proverbial elephant in the room, at least as far as Selena was concerned: her totally inappropriate sexual attraction to the man.

Selena ate rapidly, watching the others across the table and listening to their friendly hazing of one another. Even Rainey became the subject of their amusing gibes. How could she stand to be in a whole room full of animals? they'd teased her. Even their commanding officer, Owen, was an animal. A human one. Selena knew he didn't need to shift to become a feral creature.

To Owen's credit, he jested along with them, talking about how he would use his own wild nature to mow down any of those here who dared to disobey him.

But after a few minutes of the revelry, Owen fortunately ended it.

"Okay, everyone," Owen called out. "Let me have your attention." He had finished his eggs and toast quickly and now just held a coffee cup in his large right hand. Despite the prior levity, his deep voice now resonated with authority and seriousness, and although it wasn't extremely loud, he did, in fact, appear to capture everyone's attention.

Selena put her fork on her plate though she wasn't through eating. But she wanted to concentrate on what he said.

"I'm going to start at the beginning," Owen said. "I'll give a quick recap of why those of you who are now part of the Canada Alpha team have been recruited, both to refresh your recollections and to make certain our Alpha Force visitors know enough. Then I'll tell you why what you're about to embark on is crucial to our national security. How you can help save lives."

Selena had been informed of the basics before, but hearing them from Owen, with his point of view and earnest tone, drove home the importance that she'd been told surrounded her mission here.

Yes, the recruits were shapeshifters. How they had been found and recruited into the RCMP was only hinted at, but their ultimate objective was a matter of Canadian national security as Selena knew.

"We're all very pleased to have found each of you and look forward to your justifying the trust we've placed in you." Owen's gaze moved slowly from Sal to Andrea to Craig to Tim. In exchange, they each peered solemnly toward him and nodded.

He then looked toward Rainey and, finally, at Selena. Those eyes of his were gleaming and blue and grave. They didn't turn her on at that moment, but they definitely made her take notice. Made her want to fulfill whatever they commanded.

Which, right now, was apparently just to listen.

"I believe you were told what we need to accomplish, how we got the attention of the US military and why we were let in on the highly secret existence of your Alpha Force, but just in case, here's the story."

Owen took a sip of coffee, then reached toward the carafe that sat on the table not far away.

"I've got it." Selena reached for it and then poured coffee into the nearly empty cup that Owen held out. She warmed her own, and Rainey's, too, before passing the carafe so the CAs could take more as well.

"Thanks," Owen said. Then he finally dived into the crux of what they all needed to hear. He described the horrific serial crimes taking place in Canada. Family members of some of Canada's most successful business magnates, or even the magnates themselves, had been kidnapped to extort tremendous amounts of money. "There were four prior abductions that we're aware of, and you'll recognize the surnames of the victims—or at least those of you who are Canadian will."

Selena hadn't heard of three of them, but the fourth, Marc Wagnere, was well-known in the States as being the originator of an internet search-engine site that competed easily with Google and others. She'd heard something about the senior guy's illness, but as far as she'd known, that was all that had gotten into the news—not anything about an abduction.

"Of course, this is all confidential information," Owen continued, "and you're not to discuss it with anyone except among yourselves. And now there's another victim."

Before he continued, Selena heard a noise outside. Lupe did, too, since the large, furry dog stood up and barked.

Selena couldn't help glancing at the other three wolf shifters in the room. They appeared both alert and confused, looking from one to the other. She suspected they'd heard the outside sounds as well.

Was there some jeopardy here? No, she knew who had just driven up the driveway to the headquarters.

"Let's pause for a moment, okay?" she asked Owen, whose hearing probably hadn't been tweaked. "And I think you ought to get someone to brew some more coffee."

"Why?" He looked concerned and not exactly happy.

Before Selena could explain her assumption the doorbell rang.

Lupe barked once more even as Selena hurried from the dining room and down the hall to the front door. She had just grasped the knob when she felt a hand on her shoulder and Owen pulled her away.

"What the hell are you doing?" Owen demanded. "We don't know who's out there. It could be dangerous."

Selena hesitated. She could be wrong. She moved away from Owen's grasp and again approached the door. This time she looked through the peephole viewer.

Sure enough, she saw whom she'd expected to see.

Staying out of Owen's reach, she pulled the door open, then grinned at the men who stood there—her fellow Alpha Force members assigned to this mission. No cover dogs, though. Lupe was the only one on this mission.

"About time you gentlemen got here," she told them with a smile, although they had appeared earlier than expected.

"Easy for you to say," retorted Patrick Worley. "Wait until we tell you all we went through to arrive early."

"Hold that thought," Selena said, "and come inside. We're in the middle of a report on why we're here—

and something that just occurred." She was a little annoyed that the last time she'd spoken with Patrick, he'd indicated there was no way they could arrive this early.

Was this an attempt to make a good impression on the CAs, by demonstrating that the importance of this mission to Alpha Force made them pull out all the stops to get here fast?

Maybe. But Selena doubted it would have that effect on Owen.

It certainly didn't on her.

Nevertheless, she was glad to see them.

"Sergeant Major Owen Dewirter of the RCMP," Selena said, assuming all the formality expected of a US soldier on duty, "I'd like you to meet Alpha Force members Captain Patrick Worley, Lieutenant Marshall Vincenzo and Captain Jonas Truro."

As the group shook hands, Selena smiled, feeling all kinds of relief circulating inside her.

Formality be damned. These were people with a job to do—herself included.

A job for which they all needed a briefing.

"Hey, everyone," she said. "C'mon back inside so we can talk."

In a few minutes, they were all seated around the dining room table and Owen first introduced the CAs.

"They're our shifters," he told Patrick, "but I'd imagine you know that."

The senior Alpha Force member nodded. Patrick was a tall man, square-shouldered, with light, cropped hair. His face was long, and he had a cleft in his chin. As with the rest of Alpha Force, Selena was used to seeing him in camos, but today he wore a black hoodie. "I assume you can guess that two of the three of us are shifters as well. That's Marshall and me."

Selena saw no expression on Owen's face at that news, but she made a mental note to warn her fellow Alpha Forcers that though he believed in shapeshifters, he didn't appear to like them much.

Despite his reasons, though, he had been behaving utterly professionally—at least if she didn't count his sexiness and those stolen kisses. She certainly wasn't about to mention any of that to her fellow soldiers.

"I'll explain now why we need Alpha Force's help," Owen continued, "both to teach our people how to shift when there's no full moon, and also to stay aware of who and where they are, and why, which I understand our CAs need help with."

"I'll say," Tim asserted, and the other CAs nodded. Selena nearly grinned at the eagerness on his pudgy face, the way he clasped his hands on the table in front of him. "And let me say that I really appreciate this. I want to help my country, and to do it in a way that will help me, too, in ways I never knew were possible before—"

"Hold that thought," Craig interrupted. "Let's let our commanding officer speak."

"In other words," Owen said, his tone slow and droll, "shut up and listen."

Selena smiled and said nothing.

Chapter 7

"First," Owen said, "let me repeat what I started before and give some further explanation."

He was glad that the Alpha Force team was now fully present. That way, he could be certain they knew the appropriate details, and he would not have to repeat anything again.

He mentioned those kidnap victims' names again and then he went into some detail about the abductions that made Selena visibly cringe. Each victim had been treated horribly, denied sleep and food. A couple had been physically abused—beaten and even whipped.

And all were threatened with death should their ransoms not be paid. Their treatment made it clear that this was not an idle threat, but a promise by their abductors.

"They'd been allowed to speak to their wealthy family members now and then, to encourage them to fulfill the ransom demands. And when the money was eventually paid and the victims released, none had enough information as to where they'd been held. But their physical condition—especially that of the elderly Mr. Wagnere—was terrible. And now… Here's what I learned a little while ago." Owen picked up his phone from the table. "I received a call from one of my superior officers in the RCMP who knows about what we're doing—Anthony Creay, deputy commissioner of general policing services. Selena met him when she first arrived in Canada." He glanced toward the woman at his side.

She nodded. "That's right. I had to prove to him, as well as to Owen, that I was a shifter." Her grin was ironic as she leveled it first on him, then looked from one Alpha Force member to the next. They all grinned, too, as if in empathy. Owen wouldn't have been surprised to learn they'd each had situations where they were with nonshifting humans who didn't believe in their…unusual capabilities.

In some ways, he wished he'd had no reason to believe, too.

But he did believe. And at this moment, that was actually a good thing.

"Anyway, there is a new situation. One we need to move on quickly. Someone near the top of our organization—maybe the RCMP's commissioner or an assistant commissioner—somehow became aware of your Alpha Force. How they did doesn't matter. What does matter is that we've had that rash of kidnappings in Canada, where the victims are either the heads of some of our most esteemed and lucrative companies, often in high tech, or a relative of one of those top executives." He had identified them before, but Owen now added details on the victims and their businesses to further explain the urgency.

"I've heard about some of that," Patrick stated, "but not all." His fellow Alpha Force members nodded.

Owen had no doubt that at least some information about the kidnappings would leak and thereby make it into American news reports, as some had in Canada as well. Many crimes that went on here might not have been as interesting to the neighbors to the south. But these, where high-profile companies that also did business in the United States were involved, might get more attention. Particularly if the stories could be considered sensational. Titillating. Scary and exciting.

And unfortunately these could.

He hazarded a glance toward Selena. Was that sympathy he saw in the slight inclination of her head and a touch of sorrow in her lovely amber eyes?

He looked away quickly. He didn't need the distraction. He had a story to relate.

"Each time, because of who the victim was, the companies they headed anted up and paid some pretty colossal amounts of ransom. Meantime, the RCMP and even some government groups attempted to locate the kidnappers to bring them down—with no success so far. Except that…well, we think we might know their location now and where they go with the people they abduct."

"But you haven't stepped in and arrested them?" Selena asked.

"No, because our investigation has been hampered by that believed location. The victims, after being ransomed and released, say they were kept chained to walls and blindfolded, so they haven't been able to say much about their environments."

"But what's your speculation?" That was Patrick, who had leaned forward at the table. Good. The guy in charge of the Alpha Force group now looked intrigued.

So did Selena, although Owen didn't glance sideways at her this time. But she, too, had turned to face him even more. That he could tell.

"Well, there's an area near the border of British Columbia and the Yukon, miles from the nearest village, where satellite sensors have picked up more activity than usual lately, often around the time of a kidnapping. In fact, there used to be almost no activity at all in that very remote location, and what's there now disappears quickly. The place is impossible to reach except by helicopter or plane—and landing anywhere nearby would be difficult, though possible if we know that really is our target. The camera surveillance we've attempted so far was somehow jammed. We believe the victims are taken underground into caverns, but it has been impossible so far to confirm whether this is the actual location."

"How about drones?" asked Tim, leaning forward with a look of fascination on his pudgy face.

"Yes, we've sent drones into the area, but those that haven't disappeared have been retrieved with mechanical difficulties. We're still not sure what caused the problems, though." Owen moved his gaze around the table, trying to gauge the others' reactions.

They all appeared interested—some, like Tim, more than others.

There was something in Selena's look, though, that suggested she knew what he was driving at. The other

Alpha Force members, too, seemed to be sitting straighter, anticipating what he would say next.

"Anyway, here is the current situation. There has been another kidnapping—you might have anticipated that from what I said." Nearly everyone in the group nodded.

"Who is it?" asked Andrea Willburn, perhaps the first time she had talked since the meeting started. She might be of particular use to finding a solution, considering she shifted into a falcon and could potentially do a flyover—but Owen hadn't gotten there yet.

"It's the wife of Rene Brodheureux, the founder and chief executive officer of Xanogistics. Her name is Berte, and she went missing three days ago. Mr. Brodheureux has already received a ransom note via electronics—one of the programs his company developed, by the way, and even so, they can't trace the source. If he doesn't come up with fifty million Canadian dollars within five more days, Berte will be executed."

Xanogistics. Selena believed that everyone who had a computer, tablet or smartphone had heard of the Canadian company. It was in some ways that country's equivalent of Microsoft, known for a variety of consumer-friendly programs.

Xanogistics was so well-known, so successful, that Selena had no doubt its CEO had nearly unlimited resources. He could afford to pay to save his wife.

But he shouldn't have to do that.

Not if there was anything she, or the rest of Alpha Force, could do about it.

"I'm going to guess that the RCMP, or at least those in charge of the Canada Alphas, believe that wildlife can get in and surveil the area where technology can't," she said, looking straight at Owen.

His eyes lit up, and the grin he aimed her way almost caressed her—not anything sexual, she told herself. Certainly not with everyone around. But his look showed a touch of admiration that she'd correctly guessed where he was heading. Or was she just projecting that?

Still, she found herself basking in the gaze as he exclaimed, "Bingo! That's exactly it. The area we suspect supports a lot of different kinds of wild creatures—and they just happen to include wolves and falcons."

"That'll be us, then." Selena glanced to her right as Sal Emarra, who'd spoken, stood and clapped his hands. The young man gazed at his fellow CAs and they all rose and smiled at one another.

Selena glanced at Owen. He was scowling, and his expression wasn't unanticipated.

What he had described was far from a game.

But he said nothing to challenge his CAs' attitudes. Maybe he figured that allowing them to react this way only encouraged them to perform as he needed them to.

Nor did Selena want to spoil their premature celebration by reminding them that their assistance wasn't possible yet. They needed instruction by Alpha Force—and, most important, access to the very special elixir that allowed shifters to choose when they shifted and to keep their human awareness.

Otherwise, if this group simply showed up in the remote area where the abductors were thought to be, they'd have to do so during a full moon, which wouldn't occur for another couple of weeks—beyond the date the ransom had to be paid.

Presumably Rene Brodheureux would have paid to rescue his wife by then, assuming she was still alive.

Plus, the shifters would simply act like any other wolves or falcons in the area—roaming wildly without searching for a way to help any kidnap victim, with no human understanding of who they were or why they were there.

Or, worse, they would be no better than the aircraft sent to learn what was going on and would be unsuccessful, discovered and potentially taken out. So far, the RCMP apparently had no idea how many suspects there were, how well armed they might be and whether they considered themselves hunters.

Sure, the shifted animals sent in would be equipped with some highly special, new-generation video cameras that should not be jammable like the other equipment that had been tried, but those wearing it would need to recognize where to aim them—which meant the Alpha Force elixir and assistance.

She shot a glance toward her fellow Alpha Force members. Judging by the way they sat unmoving, except for trading glances at one another, their minds were on a similar wavelength.

Owen finally replied to Sal, but it wasn't the criticism she figured he felt. "Yes, we hope it will be you—all four of you. But in some ways a very different kind of you. What we need is not simply for wild wolves and a falcon to converge on the place sometime. We need shifters who know what they are and what they need to accomplish there."

"Like you guys?" This time it was Craig talking. He looked at Selena first, then the other Alpha Force members. "You can do that, can't you? That's what we were told."

Selena smiled, but she let Patrick reply. "Yes, we can do that, thanks to our amazing elixir. And it'll let you do it, too."

"That's fantastic!" Sal exclaimed.

"Yes, it is," Rainey said. "Even just to watch."

Selena was aware that Rainey loved Alpha Force. She even admitted to Selena that she'd once hoped the elixir would help regular humans shift, but she was happy enough, since it didn't, just to work with shape-shifters. And Selena was happy to have her.

"Since we now know that acting fast is crucial—" she looked at Owen, who gave a slight nod of his head, as if he knew just what she was going to say "—I think it's time for us to give our new protégés a demonstration of what Alpha Force is all about."

"You're reading my mind," Owen said. Selena couldn't help thinking about the last time she shifted to prove to Owen and his superior officer that she was, indeed, a shapeshifter.

This time, there were men around who could give an even better demo to Owen and his fellow male CAs, while Selena could show Andrea how it was done.

No need for any sexual implications or awareness that way.

But as Selena continued to observe Owen, his small, cocky grin, which disappeared nearly immediately, told her that he, too, must be thinking about humans going nude before a shift.

In a way, Selena regretted that this time, now that she knew Owen better, she was unlikely to have an opportunity to tease him about what he wasn't about to see.

* * *

A short while later, Selena watched as Owen strode out of the dining room behind Marshall and Jonas. She wondered what he was thinking. He was about to actually see a shift, but not hers.

A pang of slight regret pulsed through her, and she ignored it.

She turned back to regard the others remaining in the dining room with her. Patrick was still there, along with Rainey and the CAs plus Lupe, who woke at the sound of slight activity.

Before the three men had left, Selena had stepped to a corner of the room with Patrick for a few minutes.

Selena had first asked Patrick why the other Alpha Force shifters hadn't brought their cover dogs, and he'd responded that they'd chosen not to in the interest of a speedy arrival, notwithstanding the delays they'd encountered thanks to some inclement weather. And there were logistical reasons, too—they didn't have to prepare the dogs or select planes for transport that would be safe for them. Besides, the Alpha Force team here wouldn't be around civilians much, especially not while shifted, so they wouldn't need the cover provided by their look-alike canines in the event they were seen.

Patrick had then given Selena instructions on what she was to do while Owen watched Marshall shift.

"You're our teacher," he'd said. "Time to give this group a lesson on what to expect, especially when Marshall returns to this room."

She had smiled, glad to know her special career skills were about to be put into use here. And now it was time.

She glanced at Patrick, who nodded. His light brown

eyes shone a bit and his mouth curved in a small, encouraging grin. If Selena read the expression correctly, he believed in her.

She wouldn't let him, or Alpha Force, down. Not now and not ever.

"Hey, everyone," she said, standing to get their attention. "I'm going to tell those of you who don't know exactly what's about to happen in the other room."

"You mean Marshall's shapeshifting without a full moon and still knowing he's also human?" asked Craig, who regarded her with his dark brows lowered quizzically. "Isn't that what's going on?"

"That's the summary," Selena agreed. "And you'll all experience it eventually, but it's better if you have some detailed sense of the procedure."

"Then tell us," Andrea said enthusiastically, a huge smile radiating beneath her prominent nose. "I can kind of imagine it, but you can tell us with the voice of experience."

Selena laughed. "You could say that." She then looked at Tim, who regarded her with his small eyes wide, apparently also interested and not, fortunately, flirtatious this time.

And then she looked at Sal. The kid had the biggest, most interested smile of all of them.

"Okay," she said. "Here it is. You probably know, or can guess a lot of it, but I'm going to describe what'll happen moment by moment. That way, you'll all know exactly what to expect when your time comes."

Too bad she didn't have photos or even a chalkboard where she could draw illustrations, the way she had when actually teaching classes. But Alpha Force was such a covert military unit that any physical evidence of what it did, even temporary, was frowned on.

It didn't really matter. She just needed to describe it. They'd all see—and experience—what she explained to them soon.

She started out by pointing to Lupe, who had lain back down on the floor. "You all may know that Lupe is my cover dog." At her name, the dog rose and came over to Selena, who petted her. "Marshall's cover dog is Zarlon. They didn't bring him, but if they had you'd see right now what Marshall will look like when he returns to this room. And here's how he'll get that way now, during the day and with no full moon for another couple of weeks."

She described the steps of shapeshifting the Alpha Force way. The shifter's aide, in charge of carrying the very special shifting elixir, would uncap the small bottle and hand it to the person they assisted. That person would drink it. Then the aide would grab the special, battery-operated light that resembled the illumination of a full moon when turned on and aim it toward the shifter.

Then the shift would begin.

"Do I have to describe a shift to any of you?" Selena asked as she looked from one CA to the next. Since they were all shifters, the answer had to be no.

Instead, Sal asked, "What does the elixir taste like?" He looked concerned.

"It can vary since it is always being researched and changed and improved," Selena said. "Mostly, it's mildly citrusy in flavor. Not bad, in any of the formulations I've ever tasted. How about you, Patrick?"

He had been a member of Alpha Force longer than nearly anyone else. "I wouldn't say I'd ever choose to drink the stuff just because it tastes good," he said, "but I've always gotten it down just fine. Now how about telling them—"

"About what happens once the shift is over? I was just getting there." Selena smiled broadly. "This is one of the reasons I just love Alpha Force. And you'll surely love your CA group even more once you've had access to the elixir."

Selena began talking briefly about how shifting had felt to her when she'd been younger and before she had even heard of the elixir and the discomfort while the shift had occurred. And how she'd transformed into full wolf form when it was over.

"And now—now I'm fully aware of all that's happened, all that's around me, as if my mind is still human. But I'm completely in wolf form then. Plus, I have some control over how long I stay shifted. I can choose to shift back at any time, but otherwise the elixir will wear off, depending on the amount I drank, and I'll shift back automatically. Either way, it's wonderful."

"That sounds so amazing," said Andrea, still grinning. "I can't wait."

The door had just opened. Owen walked in first. "Amazing? Oh, yeah," he said. Selena hesitated to meet his gaze. He had now seen not only the result of a shift, but also the shift itself. Was he disgusted?

Would he despise her for what she was and how she got there?

Instead, his expression seemed full of awe. But she couldn't ask him any more now about what he thought, what he felt. And not just because of all the people around.

As he strode through the door, he was swept aside by the large, shepherd-wolf form.

"This," Owen told the CAs, "is Marshall now. And how he got like this? Wow."

Chapter 8

Wow wasn't really a strong enough word for what he'd seen, Owen thought as he watched the CAs look over the canine who'd just entered the dining room with him. Jonas Truro edged up to Owen's side. Owen was glad that Alpha Force had sent two doctors—shifter Patrick and nonshifter Jonas—just in case the shifting of his CAs led to some kind of medical issue.

"You okay with all that?" Jonas asked him softly.

"You mean the…shift? Yeah, I'm fine with it, though it's like watching a sci-fi movie with special effects." *Really* special effects. Owen didn't look at Jonas as he talked. Instead, he watched Selena, who was speaking with his CAs.

From what he had understood those years ago, the shifter who had married into his family had changed like this, yes, but under a full moon. And had turned wild—all wolf with no human characteristics.

If his shift had been like this, into a calm canine, there would surely have been a different result—and his blood family member would undoubtedly have survived.

Fortunately, the shifter and his wife had had no kids.

And Owen hadn't seen any shifting back then at all.

"Now since you all are shifters," Selena was saying, "I'm sure you're not at all surprised that this is Marshall. But what you may be unfamiliar with is what I told you about before. I'm going to give him some instructions that a true canine wouldn't understand—and neither would you while shifted."

Owen grasped what she was saying. But the vision of Marshall's change from a naked man who grew fur while his body morphed into this form... *Wow*, he thought again.

"Yeah, I remember the first time I saw a shift happen," Jonas said to him.

"Me, too," said Rainey, who'd joined them. They were all standing at one end of the dining room by then, away from the table.

"Sci-fi, weird, unbelievable," Jonas continued. "All those thoughts went through my mind. I assume they're going through yours, too."

"You could say that," Owen agreed. And they weren't the only things.

His mind, as well as his gaze, was on Selena.

He had no trouble visualizing her nude. In fact, he'd much too often ached to see her that way. And touch her. And...well, more.

But she was a shifter. She periodically went through the change he had just seen. In fact, she'd done it in that closed-off room before they'd left Vancouver—unseen by him, but imagined just the same.

And despite being amazed by what he had just seen, oddly enough he now hoped to watch Selena do the same thing.

To see her without clothes—oh, yeah. But also to see her go through that incredible process that should be a complete turnoff, yet was somehow stimulating his curiosity. And more.

"Lupe, you come here and lie down," she told the dog she'd traveled with, and Lupe obeyed. Then she turned to the dog-man who'd just shifted and come into the room. "Okay, Marshall, let's first do what regular dogs do. Sit."

Her voice intruding into his thoughts brought him back to reality. Odd reality, to be sure, but he focused on this room. On her.

The canine before her sat. That didn't surprise Owen, nor, apparently, any of the others who circled around him.

"Now get up and slap Craig on his hip with your left front paw," Selena directed.

No regular dog would understand all that, although presumably one could have been trained to make that move on a specific command. Once again, Owen wasn't surprised to see the dog obey.

He again considered how different things might have been in his family if the Alpha Force elixir had been involved.

"Next, I want you, Andrea, to tell Marshall to do something that ordinary dogs aren't likely to under-stand."

"Great!" The only woman CA was smiling once

more. "Let's see." She moved her slender body, clad in sweatshirt and jeans, near him. "Marshall, my phone is in my pocket. Can you sniff out which one?"

The dog nodded, then raised his nose in the air. In moments, he approached Andrea's right side and nuzzled her hip gently. She reached into the pocket on that side and drew out her phone.

"Good job," she said. "Now, I'm originally from Quebec and my area code is four-one-eight. Can you bark that out? I mean, first bark four times, then once, and then eight times."

Marshall obeyed and the CAs applauded.

"This is so cool," Sal exclaimed. "I can't wait for us to try it." He'd knelt on the floor near Marshall and then rose. "Can we do it today?" he asked Owen.

"Tomorrow," he responded. "Right?" He looked at Patrick.

"That'll work," the captain agreed. "And once all you CAs have your first planned shift, we'll really need to get down to work training you for your mission. This'll probably be your last free evening for a while, so you might as well enjoy it."

"Can we party first, tonight?" Sal asked, looking hopefully toward Owen.

"I thought you partied last night," he responded.

"That was just a visit to a bar for a couple of drinks," Andrea said. "I'm up for a real party."

"Especially if it'll be our last for a while," said Tim.

Owen mulled over the idea quickly. That might actually work well to maintain their cover in this town, where they were just supposed to be tourists hanging out for now until deciding to move here.

"Sure," he said. "Let's party."

* * *

Selena was glad to plan on partying, too. That meant she would be around the entire group and unlikely to be alone at all with Owen. That was good.

Even though she was dying to ask him what he thought of the shift he had watched.

"Let's start out early evening," Patrick said. "I don't want the party to last too late. We should all get up early tomorrow morning."

"Fine with me," Owen agreed.

It was also fine with Selena. With all the discussion and shifting, it was now midafternoon, so the party wouldn't start for a few hours.

Except for Rainey, this would be the first night that the other Alpha Force members slept in the house in this small compound. They would all be upstairs except for her, but she would be well aware of them. She needed a good rest to prepare for all that would happen tomorrow.

She'd done some teaching today, but what she and the others would provide as instruction tomorrow was likely to be pretty taxing. As well as a lot of fun. These shifters had much to learn about the Alpha Force elixir and what it could do for them.

And how it could allow them to help their country.

Facing Owen, Jonas asked, "Do you want to watch Marshall shift back?"

"Yeah," he said. "Definitely."

What was his mind-set? Selena wondered, not looking him straight in face. Did he find it fascinating or horrifying? Was he trying to get used to the terrible reality he would need to deal with as the commanding officer of the CAs, or was he actually drawn to it?

She couldn't help hoping for the latter, but suspected the former was the truth.

"Great," she said. "In the meantime, I'll go check out some things on my computer and change clothes. Rainey, you going to town later, too?"

"Absolutely. Looking forward to it. Last night was fun. Are those friends going to join us again?" Rainey's gaze was on the CAs, who'd taken seats on the living room sofas and chairs.

"Friends?" Owen, who hadn't yet left the room, asked.

"Just Craig's girlfriend and my sister," Sal said. "We knew our cover was to be like tourists, so we invited them to come to town for a little while. They joined us last night for drinks but left early."

Worry shot through Selena. Had the CAs' cover been broken? Had Alpha Force's?

"Who gave you permission to ask them?" Owen's voice wasn't loud, but it was strong enough to make his recruits blanch or look down or both.

"Really, sir, it's okay," Craig responded, meeting Owen's gaze briefly before tearing his away again. "My girlfriend, Holly, knows I'm a shifter, even though she isn't. She also knows I'm joining the RCMP but thinks I've found a way to hide what I am, not use it, and that I've met some friends who're doing the same thing. I just told her that the group of us had taken a short leave and were meeting up for a vacation here, and she asked if she could come."

"Same goes for my sister, Yvanne," Sal said. "I told her not to mention to anyone that we're RCMP, and she promised not to. And I figured her being here would only help with our cover here as vacationers. She's rooming with Holly in the same hotel as we are and only staying for a few days."

Owen looked as dubious about the situation as Selena felt. Patrick's expression suggested he, too, didn't like it.

"Well, what's done is done," Owen said. "And yes, you'd better make sure they both party with us tonight so I can check them out. If they're as you say, no harm, no foul. But you both might have compromised the entire mission."

"It's not like that at all, sir," Craig said, his face drawn into a worried frown. "Holly's been my girl for a long time. She's trustworthy. She'd never do anything that could hurt me."

"Same with my sister," Sal said. "I promise."

Selena could only hope that they both knew the women well enough to know that trust was merited.

As they left the room a little while later, Rainey apologized not only to Selena but also to the other Alpha Force members. "Sorry," she said as they stood in the hallway. "They all told me that Owen and the RCMP knew they were coming and were okay with it, or I'd have mentioned those women first thing."

"It should be fine," Patrick said, "since we're all meeting with them tonight. We'll make it clear that it's in their loved ones' best interests not to talk about them, or even visit here, at all."

Selena just hoped they'd understand that lack of discretion could result in nasty consequences for those loved ones—and possibly the rest of them, too.

They had all been in the Yukon's main bar area for nearly an hour now. Owen had helped, on their arrival, to push three tables together for this somewhat sizable party: the five members of Alpha Force, the five CAs including him…and the two outsiders.

Or sort-of outsiders, he reminded himself while taking a long sip of the second bottle of his imported US beer.

The place was crowded and noisy, every table taken. The TV hanging above the bar was muted but showed a football game being broadcast from the UK—soccer in the US. One of the teams was Manchester United, a huge and global fan favorite.

Owen hadn't paid much attention to the screen or the rival team, though. Instead, he listened to what was happening with this group. His group.

The group he had to ensure remained in sync with one another while one part taught the other what was necessary for its members to fulfill their assignment. Their very critical assignment.

Then there were the other two people who, despite being outside his control, had the potential to blow their whole mission. But he wouldn't panic. For now all he had to do was listen.

Selena, bless her, was doing all the rest.

"So on a scale of one to ten, what's your skill at keeping secrets?" she had just asked Yvanne. Selena's voice was a bit slurred, her head tilted so her light brown hair hung lower on her left side than her right. Owen was rather surprised that the highlights in her hair shone even in the bar's low light—but that was probably a result of its unusual nature. *Her* unusual nature. Her amber eyes, too, gleamed despite the lack of illumination around them.

Of course, most of the man-wolf shifters at the extended table also had similar characteristics, but Selena's intriguing feminine features trumped them all.

And her apparent high brought on by too much alcohol? A pretense. He was sure of it. He had observed what she had actually had to drink, and it hadn't been that much. No doubt she wanted the others to think she'd overimbibed so they'd lower their guard around her.

"I'm quite good at keeping secrets," Yvanne responded. She was apparently Sal's older sister, maybe in her midtwenties to his nineteen years. She was slender, too, and her hair was longer and blonder than his. It, like Selena's, sparkled now and then in the scant light in the bar. "On the scale you mentioned, I'm at least a ten. Maybe higher."

"That's my sister," Sal said. He reached over from where he sat next to her and rubbed her hair in obvious fondness. She responded by making a fist and giving him a brief Dutch rub that made her bro laugh and stand as if he wanted to tackle her. That lasted for only a second, though, before he again sat down and took a swig of beer.

Good show, Owen thought. And since Yvanne, too, was apparently a shifter, he believed what she said—at least with respect to some things. Would she keep silent about her brother having joined the RCMP, and the nature of the unit he was now part of if she happened to figure it out? They'd been told that these two women thought their men were hiding their special abilities from the RCMP, but they might suspect otherwise. In fact, Owen felt fairly sure Yvanne knew the truth, and perhaps the other woman did, too.

He hoped, in any event, they would remain discreet, but he would keep his eyes and ears open.

Selena had already turned toward the other complete stranger in their midst, Craig Neverts's girlfriend, Holly Alverton. Holly was petite in stature but curvaceous. She seemed attached to Craig's left side and was either holding his arm or rubbing up against him. Her eyes were huge and blue, her smile nonstop except when she took a sip of her white wine.

"How 'bout you, Holly?" Selena said, still slurring her words. "You know your boyfriend's…special, don't you?"

Owen knew just what Selena's slight hesitation meant. Did Holly?

"Oh, yes," Holly said, her voice ringing out despite the noisiness of their surroundings. "There's a whole lot that's special about Craig." She snuggled even closer to him, if that was possible.

Craig turned toward her and kissed her cheek, then rubbed his own, with its dark beard shadow, against it. "Holly's pretty special, too," he said.

"But not as special as you," Selena persisted. "Not the same way, at least."

"That's right," Holly said. "I know how very special Craig is." She turned and kissed him back on his rough cheek.

"Then I'd love to hear, on my scale of one to ten, where you fit, Holly," Selena said. "Keeping secrets or not? What's your score?"

"She's great at it, aren't you, love?" Craig said. His

glare at Selena was nasty enough that Owen considered intervening.

He must have moved a bit on his chair, since Selena glanced at him, gave an almost imperceptible shake of her head, then returned her attention to Holly, even as she took another sip of beer.

"It depends on the secret," Holly said, her voice more muted now. "There are certain ones, one in particular, that really have to be kept to myself. On that one I'm a ten." The gaze she turned toward Selena appeared almost defiant, as if daring her to guess which one she was talking about.

But Owen knew which she meant. Obviously Selena did, too. Craig certainly did. This time the kiss he gave his girlfriend was right on the lips. A long one that appeared deep and hot and a bit too sexy while in the company of other people.

It made Owen think of Selena. He looked toward her...and found that she was looking at him, too. That made a certain part of him tense up and thicken—good thing he was sitting down. Selena's expression suggested she could see his reaction anyway, or at least anticipate what he was going through.

Did that mean she felt a similar heat, similar attraction, similar...desire? That only made Owen's erection thicken even more.

She took a much longer swig of beer this time—one he believed might actually lead to the intoxication she'd been feigning if she followed it up with many more. When she put her bottle down, she pulled her gaze quickly away from Owen and looked again toward Holly.

"Excellent," Selena said. "Secrets can be a lot of fun, can't they?"

"Definitely," Holly responded, then started to kiss Craig once more.

This time Selena smiled at Owen before reaching again for her beer.

Chapter 9

If only she were as inebriated as she pretended, Selena thought, taking another small sip of her beer while making it appear as though she was swallowing a lot.

Maybe then she'd simply be having a good time without trying so hard to read the thoughts behind every expression Owen leveled at her.

She saw lust in his intense blue eyes beneath lowered brows, or so she believed. Was it true? A touch of amusement and admiration, too. She could understand his appreciation of her attempts to get usable impressions of the two visiting women, a feel for whether either or both were trustworthy with the very important secrets hovering around this group.

That knowledge was critical to the success of their mission. Not to mention Alpha Force's need to remain covert.

The CAs also had reason to keep silent about their nature and Alpha Force's. But outsiders, even with relationships?

She knew better than to believe either woman's assertion of her ability to keep confidences. But at least this way both Yvanne and Holly had to be aware that secrecy was expected of them—as if they hadn't known it before.

"So who'd like another round?" Selena waved her half-full bottle in the air as if it was empty.

"I think we've all had enough," Owen said. He looked not at her but toward Patrick, who was in charge of the US contingent here.

Patrick clearly got the message. He took what appeared to be a final swig from the bottle in front of him. "Agreed," he said. "We have a big day tomorrow."

"We sure do." Sal looked at his sister and grinned. Was he going to talk with her about what was planned for the CAs? Selena figured Yvanne probably knew, at least in general, despite claiming otherwise. From what she'd gathered, Yvanne was a shifter like her brother. Would she be jealous of his upcoming ability to shift at will and keep his human sensibilities?

Maybe. But if all went as hoped, the CAs might even recruit other shifters into their ranks.

Later. If this mission was successful.

Which it had to be. A life was at stake—and maybe more lives in the future.

Selena shot a glance toward Owen. "Well, then," she said, "let's all go back to our quarters for the night so we can get up early."

Soon everyone was standing, their bar tabs were paid and they headed toward the Yukon Bar's exit.

Outside, beneath the glow of the bar's bright neon signage that lit the darkness well into the adjoining street, Selena wasn't surprised to find Owen beside her. He leaned down and said softly into her ear, "Good job."

She ignored the warmth that flowed through her at his approval. "What time are we having breakfast?" she asked. She half hoped he would offer her a ride back to the CAs headquarters, but Patrick had driven one of the vehicles rented by Alpha Force here, so she didn't actually need other transportation.

"Seven o'clock sharp," Owen said. "As soon as we're done we'll do a quick recap, then begin our exercises." His eyes glistened in the light for a moment before he looked toward his group of RCMP members. They all stood together watching him, with the two outsider females behind them. Selena could read the excitement in the expressions of each of them.

"We'll be there right on time," Craig said, his smile huge.

His girlfriend behind him smiled, too, but her expression seemed a bit puzzled, as if she didn't really know why he was so eager to leave her early the next day.

Whether that was real or feigned didn't matter. Tomorrow was going to be a thoroughly enlightening day to the CAs—and possibly to the Alpha Force members, too, as they did their first training of the outsiders.

"Good night, everyone," Rainey said. Her aide slipped beside Selena and faced the others. "Sleep well."

Selena glanced toward Owen again. Did he actually wink at her, or was that just an illusion under the light?

"Yeah," he said, his gaze still on her. "Sleep well." Was that a challenge? Did he assume she'd stay awake all night thinking of him?

Or was that just her own assumption?

He looked away from her then and again faced the CAs. "You'll all need a good night's sleep." With that, he headed down the street while the recruits started off in the other direction.

Where was Owen staying while here in West Columbia?

And why did Selena suddenly want to visit his quarters?

She tamped down her absurd yearning and followed the other Alpha Force members as they crossed the street toward where their car was.

After Selena walked Lupe for the last time that evening, she stepped into her room. She couldn't help the images that bombarded her mind. Images of the first time she'd entered this room, with Owen. Even then she'd sensed something between them.

Shaking off the memories, she plugged her phone's charger into the wall. Just as she did, it rang.

It was Owen. She had programmed his number into her caller ID. "Hello," she said, wondering if he was going to do something to keep her wide-awake after all.

Like saying things that were suggestive and hot and—

"Hi, Selena," he said. "I just wanted to let you know that I've spoken with both Craig and Sal independently this evening. I called each of them to once again underscore the importance of their making sure that Holly and Yvanne keep their mouths shut about whatever they happen to know, even if it isn't much. As it turned out, and unsurprisingly, Yvanne knows it all."

Selena sat down on top of the bed. Lupe came over

and laid her muzzle on top of Selena's knee, and she petted the dog's head distractedly.

"And as a shifter she's jealous?" Selena made it a question despite being fairly sure of the answer.

"Yes, but according to Sal, she's concerned for his safety and won't say anything. Plus, she's hoping to join the CAs in the future."

Exactly as Selena had figured. "So she'll keep her mouth shut for that as much as anything else."

"Right."

"And Holly?" Selena asked. She was a little more of an enigma, but since she apparently knew that Craig was a shifter, she was unlikely to do anything that would harm him.

Unless they were arguing, and that certainly didn't appear to be the situation. Not the way they'd had their hands all over one another at the Yukon Bar.

"From what Craig said, she's fascinated by the fact he's a shifter. Can't wait until they're married and have shifter kids. He vouches for her unequivocally."

"Still...well, even if those two women are perfect, we should nevertheless remain cautious about all the CAs and what they do and who they tell." She didn't say so, but in her mind that included Owen.

She was an Alpha Force member and a shifter. He wasn't—no matter that he was the RCMP member in charge of his newly formed group.

And also no matter that she found him attractive. And sexy.

And way out of her reach. He was Canadian. She was American. He was a high-ranking police officer in the RCMP. She was a lower-ranking officer in the US military.

Most of all, she was a shifter, and he wasn't. If nothing else erected barriers between them, that certainly did.

"You're entirely right," Owen said. "I'll be cautious on my end, and you might remind your fellow Alpha Force members to observe as well as teach."

"Will do," she said, then paused. "Thanks for calling, Owen, and giving me at least some sense of reassurance."

"You're welcome. And like I said before, sleep well. Just remember, though, that I'll be thinking of you." His voice grew lower and hoarser. "And wishing you were here. Good night, Selena."

Before she could say anything else, he hung up.

She fortunately didn't have time to mull over what he'd said and how he'd said it—with that deep, sexy tone. Not then, at least. A knock sounded at her door.

She opened it to find Patrick standing there. "Want to go on a brief patrol with me?" he asked. "I want to shift and walk around this compound to check for any apparent dangers."

A pleased feeling coursed through Selena. He had chosen her over those who'd been with Alpha Force longer, whom he knew better?

"Of course," she said, smiling.

"Since you've been here an extra day, you might have a better sense of what's supposed to be around here."

Well, all right. That made sense, although it burst her bubble a little. Her commanding officer had a rational reason for selecting her above the others. But that still was good. She would get to shift that night. Soon, in fact.

And wouldn't have time to think any more about Owen. At least not now.

He hadn't meant to add those last comments as he'd said good-night to Selena, Owen thought after hanging up the phone.

He knew he wouldn't sleep. Not yet.

Instead, he decided to take one last drive to the CAs compound now occupied by the Alpha Force members. That included Selena. He wouldn't drop in on her, though, or any of them. He wouldn't even go into the meeting house to make certain it was ready for tomorrow.

He simply wanted to ensure that everything looked okay around that important training area.

Or so he told himself. He wouldn't see Selena, after all. That would be a bad idea.

But he knew she was there. And he hopefully would confirm that she was safe.

As if she wouldn't be, with a whole team of Alpha Force members—her own kind—backing her up…

The drive through West Columbia was fast this time of night. Most of the downtown stores were closed, and the bars that remained open—the Yukon and others— even seemed fairly quiet, judging by the few cars parked along the street. It wasn't long past midnight, but apparently this town went to bed early on weeknights.

A good thing to know, especially considering the types of training sessions the CAs would soon be holding.

Owen drove slowly so no one would notice him. In a short while he turned into the driveway up to the compound.

He stopped there. Maybe it wouldn't be a good idea to drive up the hill. Any Alpha Force members would recognize his car and question his being there.

Even *he* questioned his being there.

He parked along the street in front of a nearby house. If he walked up the driveway in the dark to check things out, he was less likely to be noticed.

By normal people, at least. But most of the Alpha Force members there had extraordinary senses for humans, or so he'd been told. Plus, the cover dog Lupe, too, might catch his sound or scent.

As a result, he decided to compromise. He wouldn't go all the way to the top of the hill. Instead, as quietly as he could, he would stand at the bottom of the driveway before deciding how far up it he would go, and he would let his own, very normal senses work on seeing and hearing anything that might be even a little beyond usual.

Good thing his sweatshirt and jeans were dark colors. He got out of the car quickly so as not to be illuminated long by its inside lights. He glanced around and saw no movement, no indication anyone was aware of his presence.

After waiting for only a minute or two, he started walking up the hill.

She led Patrick out the back of the house, leaving Rainey and Jonas inside.

Their shifts had been fast and hassle-free, as always. Selena had recalled, while drinking the elixir, how Patrick had accurately described the most recent taste as somewhat citrusy. Then Rainey had shone the bright battery-powered light on her, and now she was in wolf form.

So was Patrick. Together, side by side, they prowled down the porch steps, circled both houses, then entered the surrounding woods.

As before, even when not shifted, Selena heard the sounds of small nocturnal creatures. Scented them as well—mostly rodents and owls. The feel of fallen leaves and pine needles tickled the bottoms of her paws. She turned her ears one way, then the other, still listening. The lights from the houses illuminated the clearing, but not here, beneath the trees.

A sound! A footstep? A human?

It seemed to come from the base of the driveway. Patrick must have heard it, too, since he stopped walking and looked at her. She nodded quickly, and then the two of them, still within the cover of the forest, headed in that direction.

Then Selena picked up a scent. A very familiar, very appealing scent. Human and tangy, not sweaty or menacing or anything that suggested a need to approach and attack.

Owen's scent.

She moved slightly sideways as she continued walking, butting gently against Patrick. They both stopped, and she stared into her CO's pale brown eyes, looking down, then shaking her head slightly. Telling him by motions, not words, that there was no danger.

Or so she believed. They had to check, of course, and so she took the lead.

In moments, as she stood halfway down the driveway, remaining tucked into shadows, she saw him.

At the same time, he saw her. His chin rose, his eyes

widened, and she heard him mutter something, although she could not make out the words. Despite her acute hearing, he was too far away, his voice too low.

Was he saying her name?

He had seen her before like this, before they had departed from Vancouver. But even if he might recognize her, could he here, in the darkness?

She wasn't certain. Even so, she walked slowly from beneath the cover of the trees. She nodded her wolfen head slightly, as if in greeting. Heard Patrick's growl behind her, a warning to be cautious.

She was. That was definitely Owen, and he was no threat to her or to any of the shifters.

Owen remained motionless where he was, except that he, too, nodded at her.

And then he turned and walked back down the hill.

Chapter 10

It was her. Owen was certain of it.

He could think of nothing else as he drove cautiously back toward his hotel.

Certainly wild wolves could have shown up in this area, but he knew better. The animals' demeanors, their actions when they had seen him, had convinced him they were shifters.

Even so, there were three Alpha Force wolf shifters. The two canines he had seen could have been the two males who had come here together. One could even have been the cover dog Lupe, he supposed.

Yet the way the one wolf had looked at him, had appeared to react to him, had seemed to communicate with him...

That had to have been Selena.

He turned onto West Columbia's main street once more.

He was tired but doubted he would sleep well that night.

Not after seeing those two shifted wolves.

Not after seeing Selena.

Of course it had been her. It hadn't just been her actions that convinced him. He had worked with dogs at the RCMP police-dog service. Many of the German shepherds who were part of their canine force resembled one another, yet Owen had taught himself with no effort at all to tell them apart.

That canine who had appeared at the edge of the forest near the CAs' enclave had looked exactly as Owen recalled Selena appeared after she had shifted in the isolated room in Vancouver. Like Lupe but more aware, more connected.

He hadn't been close enough, hadn't been at an angle to confirm it was a female wolf, but if nothing else the resemblance to Lupe convinced him who it was.

He had anticipated seeing Selena changed again someday as she helped to train the CAs in his charge. He just hadn't anticipated it here and now, this night. But he'd been the one to show up at the enclave unannounced. Why wouldn't she have shifted while anticipating no Canadians would be around to spot her?

She—

Damn. He had overshot the entry to the parking lot for his hotel. He was overthinking this situation.

As if he could do anything else.

Well, tomorrow would be a big day. The first training day. That was what he needed to concentrate on—and how vital his team would be in rescuing the latest kidnap victim and preventing any more.

Pulling into another driveway, he turned the car around to return to his hotel.

They hadn't talked about it at breakfast. They hadn't talked about it at all.

Now Selena was in the meeting house's closed-off study with Rainey and Lupe, sitting on the small sofa while waiting for their morning's assignment to begin.

She was no longer in Owen's presence and wouldn't see him again until sometime later.

Had he known she was one of the wolves he had spotted last night? Somehow she didn't doubt it.

The fact he hadn't mentioned it, had simply acted cordial this morning with everyone else around, hadn't erased the likelihood from her mind.

Would he confront her with it sometime?

Would he simply ignore it because though he might need shapeshifters to fulfill his professional assignment, he didn't especially like them?

Didn't especially like her?

"When can we get started?" Andrea had just hurried into the room and shut the door behind her. As she'd been directed, she wore a loose T-shirt and jeans that could be removed quickly.

Rainey and she were also dressed casually, though Selena had no intention of shifting today.

No, this was the day to start training the CAs.

"Right away," Rainey said, then looked at Selena questioningly, which was entirely appropriate. Selena was her commanding officer.

But for what was about to occur, Rainey was in charge.

"Fine with me," Selena responded, glad her focus

was now redirected as it should be. "Rainey's going to be the one who'll help you, Andrea. She's not only my aide—and now yours—but she has also checked with another Alpha Force aide who's worked with our avian shifters." That was Ruby Belmont, whom Selena hardly knew. "As you've probably already been told, there's only one right now, a hawk." Autumn Kater, whom Selena didn't know well, either. "The amount of elixir she takes to cause her change is different from what a shifting wolf takes."

"Should a falcon take the same amount as a shifting hawk?" Andrea asked Rainey, her thick brow angled into a worried frown.

"We'll start with a little less, just in case. But it should be quite similar. Your human weights are around the same, less than ten pounds' difference." Rainey's smile was reassuring beneath her curly, dark hair, and she undoubtedly knew what she was doing. "Are you ready to give it a try?"

"Absolutely!" Any hesitation on Andrea's part had disappeared. She looked excited and ready to go.

Selena remained seated, holding Lupe's collar. Her dog had been present while she and others had shifted into wolf form, but Lupe hadn't seen shapeshifting into other forms. On the other hand, she was a very sweet, fairly calm dog who had never been known to chase other animals.

"Okay, here's what we do." Rainey had gotten a sealed container of the special elixir from the basement refrigerator and brought it into the room along with a wrapped plastic glass. "First, please take off your clothes. We're not sure how soon the process will start after you drink the elixir, so it's better for you to be ready."

That was why there were only women in this room. All the men CAs were in the basement with the male Alpha Force members.

Andrea barely took a minute to strip. Though Selena turned away, the glimpse she got told her that Andrea was as reed-thin as she appeared in her clothes.

Rainey handed Andrea a half-full cup of the liquid. "Now drink this, not too fast and not too slow." Andrea did so. That was when Rainey removed the battery-powered light from her backpack, turned it on and aimed it at the nude woman. "Now we'll wait," she said.

Selena's shifts always began as soon as the light was focused on her. The same thing happened with Andrea. It worked just fine. Despite the length of her limbs, they began to contract nearly immediately. Her face contorted and shrank as well, and feathers began to emerge from her skin.

Fascinating, Selena thought. But then, she thought all shifting was fascinating. She was just a lot more familiar with the change to and from wolfen form.

Lupe moved slightly beside her, but didn't otherwise react. Selena patted her. "Good girl," she said in a low, fervent voice.

In less than five minutes, it was over. A gorgeous falcon of no more than a few pounds, with a determined stare through golden eyes and a curved, sharp beak, perched on avian legs on the far edge of the sofa that Selena occupied.

"Wonderful!" Rainey exclaimed. "Do you feel okay?"

The falcon's head, covered with mottled gray-and-white feathers, bobbed as if nodding yes. Her throat was white. In a moment, the bird raised her wings and began flying around the room making the sound "cack, cack," as if triumphantly calling out in success.

"I'll take that to mean yes." Rainey smiled at Selena, who could only grin back. "Then let's go out to the living room and wait for the men."

"Good idea." Selena looked toward Andrea, who seemed to be listening despite her flight, and as soon as Rainey opened the door the bird soared through.

The living room was empty when the female contingent arrived there, but Selena was pleased that Lupe soon wasn't the only canine present. In fact, three dogs resembling wolves with different backgrounds, including possibly a shepherd, a malamute and an Akita, loped into the room and sat near one another on the wooden floor. As they panted, their mouths resembled smiles. Not surprising, Selena thought. She wasn't certain which was Craig or Tim or Sal—but at that moment it didn't matter.

What was important was that they had all shifted, without a full moon.

Right behind them came Patrick, Marshall, Jonas... and Owen.

"I see all must have gone well with Andrea," Patrick said, watching the bird soar around the room's ceiling.

"It sure did," Selena said. "And I gather that the wolf-shifting CAs had no problems, either."

"Right," Jonas said.

Selena stole a glance toward Owen. Had he enjoyed watching? Hated it?

Thought about her as the humans morphed into wolfen form?

Wondered about possibly having seen her shifted last night?

Her mind was back on that subject. Maybe Owen and Patrick had already discussed it, since her commanding officer had been shifted and at her side. She wasn't about to ask, especially not now.

"Time for you to give a few instructions, Selena," Patrick said. "You're our teacher, after all. It'll all work better when we do this sometime at night, but for now teach these shifters about their human cognition while in animal form."

Selena had known Patrick would direct her to do this. In fact, they had discussed it last night—once they had both shifted back into human form.

Patrick had mentioned seeing Owen at the base of the hill. He hadn't expressed an opinion or anything else, though.

Now Selena turned her attention to her charges, who'd just had their first experience with a shift brought on by the Alpha Force elixir. She started with Andrea. Selena told her to go and gently alight on Rainey's head.

Her aide laughed. "Good idea, but don't even think about providing me with a bird-poop sample."

The other humans laughed, too. The falcon who was Andrea immediately followed orders and perched atop Rainey's head, then squawked once more.

"Good job," Selena said. "Now see how gently you can fly away. No pulling hair. Next, go perch on Owen's shoulder."

Selena met his gaze with a smile. He looked fine with it. He looked fine, period, in his navy sweatshirt and jeans, his blue eyes sparkling over his aquiline nose and strong chin. Selena kept her expression neutral and pleasant.

No need for him to realize he was stoking her sexually just by being there and being a good sport around shifters.

"Now, if you know what I'm saying and you like your current shift, Andrea, give Owen a kiss on top of his head."

The falcon turned her head and lowered her beak to touch Owen's short black hair. She obviously was cognizant of what she did, since her touch was gentle despite the pointed end of her beak.

Selena let herself sigh softly in relief. She certainly wouldn't have wanted the bird to hurt Owen in any way. But she did want to prove to everyone in the room who had human cognition—which should be everyone but Lupe, who lay on the floor near the sofa—that Andrea knew what she was doing.

"Okay, next I want each of you shifted wolves to do as I say." She told the three canines to stand and turn around, one at a time. Next, they were to sit beside one another, then each stand up on hind legs, turn around and sit again. "Then, if you like being shifted thanks to the Alpha Force elixir and know what you're seeing and doing, I want you to each bark, in this order—Sal, then Tim, then Craig."

They did so, and everyone who still had hands clapped in glee.

The plan had been for this first shift to last for about an hour, and the amounts of elixir had been given accordingly—and so had instructions about how to will themselves to start changing back.

When the hour was up, the groups separated to the

locations where they'd been before. As soon as they all were in human form once more, the entire group was to meet back here in the living room.

Selena followed Rainey and Lupe into the study with Andrea flying overhead as the men headed downstairs.

She looked forward to the next part of today's experience.

She'd grown up with a little access to the elixir, having known the family who'd invented its first incarnation, but she looked forward to the delighted expressions she knew would come.

Controlling the change, and one's own mind-set, was an inevitable and endless thrill. It made all the shifters she knew who experienced it feel overjoyed and eager for more.

Even she still felt it.

And the CAs who'd just had their first such experience…?

Selena knew they'd be jazzed and excited and full of anticipation for the next experience.

That would be a good time, she figured, for the men in charge—Patrick and Owen—to remind them of their underlying assignment and its potential danger.

Owen wasn't certain why he felt so drawn to watching the shifters change, but he did. In both directions, from human to wolf, then back again.

Now the reverse process seemed to take even less time, and he observed the wolves' fur absorbed beneath their skin as the forms of their bodies changed, too, while they lay on the floor.

He heard the Alpha Force members cheering them on, a nice gesture on their part, he thought. Or maybe the two who were shifters themselves believed their kudos somehow helped the others engage in their new shifting processes.

He didn't need to wait down here forever in the cool underground chamber with concrete walls and floor, though. He'd seen what he'd wanted to.

While the three CAs lay on the floor in human form, grinning as they received their clothes from the Alpha Force members, Owen slipped up the wooden stairs into the kitchen.

Selena was there.

She clearly heard him coming up the steps since she was watching the door when he opened it. She stood near the refrigerator, a bottle of water in her hand.

"How are things downstairs?" she asked, her tone as cool as the drink she held.

"Shifting is… Well, it's amazing," he said, shaking his head as if that action would underscore his words.

That thawed her a little. "You could say that. In fact, you did. I shift often, and I'm still amazed by it, particularly now that I have complete access to that wonderful elixir."

"I wish I could try it sometime." Owen stopped, wondering where that thought had come from. Him, interested in shapeshifting?

Of course he knew the impossibility of that. Not even the magic elixir would give nonshifters the ability to shapeshift.

Selena had taken a couple of steps toward him, as if wanting to soften what she was about to say. The soft, sad look on her lovely face seemed compassionate, even sympathetic. "You know you can't, don't you, because—"

"No, no, I realize that. I'm just expressing my wonder at what you do."

Her eyes widened, and he felt utterly captivated by Selena. He took a couple of steps toward her, too. His arms began to reach out, but then he heard a noise behind him.

He turned as the men exited from the basement.

"Hey, where's Andrea?" asked Sal. "We want to compare notes on our experiences."

"Here I am." Andrea strode into the kitchen from the other side, with Rainey and the dog behind her. "And wow!"

"Exactly," said Craig. "Wow."

Owen realized that his brief time alone with Selena had ended. It was better that way. He had probably said too much already.

He might need the help of Alpha Force for his assignment, might have to work with these CAs in ways he could not possibly have done on his own.

Admiring who they were and what they did was okay, too.

But that was enough.

"Okay," he said. "Let's all get together in the living room and discuss what you experienced."

Chapter 11

Selena wasn't surprised to hear each of the CAs attempt to top one another in their descriptions of their shifts.

The three men were outspoken about how different this felt from their uncontrolled changes under a full moon, when they stalked outside until it was time to change back again, only to await the same scenario the following month.

Then there was today. They'd felt the same discomfort during the change, but it was definitely worth it, each asserted. Tim was the first to talk about it, and he seemed so thrilled, so excited, that he could hardly find the words to describe his experience. Selena couldn't help wondering if his slight pudginess made his shift more strenuous and difficult than the others', but he wasn't complaining. No, he had clearly loved it.

Then young Sal gave his description a try, and he was passionate if not clear about what it had felt like not just to shift, but to realize what was happening. And then to be fully cognizant of who and what he was once the change was complete. "It was so, so, so amazing!" he asserted, giving a fist pump of delight into the air.

Craig was less vociferous but no less enthused. "I can't begin to describe how it felt," he said, "but I can't wait to do it again. And again."

"My turn!" Andrea interjected. "I'm sure all you guys had a great time. But can you even begin to imagine what it's like to soar and see things and understand them from the air just like you see and understand things now? I can." Her falcon-like face beamed.

Selena felt her own smile broaden. Oh, yes, she understood all of what they described. Well, almost all. She'd never soared while shifted like Andrea did. But the experience, the sensations and the knowledge were all incredible.

She glanced around, seeing similar pleasure on the faces of Patrick and Marshall. Their two aides, Jonas and Rainey, looked nearly as happy. Maybe they felt some kind of empathy while being part of the process. Or maybe they were just nice people, military souls who derived pleasure from doing their jobs well.

Then there was Owen, who she had just learned might be experiencing some kind of envy of shifters. Or not. He had to work with them now, so maybe he was just pretending to cast aside his original feelings about them and to like them.

Yet when she hazarded a glance in his direction, he was looking not at his own delighted CAs, but toward her. She made herself keep smiling, and she nodded a little as if she had said something that he should now accept as true.

"I'm really glad to hear about all this," he finally said, not just to her. "In fact, as you all know, this was just step one. Step two, tomorrow, will involve all of you shifting again and then starting to learn the procedures you will need when you are set loose in the area where we believe the kidnappers are hiding out. We'll decide whether to try it at different times in the day and evening and maybe the night since we don't know when you'll actually need to conduct your mission."

"Sounds great!" Sal exclaimed, then lowered his head and stared up at his CO with inquisitive eyes. "Don't suppose we can do it tonight, can we?"

"No," Patrick interjected from beside Selena on the sofa. "This was a partially new experience for all of you. Your bodies will need to rest. But our experience with new Alpha Force recruits using the elixir indicates that you should all be fine for a new shift tomorrow. Of course, if you have any reactions that feel different from when you shift naturally under a full moon, you should let us know right away."

"Of course," Andrea said, and the expression on her face seemed to indicate she was trying to be serious and professional, but wasn't quite able to hide her continuing excitement and triumph about her falcon shift.

Quiet Tim surprised Selena with his next request. "Since it sounds like we'll be busy at night from now on, at least some of the time, and we can't shift again now, is it okay if we have just one more little party tonight?" He looked at Owen. "It'll help in our cover here as temporary visitors. We'll need to come up with a good story about why we're not partying for a while—nighttime hikes or stargazing in the mountains or whatever—and we can mention that at the bar tonight, just in case anyone's paying attention to us." He sounded rational—and eager.

Selena wasn't surprised at Owen's response. "You make a good case for having some fun tonight, Tim," he said. "Anyone else up for it?"

He looked at her, even as his CAs all issued positive responses. She felt a flush of discomfort redden her face, even as she glanced toward Patrick, then her other Alpha Force comrades. None objected, and she couldn't think of a reason to deny the CAs a final evening of fun before their work notched up to a new level.

"Good idea," she added to the replies.

Good idea or bad, Owen looked forward to what could possibly be their final bar outing while in West Columbia. After all, it might be the final opportunity for fun around here for at least a while. If all went well, his team would learn how to conduct its necessary operations over the next few days and nights, and then they'd finally be deployed for the field assignment for which they had been recruited.

No more partying.

Which would probably be a great idea. If he continued to see Selena only in training ops, maybe he would stop thinking about her in anything but her official role here, as an instructional officer for his shifting CAs.

Entering his hotel room back in town, he dialed his commanding officer for an update on the kidnapping situation.

"Dewirter? Glad you called." Creay's voice sounded tense. "I was about to text you to call me whenever you could, since I didn't know what you might be engaged in at the moment."

"Is there any news I should know about?" Owen studied the wall in front of him as though he could view the faceless, nameless kidnappers. He wanted to strangle them. Did he love billionaires? Not particularly, but he loved his country. And he hated anyone who would harm another person for greed or any other reason.

"Rene Brodheureux received another ransom note. It pretty well followed the last one, nothing new, just a reminder that he has only another four days to pay or his wife will be toast." A pause, then Creay continued, "So how are things going with you?"

"In other words, what's my timing? Things are progressing well, but I'll need at least another couple of days before we can deploy." Owen purposely kept his comments general. Not that he believed anyone was monitoring his calls or Creay's, but he wasn't taking any chances.

"Just keep it moving," Creay said. "Fast. And keep me informed."

"Got it," Owen said. "I'll be in touch again soon."

"Real soon," his boss responded. Then Anthony ended their connection.

Good thing Owen had a party to prepare for, he thought. Otherwise he might focus on the implied criticism from his commanding officer.

Things were progressing, on his part, at a fair speed. He knew that pushing his new recruits any faster wouldn't necessarily make them perform better. In fact, it might discombobulate them enough to send them into a tailspin. He wouldn't do anything that would hamper their ability to do what was asked of them: act like the wild animals they sometimes were, at different times and in different ways than they ever had before.

Good thing they were given clear instructions along with the elixir that allowed them to change better.

Instructions largely from Selena Jennay.

Whom Owen looked forward to seeing again tonight. Partying with…for the last time.

While back in her room a short while later, Selena decided to drive herself to the Yukon Bar that evening. She suspected she wouldn't want to stay as long as the rest of the Alpha Force members. And fortunately, Jonas had rented a second car for the convenience of the Alpha Force members, setting things up so that any of them could drive it when necessary. She called him to make sure her using it that night was okay. It was.

"Is that okay with you, too?" she asked Lupe. Her cover dog wagged her tail as Selena patted her head. She'd feed Lupe now, in any case.

Selena decided to wear one of the few dresses she had brought along on this trip. She'd needed them as part of her cover on her last assignment before she had been told to head to Canada. She hadn't really anticipated having to get dressed up while instructing the CAs about what they needed to know as flexible shifters. Nor had she figured she would wear the camos she wore while on duty at the Alpha Force headquarters at Ft. Lukman on Maryland's Eastern Shore. Instead, she'd spent the past few days in casual civilian clothing. Getting dressed up tonight would be a bit of a treat. She selected her black, knee-length dress that had a silky gray jacket that would fight off the after-darkness chill. It was one of her favorite outfits.

She put it on, then quickly checked her hair and makeup. She wanted to look okay, but the idea was just to be one of the partying gang tonight. She had no intention of trying to look especially good for this group. Not even for Owen. Especially not for Owen. Even if she felt some attraction toward the man, she certainly didn't want to appear as if she was coming on to him. That would be unacceptable in so many ways.

A short while later, she exited her room with Lupe and met up with the rest of the Alpha Force members, who were congregating in the kitchen.

"Ready to go?" Patrick asked.

"Sure." But Selena let him and the others know she didn't expect to stay long so she was going on her own.

She shut Lupe in the kitchen, then invited Rainey to ride with her into town.

"You look good," her aide said as she slipped into the passenger seat. "You planning on having some extra fun tonight with Owen?"

Good thing Selena was already driving. Otherwise, she might have slunk beneath the seat. As it was, she felt her face redden. "No," she said. "I'm not."

"Well, in case you change your mind, it's fine. You know I'll always take care of Lupe if you happen not to be around. I'll cover for you, too. Say that you wanted a night somewhere nearby on your own before things get more intense tomorrow, whatever."

The car had reached the bottom of the driveway. Selena considered confronting her sassy, sweet aide and telling her that her duties didn't include such impossible silliness—and that she was being awfully presumptuous about Selena's supposed interest in the RCMP leader.

Instead, she realized she appreciated Rainey's promise to go the extra mile for her, even when it was unnecessary.

"That's very nice of you," she said, turning to look at Rainey before heading onto the road. She hadn't paid particular attention to what Rainey was wearing before, but now she noticed that her aide had put on a nice dress, too. Her dark hair seemed even curlier than usual, and she wore more makeup. "But are you the one who has other plans for the evening?"

"Not at all. But I'm like you. I wanted to make some men in our group notice that female Alpha Force members are a force to be reckoned with on their own, too."

Selena laughed. "You'll do a great job with that," she said.

"So will you," said Rainey. "And if you happen to change your mind, you won't even need to tell me about it. I've seen the way Owen looks at you. And your looks back at him? Well, like I said, you don't need to tell me if you change your mind."

Selena found a parking spot about a block from the bar. She and Rainey strode quickly along the barely occupied sidewalks, and Selena was glad to notice the CAs arriving at the door at the same time from the other direction. She didn't see Owen with them, though.

"Hi, you two," Sal said, a huge smile on his face. "I'm ready to party. How about you?"

"Fine with me," Rainey said, pulling ahead of Selena and latching on to Sal's arm.

The other two male CAs waited politely for Selena to enter with Andrea in front of them. The moment she stepped inside, Selena saw that three tables had been pushed together in the center of the room once more.

She didn't see Owen there, either. But someone familiar sat on one of the tall stools—Holly. She must have come early to claim their spot.

One of the servers Selena had also seen here before stood right beside Holly. He was a tall guy in a plaid shirt and dark pants like all of them, but with long, light hair that didn't quite conceal his large ears. Holly was looking straight up into his face wearing what appeared to Selena to be a sincere yet flirtatious expression, and neither appeared to notice that the CAs had entered the room.

They didn't seem to notice anything else around them in the bar's dim light, for that matter.

Selena felt, as well as saw, Craig move quickly from behind the group and practically fly around the other crowded tables until he, too, stood beside Holly.

Wondering whether there was going to be some kind of unwelcome confrontation, Selena glanced toward Rainey, and they both turned and hurried to join Craig with the others.

"Hi, Holly." Craig's tone was calm, but he butted up against her side, put his arm around her and regarded the server belligerently. Selena could almost feel his feral wolf nature.

"Oh, Craig, I'm so glad you're here," Holly said, almost gushing. "Boyd and I were just talking about how much fun it is to sightsee around here, especially if you like hiking. There are some trails with spectacular views, and I'd love to visit them with you. We could hire Boyd as a guide, you know." She angled her head now to share a quick kiss with Craig.

Selena hadn't only been watching Craig's reaction. She had wondered how the server—Boyd—would react to having the woman he seemed to have been flirting with do a complete reversal now that her boyfriend had appeared.

At first, Boyd's light brows had risen as if in complete bewilderment about what was happening. But was that real?

Apparently not. Those brows lowered, and his expression became friendly, like a server who wanted a substantial tip. "Right," Boyd responded. "Holly and I have talked about this before. I could show her, and the rest of you, a whole lot of fun things about West Columbia. I know you've got a group visiting here. How long will you be in town?"

Instead of Craig, it was Patrick who answered.

"Unsure so far," he said. He and the rest of the Alpha Force members had just walked in and joined this group, making Selena feel relieved. Her CO was in charge once more, as it should be. "But we'll keep your offer in mind. Now, I'd really like a bottle of that locally brewed Canadian red ale I tried the other night." He looked straight at the server, who nodded.

"I'd like to try it, too," Selena added, and she was glad to see Boyd remove a pad of paper from the pocket in his leather belt and start making notes.

"Gin and tonic," said Craig, sitting down on the stool beside Holly. "Lots of gin. And I'd like it fast." The look he directed toward Boyd was clearly designed to put the server back in his place.

"Right away," Boyd said. "As soon as I get everyone else's orders." His expression was a touch less friendly than before, but Selena felt fairly comfortable that the confrontation had ended.

"Hi, sorry I'm a little late," said a deep and very welcome voice from beside Selena. "I had to respond to a couple of phone calls."

Fortunately, the stool beside Selena had remained empty. Or maybe the others knew where Owen would want to sit. In any event, he slid onto the stool and leaned forward on the table. "I'd like whatever she's having," he told Boyd.

"Let the party begin," responded Selena.

Chapter 12

Owen wasn't happy that he'd missed the earlier interplay between Craig and the server. It was now being whispered about around the table. He heard the comments, despite the noise in the bar and the fact that his hearing was the ordinary sort that mortals had, unlike some of those around him.

He listened closely. He needed to know and understand all the interactions between those in his command and anyone else they spoke with around here, both to understand who they were and for the security of their operation.

He considered ordering Craig to send his girlfriend back home, or at least away from West Columbia, but that wouldn't improve his relationship with Craig or even the other CAs.

Sal might even start to worry that Owen was about

to order Yvanne out of here. The young CA might still follow rules, but he would undoubtedly feel resentful. Or at least that was the impression Owen now had of the eager yet somewhat moody kid. And that might affect his ability to do his job.

Plus, after this encounter, such a move might wind up making the townsfolk—especially this server—wonder who they actually were if no one around here could interact with them except on a business basis.

As Owen shifted on his stool beside Selena and began nursing his beer, he stayed quiet, watching, listening, thinking—and wondering how things would go tomorrow, when they got down to serious business.

Shapeshifting business. Shapeshifting business that would ultimately help achieve highly important RCMP goals.

Shapeshifting as part of the RCMP. If he'd even considered such a possibility as recently as a few months ago, he'd have thought he was going nuts.

Maybe he actually was—especially since one of those shifters in particular fascinated him, despite all his good sense telling him to back far off.

As he sat there, Yvanne joined them, taking a seat near her brother.

"How did you happen to book rooms in the hotel where we're staying here in West Columbia?" That was Holly talking to Craig, apparently on a subject other than her flirtation or what else might have been going on around here. "It's such a nice place for this town. I mean, there are other good places, but I especially like ours."

Eavesdropping could be interesting, Owen thought. Was this an attempt at seduction, to get the guy with whom she might still need to make peace leave the party with her and go screw in the nice hotel room she shared with Yvanne?

Maybe. Owen didn't look toward her to see whether her expression said even more than her words.

But beside him, Selena made a noise that sounded half like laughter and half like disgust. Owen turned to see her shaking her head.

Why did that reaction, so similar to what he felt, too, make her seem so sexy?

Or at this point, maybe everything about her seemed sexy to him. He took another sip of his beer, then turned to her.

"How about you? Do you like your quarters here?" he asked her, loudly enough for others to hear.

"They're quite nice," she said. "I'm sure that anyone who moves in there will like them a lot."

Good girl. She was saying something that the CAs would understand—that they soon would move into the residential part of their headquarters, once they'd learned all they needed to from the Alpha Force members. But she said it in a way that anyone listening in would not understand.

"And you?" she continued. "I understand you're staying here in town all by yourself, in a different hotel. Guess you're not as friendly a tourist as you seem." Her amber eyes captured his as if in challenge. One he enjoyed.

"Friendly? Me? Heck, yes. But that doesn't mean I don't want my own space, too."

Space he wouldn't mind sharing with her, under other circumstances. The way her skirt barely seemed to cover her thighs despite the prim way she sat with her legs together on that bar stool underscored his in-appropriate interest in her. He couldn't help but notice that she even wore dressy heels instead of the athletic shoes or military boots she'd worn around him before.

Sexy.

All the more reason for him to have space of his own, where he could retreat not only from those under his command, but also away from Selena.

Not now, though. He let his eyes alight on her as he continued to nurse his beer and glance around the crowded bar, listening to both the Alpha Force members and CAs around him make small talk, as they were supposed to: tourist stuff and how good their beers and other drinks were and why they preferred the Yukon Bar over the town's other drinking establishments.

Every once in a while he joined in the conversation, offering a platitude or general comment that meant nothing but added to their pretense.

He actually enjoyed it, and it appeared that the others did, too. Even Craig and Holly seemed to settle down and return to the same kind of flirting Owen had seen between them previously. That was a good thing.

So was his eye contact with Selena.

Lord, was she beautiful, especially now, all dressed up for the evening out. Her light brown hair was loose, framing her smooth and perfect face. She seemed to be teasing him without saying a word, shooting glances toward him with those intense amber eyes.

What was she really thinking?

Was she goading him nonverbally about the fact that his charges had now shifted during daylight, that they would do even more tomorrow and in the following days so they could accomplish their mission?

Or more likely, about the fact that she, too, was a shifter?

"Everything okay with you?" she finally asked him in a low voice. "You look like you're thinking a lot."

"In other words, I'm not entering into the conversations?"

"Exactly." She smiled. "Care to talk about the weather? Or what's on TV tonight?"

"Not really. How about you? Care to talk about how much you're enjoying visiting Canada?"

"Absolutely!" She seemed to beam and in fact did start describing things she liked about this country—its coolness, the friendliness of its citizens, the remoteness and beauty of some of its towns and countryside.

She stopped after a while. "Your eyes are glazing over."

"I'm enjoying what you're saying, but I'm actually quite tired. And as we've all said, tomorrow's going to be a big day."

Her expression grew sober. "Yes," she said. "It is."

"In fact, as much as I'm enjoying myself, I think I will become a party pooper and head back to my hotel." He stood, hoping his departure would in fact inspire the others to take their leave. "Good night, everyone. See you all bright and early tomorrow."

"Good night, Owen," Selena said as he started to walk away. "Sleep well."

Selena meant it. She hoped Owen would sleep well that night.

She doubted she would.

Yes, the first really major step of teaching the CAs what they needed to know had been accomplished that day. But what would evolve over the next days would be even more important to their assignment.

Her training plans would potentially keep her awake.

So would her darned attraction to Owen. She'd already been wondering what he really thought of her. Apparently he found shifters intriguing on some level—most likely only professionally, not personally.

That was okay. Or it should be. But in actuality…?

No matter. The fact that her most private human areas warmed and ached when he was around was irrelevant.

But she was curious about him on that personal level. Heck, she even just wanted to know where he was staying, what kind of place he had chosen to remain far from his own subordinates as well as the Alpha Force members.

She'd had enough to drink. She'd had enough talking and bantering and pretending to enjoy the party that would be this group's last—at least the last any Alpha Force members would attend.

It was time to leave.

It was only minutes after Owen had left. She had an idea. A dumb one, yes, but it would help to satisfy her curiosity.

It would potentially even help her sleep that night.

She stood, raised her hands into the air as she stretched and looked around at her coworkers. "Hey, everyone. I'm tired. And like Owen said, there's a lot we're going to do and see tomorrow. I'm going to leave, too. Anyone care to join me?"

She glanced at Rainey. Her aide had been busy chatting with Tim and Sal and Yvanne. Rainey looked at her and gave a small, catlike smile as if she assumed

Selena had things on her mind besides heading to the compound to sleep.

Which she did, but not the one Rainey probably thought: seducing Owen. Although the idea did hold a lot of appeal...

But no. What she really wanted was to learn where Owen was staying. And then she would return to her room—and to Lupe—and go to sleep.

"Okay," she said. "I don't see any takers. I'll see you all tomorrow morning." Then she left.

The sidewalk outside was dimly lit, but she nevertheless saw Owen walking briskly about a block away, in the opposite direction from where the CAs' hotel was.

This was dumb, she thought. But he hadn't told her where he was staying, and she wanted to know.

Carefully, staying in the shadows, she followed him. She needed to keep him within her vision, yet not allow him to see her.

There were at least a couple of small hotels down this street, plus a bed-and-breakfast or two. She'd just watch to see where he turned to go inside and then she'd come back here for her car. An easy plan. What could go wrong?

Owen liked the briskness of the air as he strolled toward the WestColum Hotel, a small, independent place that was a little more elite than the chain hotel where his subordinates were staying. Fortunately, it wasn't much more expensive, and he was paying the difference in price to avoid any issues later.

He was about a block away when he felt someone following him.

He wished, for that moment only, that he had some

of those enhanced senses that shapeshifters supposedly had—hearing, for one. He believed he heard footsteps occasionally, but when he stopped, so did they.

He considered turning and looking around but felt foolish. And if he was actually right, that would tell whoever was following him that he knew.

No, he waited and walked…until he reached the outside of his hotel. Then he opened the door to the lobby and slipped inside.

And hurried around to leave through a side door.

Outside again, he waited in shadows.

Sure enough, someone had been following him. Selena.

She stopped on the sidewalk and folded her arms in front of her lovely, curvaceous chest, apparently taking in the exterior of the lobby's building.

Then she pivoted and started to walk away.

That was when Owen made his move. He jumped out at her and pulled her toward the building, into the shadows.

"Okay, Owen, enough," she said immediately. "Did you think I didn't hear or smell you there? Why did you come back outside so fast?"

"Because I knew you were there and I wanted to catch you."

"Why?" she demanded.

"This is why," he replied, and then he pulled her tightly into his arms, lowered his mouth and kissed her.

This wasn't why she had been following him—was it?

Selena could no longer think. All of her consciousness, her being, was drawn into the feel of Owen's hard, hot body against her, his lips moving against hers, tasting and teasing her to open her mouth by pushing gently with his tongue.

She could do nothing but obey.

After a minute that seemed like an eternity, though, she realized that very sexy mouth of his was speaking against hers. "Come inside," he said. "We have no privacy here."

Another bad idea, she knew, yet what could she do but follow him inside? Running off held no appeal.

Owen held all the appeal around here.

When he pulled away, she felt bereft but held his hand tightly when he grasped hers. He used a key card to open the door.

He led her through the lobby and into the elevator. As soon as the door closed, she found herself in his arms, his mouth on hers, involved in a kiss that was like no others she had ever experienced.

A short kiss, though. The door opened again on the second floor.

The hallway was bright and not particularly long. Owen took her hand once more and led her past only a few doors. He used a card again to open the door to room 211. She glimpsed that number for only a second before she was inside the room, the door closed behind her.

The dim light of the tiny entry area was the only light in the room. In it she could see the king-size bed, the typical TV facing it, a desk against the wall…

But it was the bed that garnered her attention. Some of her attention, at least. The rest was focused on Owen, who suddenly pulled her into his arms once more.

"Selena," he whispered against her lips. But that was

all he said as his hands began stroking her back. The dress she wore had seemed attractive enough and not especially obtrusive before. Now she wondered how fast it could be removed.

But Owen didn't try. Not yet. Instead, he bent enough to touch the backs of her bare legs, the feeling of flesh on flesh making her moan with desire.

Oh, this was a bad idea. They were professional colleagues, both with official missions to accomplish.

But, oh, it was a wonderful idea. She wanted more. She wanted Owen.

She felt his fingers trail up her legs, over her derriere, up her back. Was he looking for a zipper? She almost smiled against his mouth. He'd have to back away at least a little to get the dress off. It buttoned up the front.

Meantime, she could start undressing him. But first she wanted to tease him a little. Only a very little since she was already starting to become impatient.

She pressed herself against him, feeling his hardness at stomach level. She wriggled just a bit to get his attention.

"Selena," he said again, this time louder, in a more ragged voice.

"Yes, Owen," she managed to say, moving her hand around to latch on to his buttocks, squeeze them and pull him even closer.

Oh, heavens, she wanted him. And this was taking much too long.

She refused to think any more about how bad an idea sex was with a professional colleague—and a nonshifter. Despite how his arms enfolded her, she stepped back and looked at him as much as she could beneath the dim light.

His gaze was hot. So hot. Those blue eyes of his were molten, his mouth swollen and enticing, his breathing fast.

Selena quickly began doing what she wanted, what she needed. She reached toward him and began unfastening the buttons of his shirt—from the bottom up. That allowed her hands to drop just a bit and press against the hardness beneath his dark slacks.

The feeling, even in her fingertips, made her moan, and she hurried to undress him with trembling hands.

Owen began undoing her buttons as well. His hands on her—first skimming over her breasts, then taking hold of them—left her gasping, and she tried to hurry even more.

Somehow, in mere seconds that somehow felt like days later, Selena realized she was nude—and Owen was close. His shirt and pants were on the floor, but he still wore his shorts. They extended out in front of him enticingly, and she wanted to see, not just feel, the erection they hid.

She moved toward him just as he, too, reached for the last item he wore, and suddenly he was naked.

And gorgeous. Selena had visualized in her mind how he would look, all muscles and sinew, plus a male member that was large and erect and altogether alluring.

"Come here," he whispered, even as he began to touch her most sensitive sensual areas and lead her onto the bed.

She lay down facing him, touching him, squeezing him and pumping gently for her own benefit. He clearly needed no further arousal.

His head bent, and she felt him licking, then sucking at her bared breasts. "Owen." Her voice was husky and

needy—and then he pulled away. "Owen," she repeated—
and then realized he was moving not completely away
from the bed but reaching down to the floor, where he
pulled his wallet from his slacks.

He pulled a condom from inside the wallet. Oh, this
man wasn't merely sexy. He was responsible.

And she wanted him. Now.

"Let me," she whispered to him. She felt the heat
and shakiness of his fingers as, smiling as he returned
to face her upon the bed, he handed the condom to her.

She needed no help at all unwrapping it and placing
it over his swollen, sexy, captivating member. As she
finished, she didn't need to tell him he was ready. He
gently laid her back, pulled her legs apart, touched and
stroked her there again as if to ensure her moistness,
and then he entered her in one slow, enticing motion.

"Selena," he said softly as he began pumping gently
at first. "Are you—"

She didn't let him finish, covering his mouth with
hers even as she again grabbed at his now-bare buttocks,
as if guiding and encouraging him despite his clearly
not needing any help.

She reveled in the feel of him inside her, breathing
harder with each increasing stroke.

Hearing a loud gasp from Owen, she gave a small
scream of her own and followed him over the edge.

Chapter 13

Owen didn't move for a long while. He wasn't sure he could. His energy had been expended in an amazing, earth-moving way.

His head was on a pillow now, and Selena's was pressed into his neck. Her entire naked body remained against his, and he timed his breathing to coincide with hers, fast at first and gradually slowing.

Could he speak? What could he—should he—say now?

And if he moved, would his erection stiffen once more? Even sated as he was, he still found Selena incredibly, enticingly sexy.

She seemed all human now. Did she ever! But he knew her senses were sharper than his. Was what they shared somehow different for her? He couldn't imagine how that might be—such amazing sex even stronger and more intense?

What he had felt had been incredible. Something he would never, ever forget. And would always want to experience again.

Yet would he?

At the moment, he glanced her way and wondered whether their bareness was uncomfortable to Selena, either because she might feel chilly as her body cooled after their fantastic exercise, or because she might feel uncomfortable with his heated gaze on her lovely, curvaceous and utterly sexy body. "Do you feel okay?" he managed to ask in a raspy voice. "I mean, would you like me to put the covers over us?"

She moved back from him just a little, making him feel a bit odd. "I'm fine, but if you're chilly, I have an idea about how to warm you up." Her voice was a bit hoarse, too, yet it managed to sound teasing.

Did she mean what he thought she did?

As her eyes moved from his, down his body, stopping at his now-relaxed erection, he began to grow stiff again. Really stiff. "I think you're succeeding already," he said.

She laughed, then reached for the body part that gave his feelings away. He drew in his breath as she began stroking it again.

"Hey, you're giving me some good ideas," he said, knowing his eyes were half-closed in ecstasy.

"Then why don't you act on them?" she said.

And he did.

This time, when their lovemaking had ended, Selena found herself unable to concentrate simply on the sensations she had experienced and reveled in.

She inhaled Owen's tangy, salty, all-human-male

scent once more. She listened to his deep breathing, thought about how delicious he had tasted as their mouths had met and as she had subsequently kissed other parts of his body.

Clearly, now that they'd stopped for a while and Owen did in fact cover them both with the blanket, she couldn't keep her mind from thinking, rehashing... and wondering.

What would come next? They still had to work together. She still had to help him get his recruits ready for a very important, very covert assignment.

He hadn't mentioned that tonight, but it was surely on his mind—or would soon be again.

So would her similarities to those people, her differences from him. She was a shapeshifter. He was not.

They had made love together, a mutual decision. But now what?

She could not think of this as a bad idea. Not now. Not ever. And yet, it had surely been a once-in-a-lifetime event.

Things were changing tomorrow with the CAs, growing more definite, more intense. She and the other Alpha Force members wouldn't have much longer to work with the CAs before they had to go and fulfill their assignment. And then Alpha Force's job here was done.

As her time with Owen would be done.

That meant she had better make the most of this situation right now, while she could.

Had he been sated? In case not, she shifted beneath the blanket so that she wasn't merely against him, absorbing his body heat. No, she reached for the sexiest part of his body once more.

"Mmm." He clearly was still awake, too. "That feels good."

"Want to feel even better?" Selena asked. She drew in her breath as his hands started moving over her body again, too.

"Sure," he said. "Do you?"

This time, after yet another bout of incredible love-making, Selena slept. She wasn't sure for how long, but she pulled herself awake.

What time was it?

She couldn't stay here all night. Even though Rainey had promised to take care of Lupe, Selena didn't want to face the other Alpha Force members as she walked in the house in the morning. They'd ask questions she wouldn't want to answer—unless they made correct assumptions, which could be even worse.

Carefully, hoping not to wake Owen, she slid away from him and out from under the covers.

"Selena? You okay?"

"Fine, but I didn't mean to wake you. I need to go back to headquarters. It'd be… Well, it wouldn't be a good thing for anyone to suspect we did what we did. Not while we need to work together."

He didn't say anything at first, but in the dim light she saw him rise, too.

Lord, but he was gorgeous, still nude, with his male member at rest.

She couldn't keep looking at him, though, or she would never want to leave.

"I guess you're right," he said. "I'll drive you back there."

"I left my car near the Yukon Bar," she said. "I can just walk there."

"Not at this hour. Like I said, I'll drive you."

She didn't argue. He had already proved he was a nice guy, a gentleman, as well as possibly the sexiest man on earth. Selena was glad she'd experienced what she had with him.

They both got dressed nearly wordlessly. Selena looked around in the hotel's hallway as they exited his room. No one was there to observe them.

In his car a few minutes later, Owen said to her, "I realize that what we did might not be fully acceptable to our respective employers so we'd best not talk about it—even though I've got an urge to shout about it."

"And we both know how compelling your urges can be," Selena said with a laugh. "No, you're right. That's what I've been thinking, too. But, Owen?"

"Yeah?"

"I really had a wonderful time tonight. I thank you for that experience. I'll never forget it."

"That sounds like you're saying 'Goodbye, it's been real, but it'll never happen again.'"

"I don't know how it could, given our respective positions and how we have to work together." Selena was saying what she had to, but it hurt. She wished she could promise, or even suggest, otherwise.

He pulled his car to the curb right behind her rental. When she reached for the door handle, he bent toward her and grabbed her arm, holding it gently. "Never say never, Selena," he said. "Maybe when this is all over and that kidnapping victim is rescued and the abductors incarcerated, we can get together to celebrate—without the burden of everyone and everything else getting in the way."

"*Maybe* is a good word," she said. "Thanks again,

Owen." She opened the door and flicked the key to un-lock the rental car so she could drive away at last.

It didn't take Selena long to return to headquar-ters. Although one small outdoor lamp was lit over the doorway—*Thanks, Rainey*, Selena thought—she saw no lights on inside either building, which was a good thing. Maybe everyone was asleep.

She opened and closed the car door as quietly as pos-sible, not wanting to awaken anyone.

As she had the previous night, she inhaled to see if she could identify any local wildlife that emerged after dark. The same kind of rodent scents were around. Avian, too.

And…was that a lingering human scent as well? Too bad she wasn't shifted to see if she could be certain about it with her enhanced senses and identify whose it might be. She didn't recognize it as one of the Alpha Force members, so it had to be one of the CAs. There was something else about it as well that bothered her a bit. A hint of sharpness to it?

She was probably just tired, maybe focusing on stuff that wasn't real, or wasn't important if it was real. She'd mention it to Patrick in the morning, though, just in case.

Quietly she entered the Alpha Force residence, hop-ing that Lupe wouldn't start barking like a watchdog. She was well trained, as were all the unit's cover dogs, but she was still a canine whose instincts included pro-tecting the people around her.

Selena detected no noise, fortunately—not until she pulled out a small flashlight from her purse for illumi-nation, walked past the living room and kitchen and headed toward her temporary living quarters. She heard scrabbling nails on the hardwood floor of her room and grinned.

Lupe was being a very good girl, but she had heard her human's arrival.

When Selena opened the door and knelt down, her arms were suddenly full of the fur of a combined wolf-husky, and her face was dampened with doggy kisses.

"Hi, girl," she whispered. "It's great to see you, too. Want to go out for a minute?" She quickly located Lupe's leash—where Rainey must have left it—looped over the doorknob to the hallway. She attached it to Lupe's collar and they headed back in the direction from which Selena had come.

Outside, Lupe stopped on the porch, her ears raised, her nose in the air as if she was doing what Selena had—but with a lot more skill, with her all-canine senses. She gave a small whine. Was she interested in chasing a mole or whatever other rodent happened to be around?

Or was it something else? Did she also sense that a human had been out here? Was that person still here? If so, there was no indication—no car or light or movement except for the light breeze in the air. And Lupe didn't seem particularly upset, even if she did smell something.

Could Owen have followed her here to ensure she got back all right? It was something he would do, yet he wouldn't have preceded her here—and the first time she perceived the scent was when she had first gotten out of her car. That couldn't have been him.

It was probably nothing. Selena was just overly emotional considering her job here—and the fact she'd just engaged in the most mind-blowing sex in her life.

"Let's go back inside and get to bed," she told Lupe, who had just squatted to relieve herself, and they headed inside.

Owen didn't have to show up for breakfast at the residences that would become his CAs' local headquarters, he thought early the next morning as he exited his hotel. It was entirely his choice.

As he got into his car he remembered that the last time he'd been inside the vehicle, he hadn't been alone. Selena had been with him.

As if he could have forgotten that or anything else about last night.

He pulled out of the parking lot, heading through the now-awakening town toward the CAs HQ. He knew there would still be plenty of fixings for breakfast there, including coffee. There was no place else he would rather eat.

He thought about the day ahead. Since their next exercise wasn't scheduled until late afternoon, he'd allowed his recruits to sleep in. Later on, there'd be an informal Q&A and a general rap session with the CAs about how it had been growing up as shifters and more. A lot of that had come out in their vetting before they'd been invited to become CAs, but Owen hadn't been fully involved in that process, so not everything might have been passed along.

Plus, to work together later without the kind of assistance and supervision they were being provided now by Alpha Force, they should have full awareness of each other's backgrounds.

This was his ostensible reason for showing up early.

His real reason? To be in Selena's presence again. Not that he would even hint about their delightful evening. He just wanted to see her as much as possible while he could.

He arrived and parked and knocked on the door. Rainey answered. "Come on in. Are you here for breakfast? It's cooking right now. Selena got it started early, even though she seemed tired. She said she didn't sleep well last night." The smirk she wore suggested she knew why Selena hadn't gotten a full night's sleep. Would Selena have told her aide about where she'd been, or was Rainey only guessing? Knowing Selena's attitude, as well as her sense of discretion, Owen figured it was the latter.

"Thanks." He followed Rainey down the hall toward the kitchen, but was disappointed not to see Selena there. Marshall stood at the stove, with Jonas beside him.

"She's talking with Patrick in the other room," Rainey said, as if hearing the question in his mind.

"Who? Selena?" He didn't want to acknowledge that he was looking for her. At Rainey's nod he asked, "Anything I can do to help in here?"

"Yeah. Sit down and stay out of the way and stop moping. She'll join us here in a few." Rainey pranced toward the stove and took her place at Marshall's side.

If he was that obvious, Owen thought, he'd better stay far, far away from Selena—especially today.

"It was probably nothing, but I wanted to tell you about that scent last night." Selena had asked Patrick to come into her bedroom to talk so their conversation could remain private. "Since I wasn't shifted, I couldn't tell much about it, but it did seem human."

They stood beside the closed door and Patrick leaned on it. Her CO, in addition to being a high-ranking member of Alpha Force, was a medical doctor, a nice guy and a happily married man. She had heard about how he had come to marry Mariah, who was a noted wild-life reporter. Mariah was off on her own research study now, so Patrick apparently didn't mind being away from home.

"Our circumstances will be different tonight," Patrick said with a worried frown. "We won't be able to repeat your late-night walk around the place. You were just walking Lupe then?"

"More or less. I didn't get to sleep immediately." She left it at that. He didn't need to know that she'd been up and about and elsewhere at the time she would otherwise have gotten to sleep. And—oh, yes—having the best sex of her life.

"Would you recognize that scent again?"

She shook her head slightly. "I'm not sure. It probably was nothing, but I know it's important that who we are and what we're doing here remains covert."

"Absolutely. Well, I'll let all the other Alpha Force members know what you've said and make sure they remain alert. Thanks for letting me know."

"Of course, sir." Even though Alpha Force was a fairly informal unit because of its special nature, she gave him a regular military salute. He laughed and saluted back. "Now, let's go have some breakfast," she said.

Selena preceded Patrick back down the hall to the

kitchen. She smelled the sausage and bacon that she had started cooking—good dishes for people with canine aspects to them that made them appreciate meats.

She entered the kitchen's doorway and stopped abruptly as she nearly walked straight into Owen.

Oh, she wouldn't mind feeling that hard body of his against her once more, even this soon. Especially this soon. But it couldn't happen again—and most particularly it couldn't happen when they weren't alone.

"Good morning," she said, taking a step back. "I didn't realize that any of the CAs would be joining us this early." Good. She sounded cool and professional and totally disinterested. She hoped.

"I woke up early." He looked down at her with only the slightest twist of his mouth that suggested a smile. "Lots on my mind. As far as the other CAs, I told them they might want to sleep in since things are going to get busy later today."

"Well, glad you could make it." That was Patrick, who remained behind Selena. "Maybe we can go over how we want to handle things later. I've got some ideas that could work well to ensure that your guys jump right into their shifts independently—and move things along even more quickly on their mission."

"Great!" Owen truly was smiling now. "The sooner we get them going, the sooner we'll catch these kidnappers and let you Alpha Force people return to your own post."

Selena was certain Owen's words were intended to make the members of Alpha Force feel good—Patrick, at least. And maybe the others.

Well, it should make her feel good, too. It would mean she had fulfilled her own duties here, in Canada.

She could go back to Ft. Lukman with her mind clear, ready to take on her next assignment back in the States.

But even so, as she moved past Owen to enter the kitchen, she wished that the mug of coffee she poured for herself had something stronger in it, despite the time of day.

Something that could help her forget her feelings and move on.

Chapter 14

They sat around the nice-sized dining table—the Alpha Force team, plus Owen, with Lupe on the floor.

Selena pretended to enjoy her well-made omelet with its meats and cheeses. It did, in fact, taste good. If she'd only been hungry, she would have liked it even more.

She gave occasional bites to Lupe, who was clearly happy about it.

As her team discussed the training with Owen, she just sat there at first, picking at her food and drinking her coffee, listening. And only glancing now and then toward Owen to show interest and politeness.

She purposely kept off her face any indication of what had occurred last night—and her misgivings about what would happen now between them, even though the answer was indisputable. Nothing.

But her emotions were in an uproar. That caused her

to think too much about her last relationship, such as it had been, in which her lover had told his son that shape-shifters weren't real and the whole idea was stupid.

Owen knew they were real, and he needed to use shifters in his position with the RCMP. But what did he actually think of them, deep inside?

Especially now.

Not that they actually had a relationship. Not now and not ever.

Only sex…of the mind-blowing kind.

"Have any of you ever conducted this kind of operation before?" Owen was asking. "I mean, shifting first and then going to surveil an area?"

"I think we all have," Patrick said. "Sometimes we do that as an exercise, essentially spying on humans we don't want to notice us. Sometimes it's special-ops troops who are advised there's a covert military exercise going on near them to see if they can spot anything out of the ordinary and report it to their commanders. Sometimes it's in a regular civilian situation like an office building or a shopping center. But our kind of recon only works well if there are nearby wilderness areas or urban parklands known for containing wildlife."

Owen nodded. "I really want to start talking now about the information I'll need once my CAs start our mission."

"Fine. Let's go over it."

For the next hour or so, as the group finished breakfast, mostly Patrick and Owen talked, with the rest of the group chiming in as they had thoughts or suggestions.

That included Selena. Even though she was the least experienced Alpha Force member, she utilized both her

educational and shifting backgrounds to try to anticipate the needs of the CAs.

"When I grew up in a remote location in Wisconsin," she said as they planned how CAs who had already
shifted would do recon at the highly suspected area,
"some friends and family members who were shifters
did something similar, long before I engaged in Alpha
Force tasks after joining about six months ago. We had
access to a forerunner of the current elixir, thanks to
Major Drew Connell and his family also coming from
the same area."

Trying not to be distracted by Owen's intense scru-
tiny of her as she spoke, she described how, for fun and
not for security or rescue of anyone, they had tested
their skills.

"We would start as far from the target of our exercise as possible while still being able to use our senses
that were enhanced by our shifts. In other words, we
stayed camouflaged in the woodlands or mountains
while listening and using our olfactory senses to smell
people or places or other animals."

She paused to take a sip of coffee, then continued,
"We learned all we could before moving in to check
things out further, assuming that was the goal of what
we were doing. If any of us thought the situation too
dangerous after that, or potentially so, had it been real,
we all backed off—but usually only for a while, until
the situation seemed to improve. Plus, we mostly spread
out, avoiding each other's company in the interest of
safety. Of course, what we were doing was just a game,
so safety wasn't a real issue, but we had fun pretending."

"That's essentially how we do it now in Alpha Force
maneuvers, too," Patrick agreed, "but safety is a genu-

ine and vital concern. For your mission, just make sure that Andrea, while shifted to a falcon, is primed to circle somewhat low, or perched in trees to keep an eye on each of your wolf shifters. If a problem arises with one, she can use some prearranged signal to let the others know about it."

"And if a problem happens with all of them?" Owen asked.

"She should have another prearranged signal—as well as a way via the camera and other electronic equipment she'll be wearing to inform you and the other non-shifters on your team."

"The same should be arranged with the other shifters in the event Andrea's in trouble," Selena added.

"Absolutely," agreed Patrick.

Selena stood and got herself more coffee from the pot that remained on the kitchen counter.

Despite how little sleep she had gotten last night, she was certain that the adrenaline in her system from what she had done, and what this combined group was about to do, would keep her awake.

While she stood there, she listened to the conversation. She had no input into this part anyway. It was mostly about logistics—how and when the CA members could best be transported to the area and the best time for them to shift. They didn't yet have any aides to help in their shifting using the elixir, but that was under discussion. For now, Rainey and Jonas volunteered to help out since the timing here was so critical.

The Alpha Force members also stressed the idea of getting cover animals as apparent pets to the CAs in the future—ones who looked like them while shifted. The idea had been mentioned before, but Patrick clearly wanted to impress Owen with how useful cover animals could be. "That helps keep your unit's real purpose covert," he said. "Anyone who's met your team members and their apparent pets will most likely assume they're seeing those pets should they run into one of those members while shifted."

When that part of the discussion ended, Owen asked, "Okay, once we've got our CAs in and they've checked out the critical area and reported, via their cameras, how do we get them out? I assume we won't want to wait until they shift back. In case they're seen, it's better for them to remain in animal form, right?"

"Absolutely," Patrick said. "Especially since there are believed to be wolves and falcons in the area in question, it'll be a perfect cover for them. Once again, it's imperative that planning be spot-on. Make sure there's a meeting point fairly distant from your target area. Wolves can run fast to return there, and it should be second nature for a falcon to zoom in on the destination."

"Great," Owen said.

Selena was about to return to her seat at the table as he stood and walked toward her. Their eyes met, and he gave a small but impersonal smile. "Is there any more coffee?" he asked.

Wordlessly, she reached out for the pot and filled his cup, and they walked together back to the table. Selena hated keeping things so distant, so she said, "I'm sure I'm speaking for everyone here in Alpha Force when I say we're all cheering for you and your CAs and wish you success."

"Hear, hear!" Patrick said, and the other Alpha Force members added their good wishes as well.

The timing couldn't have been better, since there

was a noise at the front entry and the rest of the CAs
came in.

"Good morning, everyone," said Andrea, the first
to enter.

"Is there any breakfast left?" asked Tim.

"Plenty," Rainey said. She rose and led the arriving
CAs into the kitchen.

"So what are the plans for this afternoon?" Selena
asked Owen. "What time will you have them shift on
their own?"

"Probably three or four o'clock. In between, I want
to meet with them here by myself, get the latest from
my commander and pass it along, as well as discuss
more RCMP protocol."

"That'll be fine," Patrick said. "In the meantime, we
Alpha Force members will head back to the residence
house and do some catch-up of our own."

After the CAs had joined him, Owen again emphasized how important their mission was. "If you're successful, I'm sure you'll have a fantastic career within the
RCMP despite the secret nature of your unusual skills."

And if they weren't successful? He wasn't about to
discuss that with them. There was no choice. They had
to do their jobs, and do them well enough to capture
the kidnappers and end their vicious operation forever,
as well as to free the current victim unharmed—or as
unharmed as possible.

They had to achieve the necessary result, but the
world could never know exactly how they'd accomplished it. Secrecy was key. And if it took acquiring
cover animals for each of the shifters, so be it.

Since he was in law enforcement, keeping things covert was simply part of his job.

"This is all so cool," Sal said as they discussed the logistics of how everything would be handled. Maybe being a shifter enhanced this young guy's appetite, since he had been nibbling on toast since the omelets had been finished.

Chunky Tim had not stopped eating, either. "You said that the two Alpha Force aides would continue working with us for now. I thought that once we learned everything about shifting with their elixir, we'd buy a good supply of it from Alpha Force, and the RCMP would be on its own. We'd get our own aides to help in our shifts." He paused. "Maybe even you could do it for now."

Owen had considered it. Maybe, in the future, if he remained the officer in charge of the CAs, he would learn all he needed to and act in the capacity of an aide—or at least be prepared to do so in an emergency. But there wasn't time for him to learn everything right now.

Although Selena was one good teacher. She wasn't an aide, but she would certainly know what the aides did.

He wouldn't mind having her as his tutor in that or in anything else.

But he pushed that thought from his mind. Even if it was appropriate to consider, the circumstances and urgency did not make it feasible for now—if ever.

Craig spoke up. "Are there people in the RCMP, besides you and Deputy Commissioner Creay, who even believe in shifters and would be willing to step in and help that way?"

"We'll work that out in the future," Owen said, side-stepping the question. He wasn't yet certain how every detail would be handled, only that they would be—and it would be considered a lot more important if the CAs were successful on this mission.

They simply had to be.

Perhaps, for now, he should attempt to get at least one more person to act as an aide to help in the CAs shift.

Maybe not. Maybe he was just using the idea as an excuse to keep Selena nearby as this mission was carried out.

As if he had called her, Selena suddenly appeared in the kitchen doorway. She looked amazingly sexy even in her plain T-shirt and jeans—but maybe that was because his mind removed them as she stood there.

She glanced toward him. Did her complexion redden a little as if she read his thoughts, or was that just wishful thinking on his part?

What she said didn't reveal her thoughts to him, either. "I know it's a little early," she said, "but Patrick sent me. He suggested that you shifters get started now so you have more time to get used to not only your physical change, but your mental one, before it's time to go outside and work on your preparations there."

"Are all of you ready?" Owen asked.

"Definitely," said Andrea, and she was the first to rise.

Once again, Andrea went into the meeting house's study to shift, and the male CAs headed for the basement.

This time, though, only the two aides went with them.

So, once more, Selena was in the dining room, this time with Patrick, Marshall and Owen, along with Lupe.

"I guess this is something pretty different for all of you," Owen said. He sat with a bottle of water in front of him on the table, as they all did.

"How so?" Marshall asked. He looked tall even sitting down, and his thick brown hair appeared a little unkempt, possibly belying his composed attitude.

"If shifts are going on near you, I assume you're involved most of the time, either changing or helping, right?"

"You could say that," Patrick agreed. "But I think we're all okay with doing what's appropriate for any situation. Right, guys?"

"Right," Selena agreed, as did the others. She aimed a glance that was slightly challenging toward Owen. "And you? How do you feel knowing there's a shift going on with your subordinates and you're not even invited to watch?"

"Surprisingly left out. But I look forward to seeing them all later. You, too?"

"Me, too," Selena concurred.

The conversation in the dining room was friendly after that, but no topic was found that engaged everyone.

That was fine with Selena. She didn't really want to talk. Instead she barely listened as the men around her talked sports—primarily football.

About half an hour later, she heard some activity in the hallway outside and saw a flash of dark feathers in the air.

Andrea's shift was complete.

The men near her rose.

"Shouldn't we wait for the wolf shifters?" Owen asked, although he stood, too.

"They should be here shortly," Patrick said. "Surprisingly, most shifts, no matter the species, tend to take around the same amount of time."

They stayed in the dining room, waiting. Within five minutes Selena heard the sound of muffled paw falls from the stairway to the basement.

There was another noise, too. The sound of gagging or retching. *Human* gagging or retching.

What was going on?

Two wolf-dogs entered the dining room and stood there, panting. They somehow looked confused.

Rainey and Jonas came into the room then, too, but they weren't alone. Sal was with them, unshifted. He retched again, although nothing came out.

Rainey's eyes were filled with tears. "Something's wrong with Sal."

Chapter 15

Owen paced the study at the back of the meeting house, telling himself that Alpha Force was experienced and knew what they should do for Sal.

But he couldn't stop worrying. His youngest recruit now lay on the pull-out sofa in that compact room moaning and sometimes gagging. Even though that house hadn't been designated as sleeping quarters, Owen had ensured that the rooms were furnished. This room contained a desk and, fortunately, a sofa that converted into a bed. The surface was covered with a sheet that Rainey had quickly retrieved from the other house. A wastebasket lined with a plastic bag sat on the floor nearby. Fortunately, though, Sal must have gotten everything inside him out already since he was no longer vomiting. But the youngster clearly felt lousy.

It didn't hurt that Patrick Worley happened to be a

medical doctor. For humans, yes, but since he was a shifter, too, he had to know about how to cure others like him who were ill.

Owen had assisted in getting Sal to the room, where Patrick had conducted an initial exam on him. "Pulse rate high but probably okay," Patrick had said. "I need to get my bag out of my car to conduct a more thorough exam, although I wish we had some better facilities for this. Will you stay here with him for now?"

Owen had agreed and he was now waiting for Patrick's return. He knew Patrick had arrived here with some large crates in the back of his rented SUV—and that they contained a large supply of the Alpha Force shifting elixir. That had been part of the agreement between the US military and the RCMP—provision of an ample initial supply of that special, secret elixir. Considering that Patrick was a physician, it didn't surprise Owen that he had also brought a medical bag.

"How is he?" Selena's voice startled Owen, whose attention had remained primarily on the ill shifter on the bed. He looked up and saw her in the doorway, the expression on her lovely face as grim as he felt, her hands clasped in front of her.

"Not good. Or at least I don't think so, although Patrick's initial check didn't seem to indicate his life was in danger." That was what Owen hoped, at least, and he wasn't about to say otherwise anyway in front of the clearly ill young man. "Do you know what might have happened to him? Have you seen any other shapeshifters react this way after an attempt to change?"

By using that elixir was what Owen meant, but chose

not to say. Then again, it wasn't as if Sal hadn't tried it before.

But from what Owen had understood, the dosage yesterday, meant for only an hour-long shift, had been fairly small. Today's dosage had been more significant since the group had intended to prowl the compound and the surrounding hills, getting used to their ability to achieve cognition while in animal form. This time they were supposed to stay shifted for several hours.

Had that damned elixir, in this higher amount, harmed Sal?

But then, if Sal reacted this way and no one else did, was it him or the elixir that was flawed?

Without knowing for certain, did Owen, as a responsible officer in charge, dare to allow this operation to continue? As far as he knew, the other three CAs had shifted and were out prowling and flying and doing what this exercise was supposed to accomplish.

But were they all okay?

Maybe he should take advantage of Selena's being here now to find out. "Could you stay here with Sal until Patrick returns?" he asked, walking toward where she stood at the door. "I want to go outside and check up on the other CAs."

"I've done that already," Selena said, her expression wry. "I assume you're wondering if the elixir harmed Sal. So do I, and just in case the others were at risk, I went outside with them for a few minutes just to observe. I don't know of any differences, genetic or otherwise, between US and Canadian shifters, but that doesn't mean there aren't any that might mean differences in reaction to the elixir. From what I saw, Tim and Craig were doing just fine as wolves prowling the hills, and the falcon who's Andrea was soaring overhead looking pretty pleased with herself."

"Does that mean only Sal's somehow at risk?"

"I don't know what it means, although I have my suspicions." Selena appeared grim as she looked down and shook her head, her light brown hair gleaming a bit in the artificial light overhead.

"So do I." Patrick's voice sounded from behind her. He entered the room, a large medical case in his hand. "I did a quick online check of our records about your CAs. Are you aware that Tim Franzer comes from a town here in British Columbia? It's Roadwich, and it's only about thirty miles from here. I'll check Sal over a bit more thoroughly now, and if he's okay to travel, I'll take him there. I did some further research on my smartphone and made a couple of calls to some very special sources. An urgent-care clinic in the area isn't only for regular humans. It's for local shifters, too."

"Are there many shifters who live in the area?" Selena asked.

"That's what I gather, and the medical team at that urgent-care clinic also includes shifters." Patrick maneuvered past both Selena and Owen, over to his patient.

Owen stood motionless beside Selena, watching as Patrick listened with his stethoscope to Sal's chest, looked down his throat with a light—causing Sal to gag again—and conducted some more tests.

In a few minutes, Patrick asked Sal, "How are you feeling now?"

"Don't know," he said in a lethargic voice.

"I hope you're well enough to take a ride," Patrick said. "We can get you better help in a little while."

"'Kay," Sal managed to reply, then shut his eyes again.

"Can you help me get him to my car?" Patrick asked Owen.

Owen nodded and approached them immediately.

"What can I do to help?" Selena asked.

"Go in front of us and open doors," Patrick said. "And while we're getting him into the car, tell Jonas what we're up to and that I'd like him to come along."

"Of course," Selena said.

Sal was like a deadweight, Owen thought as, together with Patrick, they nearly dragged him back through the house and out the front door.

As they got him into the car, Jonas joined them, as did Selena. She had a couple of vials in her hand. "Jonas said this was the one Sal drank from," she said, raising one of them. "If the clinic you go to has any way of analyzing contents, I think you should check it out. There's a slightly different color to what's left in the bottom of this one, and a different scent, too, that I can't identify. Maybe you can have someone compare its contents to the little bit left in this one." She lifted the other vial she held.

"You think—" Patrick began, then glanced into the car toward Sal. He took the vials from her. "I'll have these checked. Thanks, Selena."

Then Jonas and he got into the car, too, and drove off down the driveway.

Selena watched the car head down the hill. Then she closed her eyes for a moment, her arms limp at her sides.

Had someone tainted the elixir? If so, was it only one bottle?

Only? One was too many, especially if it harmed a shifter.

And it had apparently harmed Sal.

Or maybe not. Maybe there was nothing wrong with the tonic he had taken. Maybe he simply had some kind of allergy to the elixir taken in normal dosage.

She didn't know. None of them did…yet.

Hopefully Patrick would be able to find out.

"Are you okay?" Owen, beside her, took her arm gently at the elbow. She was suddenly very aware of his presence, his strength, his touch.

She wanted to lean on him, take some kind of support from him.

And yet…if the elixir was tainted, who had done it? Most likely not a shifter.

There weren't many nonshifters here. Two—their aides—were members of Alpha Force.

And then there was Owen.

No. She couldn't—didn't—suspect him of anything. He, more than anyone, was the person who truly wanted a good result here.

She mentally shook herself as she looked at him. "I'm fine," she finally replied to his question, knowing it wasn't true but saying it with enough conviction that she might even convince herself. Or not.

"You don't sound like you are." He paused. "Do you want to stay outside for a while and try to see what's going on?"

"Yes." This time she was actually serious. She wasn't sure if they'd have an opportunity to check out the two shifted wolves or the falcon. But at least that gave Selena a purpose for the moment.

"Do you know where they are?" Owen regarded her

with a half smile, as if he was challenging her to use her wolfen senses. Maybe she was just reading that into it, but just in case she smiled back.

She closed her eyes for an instant, listening, inhaling, attempting to discern anything with her enhanced senses that would pinpoint the location of either Tim or Craig.

There! She heard a distant bark of excitement, somewhere within the surrounding woods but up higher in the hills and off to her left. "That way," she said. "Want to go look for them?"

"Definitely."

Fortunately, it was early enough in the afternoon that daylight wouldn't start waning for another hour or longer. Selena led Owen toward a narrow path that rose along the mountainside. The aroma from the surrounding fir trees, and the needles on the ground, sweetened the air around them.

Aroma. Selena hadn't thought about it before, but now she recalled all too clearly the smells she had sensed the other evening. Smells that suggested the possibility of other people up here around the enclave.

But even if someone had come up here, surely they couldn't be the source of any tainting of the elixir. No one in this area knew the nature of the group staying or meeting here. Even if they did, they'd have no idea about the elixir or where it was or how to modify it.

Surely the two outside women, Sal's sister and Craig's girlfriend, didn't know enough to do this, either—and they, of all people, wouldn't want to harm the shifters even if they'd been told too much.

The idea bothered Selena a lot, though. She would mull it over in her own mind, perhaps revealing her concern to Patrick depending on what, if anything, was found about the possibly tainted vial of the elixir he had taken with him.

Their trek, though largely uphill, wasn't a problem for Selena. As far as she could tell, Owen's endurance was fine, too. No wonder. He seemed in really good condition. Plus, she knew how muscular he was…all over.

The recollection made her tingle below the waist, despite where she was and what she was doing here. It also made her wonder if she could manage somehow to experience that pleasure yet again. If so, it would have to be soon, since, whatever happened, this combined group would break up within the next few days and possibly never get together again.

She hoped that Sal was okay, no matter what had caused his bad reaction to the elixir.

And that the CAs were completely successful in their assignment.

"You still okay, Selena?" Owen's voice was strong despite the slight shortness of breath it evinced.

"I'm fine. And you?"

"Doing well. So where are those wolves?"

"They should be—" She didn't finish. Her sense of smell informed her even before her sight and hearing that the two shifted wolves were nearby, in front of them on the path.

In just a few moments they were confronted by two wolf shapes bounding down the path toward them.

She sensed Owen stiffening beside her and was glad that, for this assignment, he didn't seem to be carrying a firearm, although she figured that might be standard procedure for RCMP members. Then again, the

Canadian police were far different from the US police forces. Surely, though, they needed ways of protecting themselves.

Both wolves stopped right in front of them. They were the same canines who had left the local compound— Tim, who appeared part Akita, and Craig, with what looked like a hint of malamute in him.

"Hi, guys," Selena said softly. "Just so you know, Patrick and Jonas have taken Sal to some urgent-care facility in Roadwich—your hometown, I understand, Tim."

The wolf bent his head in an apparent nod.

"Patrick examined him first and seemed to think he should be okay, but thought that he needed better facilities under the circumstances to be sure."

A whine issued from one of them—Craig, Selena ascertained. "Anyway, you two go ahead with your maneuvers. I know you're supposed to be surveilling an area as if it was your upcoming target, where you'll be heading soon if all goes well tonight. We'll have to see if Sal is well enough to go with you, but we all hope so."

"That's for certain," Owen added. "Anything you two need?" His tone sounded somewhat tentative, as if he wasn't quite certain how to handle a conversation with shapeshifters.

Selena smiled. "I gather they're fine," she told Owen, "but it's good that you asked. Right, guys?"

This time both wolfen heads bowed in nods.

A sound like "cack" sounded overhead, and Selena looked up. A falcon was circling them.

She waved. "Looks like the three of you CAs have things under control. I think we can head back to the compound and wait for you, but have fun with the rest of your maneuvers."

Both wolves turned and loped back in the direction from which they'd come.

Selena turned toward Owen. "Are you ready to go back?"

"I am," he said, but instead of turning back he gently grabbed both of her arms. His blue eyes seemed to bore into hers. "I can't tell you how amazed I am this time, Selena. With each new good experience with shifters... Well, it's nothing I ever thought could be real."

"Fortunately, that's true of most humans," she said. "Otherwise my species might be in danger of extinction."

"Not if I could help it," he said. And then his mouth came down on hers.

The kiss was brief but, oh, so intense. Selena threw herself into it, tasting him, thrusting her tongue into his open mouth and taunting his with it.

His body was once again hard against hers. Very hard, in the most vital of locations, which made her gasp and give herself even more to the kiss...and into his arms.

She didn't want to pull away, and yet this wasn't an ideal place for kissing...or anything else.

She pulled away after planting one final kiss on his hot mouth.

"I don't suppose you'd want me to come back to your hotel again tonight...to discuss shifter logistics that might work for the CAs' assignment, would you?" Her voice was soft and uneven. Who did she think she was kidding? Hold a discussion? No way.

And yet the distraction after what had happened with Sal might be exactly what she needed.

So would hot, powerful sex with Owen one final time.

"Sure," he said in a deep, raspy tone. "I think that's one hell of a fine idea."

Chapter 16

As it turned out, though, Selena did not go back to Owen's hotel, nor did he. Instead she tackled the development of ideas to assist the CAs, and that required her immediate focus. She wanted to be too busy to think hard about what had been and what could be.

It was better that way.

She now sat on the living room sofa in the meeting house, with Lupe lying on the floor beside her. Owen faced her on one of the upholstered chairs. No one had talked much, but her mind was preoccupied with worry about Sal and his recovery, plus the shifted CAs. At least it kept her mind from drifting to other things.

Outside in the hills, the plan was that Marshall—who was substituting now for Jonas—and Rainey were to remain at a clearing in the woods. If the CAs had any difficulties, they would go there for help. Once their practice mission ended, likely several hours from now, they would go to that area for any assistance they needed changing back again.

"How much do you actually know about the location the shifted CAs are supposed to observe when they're sent on their actual recon mission?" Selena asked Owen, attempting to treat him like just another coworker instead of a gorgeous, sexy man she'd made fantastic love with…and wanted to again.

"Not a lot." His black brows dipped pensively over his distantly focused blue eyes. "We've gone over the known topography of the area as much as possible with some of the nearest local Mounties, without revealing why we needed the information."

"And?"

"I described as much as I knew to my CAs before they shifted earlier so they could work on the situation to the greatest extent possible today."

"That's what I figured," Selena acknowledged.

With their minds entirely human, despite the shifted configurations of their bodies, the CAs were to head to a target area. Once there, they were to circle that location, to act as if it was occupied by the enemy, without knowing the terrain or how that occupation was accomplished— whether in aboveground facilities or underground or a combination of both.

Since the true nature of their kidnappers' compound was unknown, they needed to act as if any situation was possible so they could report back and discuss how they would act in any scenario.

"The thing is, though," Selena said, scrolling through her smartphone, "I want to do some research now, as best I can. Then, when they report on how things went for them today, maybe what I find can help them when they're actually out there performing their mission."

"I just told you I've already conducted research, even talked to people who know the area." Owen scowled at her, probably thinking she had insulted him for not doing his job adequately.

That definitely had not been her intention.

"Of course," she said, "and I've no doubt you did a good job with it. But the one thing you couldn't have factored in, at least not completely, is how someone who is in falcon or wolf form would view the area."

"That's what Andrea, Craig and Tim are supposed to describe when they return. And, of course, Sal was going to as well." He had sat back on the chair, trying to pretend as if he was relaxed, but Selena read something different in his eyes.

Maybe that was a good thing. It certainly kept them apart, both mentally and physically.

"Yes, and I'm sure the three working there today will do a good job rehearsing it," she said. "But remember this is their first outing after using the elixir and on their own. I'm not with them, of course, but having done similar kinds of operations after the same kind of shift, I might have a different perspective that could help them when they're out there for real later."

This time, Owen did seem to genuinely relax, at least a bit. "Care to explain?"

"Not yet. But I will."

Selena knew the area in question was near the border of British Columbia and the Yukon. Satellite sensors and drones had picked up more activity than usual around there lately—particularly after attempts to locate the kidnapped executives and others had begun.

Owen had also reported that there had been trouble with the electronics in the area.

Was it certain they'd been taken there? Not at all. But the location had to be ruled out...or a determination made that it should be the focus of the next rescue maneuvers.

That was what Selena had started looking for, via the internet on her smartphone. She might be duplicating the efforts of Owen or others in the RCMP, but it wouldn't hurt. Even using her fingers to enlarge the aerial views she found, though, didn't provide her with enough information to feel she was doing the best job possible.

She was determined to pursue it. Learning about the target area wasn't her job. Instructing the CAs about their shifts was. But now she had time to fill, and she also realized she might bring a different perspective to the research than the others, as both a teacher and a shifter.

"My laptop is in the other house," she told Owen. "I want to use it for a while to look further into that area. Not that you haven't done a good job, but I think the more information retrieved in various ways, the better for the mission. Okay?"

She intended to do it with or without his approval, but for the sake of maintaining some amity between them she at least asked. If he said no, she'd find another way, perhaps without letting him know.

"Good idea," he said.

"Fine." She rose, and so did Lupe. "We can talk again later. Let me know when the CAs return, and most particularly if Patrick and Jonas return with Sal, okay?"

"Of course."

Snapping Lupe's leash on, Selena headed for the door. Owen didn't follow. She felt somewhat bereft even while telling herself that her leaving now, while they were otherwise alone together, was the best thing for both of them.

Plus, she actually did want to conduct the research she'd described. She exited the meeting house, walked Lupe for a few minutes, then headed toward the residence where she was staying.

She unlocked the door and went inside. For the past few days, the house had been occupied by a number of her Alpha Force teammates. At the moment, being in this building by herself felt unnatural, but she shrugged it off.

Her concern over what had happened to Sal probably overrode her common sense. Everything here was fine, she told herself.

She headed down the hall to her room, Lupe at her heels. She got her laptop out of her suitcase and set it down on her bed, where she sat and booted it up. Fortunately, possibly in anticipation of staying in touch with the outside world as the CAs operations were going on, they had Wi-Fi available, so Selena could start her online search.

From what she gathered, looking at the border areas between British Columbia and the Yukon, a lot of the territory consisted of stark mountain ranges, with sharp peaks that were often covered by snow and ice. But some locations appeared more temperate, and she assumed they were the ones considered most likely for the kidnappers to be using.

Did Owen have a better idea which areas were key?

Most likely, considering the kind of research he had been doing.

Selena hadn't looked up the areas before, at least not past double-checking whether there were wolves and falcons in that area of British Columbia. Fortunately, there were, so the CAs should be able to act undercover, no matter what.

Still, for them to actually be of assistance if the kidnappers had taken their victim to the suspected area, Selena hoped that the vast expanse had been somewhat narrowed down and further researched. She needed that information from Owen.

Or maybe she didn't. Maybe she had just decided to do this research to get away from him, at least temporarily.

For when she was with him, what she wanted was to really *be* with him. Flesh against flesh.

Lupe suddenly stood and gave a deep woof.

"What is it, girl?" Selena stood, too, leaving her computer on the bed.

When she turned, Owen was there. "Sorry if I startled you," he said, "but I thought we should work together on this. I can tell you what I've come up with for where the shifted CAs should go once they learn what to do. And maybe you can advise me what to tell them even now to enhance their skills in using their new abilities."

"Sounds good—especially since despite all I've heard so far, I wasn't sure where to look for the target locale, let alone zero in on the particular area."

"Great. Working together makes the most sense, then." But when Selena looked into Owen's face, working together didn't seem to be what he was thinking about. Doing other things together was. His gaze was sensuous, and so was the set of his mouth.

She didn't even think about resisting. In moments, Selena was in his arms.

When their mouths met, the whole idea of conducting research on her own to avoid him flew from her mind, even as her hands went behind him and grasped his buttocks to pull him even closer.

His hardness against her was irresistible. "Owen," she whispered against his mouth.

"Good thing we're in your bedroom," he said hoarsely. "Or was this why you came in here?"

Despite herself, she laughed a little without pulling back very far. "Believe me, I came in here to avoid this."

"Nope, I don't believe you." He softened his words by deepening the kiss.

Selena moaned against him, even as her most sensitive body parts warmed and tingled in anticipation. Then she closed her laptop and set it on the floor.

She still reveled in her memories of the last time they'd made love despite recognizing what a bad idea it had been. Having sex with Owen again would be an even worse idea...and it was absolutely foolish to even contemplate it here. They were alone, except for Lupe, but who knew when the others would enter this house once more? It could be at any moment.

"You taste so good," Owen said, backing off just a little to look at her. His hands were still upon her, though, and he moved them to her breasts, making her draw in a ragged breath yet again.

"You taste wonderful, too," she said, "and beings like me can really sense the best of flavors."

She half waited for him to be the one to back off

after that. Did he care that she had reminded him who, and what, she was?

Apparently not. He didn't flinch.

"Then what do I taste like to you?" he asked, dipping his head for a quick but heated kiss.

"You taste like hot, delicious sex," she said. "Addictive sex."

"Just my kiss? What if we taste each other's bodies all over?"

Just the thought nearly made Selena have an orgasm. But at least one of them had to remain sane.

That had to be her, or so she told herself.

"It sounds wonderful," she said, even as she let her hand creep beneath his shirt and upward, caressing his warm skin with just a hint of chest hair. "But you're as aware as I am that someone could come in here at any time. As much as I'd like to indulge with you again, we just can't."

"Of course we can." His hands began to play games beneath her T-shirt, cupping her breasts, flicking his thumbs over her nipples outside her bra in a way that made her want to forget everything sensible and strip again and have hot, mindless sex with him once more.

Good thing she retained her senses. Didn't she? "But—"

"Here's what we'll do." He moved his hands away and she felt almost robbed, deprived of the sensation that had made her willing—almost—to defy all logic.

His hands moved lower, and she felt him pull her jeans away from her waist, beyond her hips and farther down, until her jeans pooled at her feet.

"What are you doing?" she began, only to have him cover her lips once more as he pulled her closer to the bed.

"Now you do the same to me. Just take my pants partly off. That way, when we make love, if we hear anyone enter the house we can get dressed again more quickly."

What a good idea, she thought. Or maybe she simply wasn't thinking any longer. It was really a foolish idea, wasn't it?

But she had a desire to play along anyway. She had desire. Oh, yeah.

"I don't suppose you have a way to communicate with Lupe to tell her to bark softly if she hears anyone, do you?"

Selena laughed. "She's well trained, and I look a lot like her while shifted, but we still haven't figured out a way to communicate with our cover animals that way. Maybe someday."

"So we don't add to our delays, I'll take care of this." He pulled back just a little and waved the package containing a condom in front of her. She heard the plastic tear, and only a few moments later Owen was stroking her body in its most sensitive and moist area, making her nearly scream with need. "Are you ready?" he whispered hoarsely.

"Are you?" she countered and reached toward him, feeling how stiff and hard he was beneath the covering of the condom. "I'd say yes."

"Yes," he repeated, and in moments he was inside her, thrusting and breathing hard.

She came nearly immediately. Apparently so did he, for he groaned as he continued to move with determination, but for only another minute. And then he was still.

They just lay there on the bed that was Selena's while she was on this assignment, in this town.

"Not bad for a quickie," Owen said after a long moment.

"Not bad at all," Selena said, but what she thought was how wonderful it had been, maybe because of the risk as well as the intensity.

That was when she heard Lupe, beside the bed, rise to her paws and give a small woof.

"Maybe she did understand," Selena said. "I think we've been warned."

Laughing, Owen responded, "Time to pull ourselves together and get back on your computer."

A minute later, Owen and Selena, fully dressed once more and no longer out of breath, walked slowly down the hall and into the entry area together to see who was there, with Lupe already sniffing at the opening door. Owen wasn't especially surprised to see who came inside.

"Oh." Rainey looked startled as she stopped and stared at them. The curls of her dark hair seemed mussed up by the wind outside, and the lids over her brown eyes were lowered a bit, as if she was in pain. She explained, "I didn't think anyone would be here. I just came back for some aspirin to ward off a headache I've started fighting."

"Sorry to hear that," Selena said. "Can I get you anything?"

"No, thanks. I always carry aspirin in my purse just in case. I'll go upstairs and get some from my room." She started past them down the hallway.

Owen asked, "As far as you could tell, the practice surveillance is going okay with the shifted CAs?"

"Yes, as far as Marshall and I could tell. He's still there, and I'm going back to where he's waiting." Rainey stopped at the bottom of the stairway to the second floor. She turned, and the expression on her face now was both inquisitive and teasing. "I didn't expect you to be here since I thought you two would be in the meeting house waiting to see what happened. Are you...working here?" She aimed a huge, catlike smile at Selena, who shifted where she stood beside Owen.

"Yes, I wanted to research some things about the target area on the internet, so I came back here for my laptop." She'd been carrying it and now gestured with it. "Owen had already done some investigation, online and otherwise. He came with me so we could compare notes and synchronize what we did."

Owen wanted to hug Selena for keeping her cool. Her response was logical and sound. But he couldn't help thinking that Rainey guessed why they were really here, or at least what she had interrupted. Those brows of hers were raised now as she regarded her boss. "I want to hear all about that...research later." She turned again and hurried up the stairs.

Owen heard Selena slowly let out her breath.

"Guess we dodged that bullet," Owen whispered to her, putting an arm around her and squeezing gently.

"Not with Rainey," Selena said, also softly. "Even though she's not a shifter, I suspect her senses help her to know everything."

Rainey returned back down the stairs a few minutes later, a small pill container in her hand. "I'll just be a minute," she said, heading into the kitchen. "I'll bring a water bottle along with me, too, this time."

Selena hoped it wouldn't be tainted, then chastised herself. She didn't know for certain—yet—if the elixir had been tampered with somehow. And even if it had been, that didn't mean there was a problem with everything stored around this compound.

At least she hoped not.

"Then I'll leave you two alone again," Rainey added, practically dancing into the kitchen on her well-worn tennis shoes.

Selena said nothing, just shook her head and sent a wry smile toward her aide that Rainey, now with her face in the refrigerator, couldn't see. Selena instead aimed it toward Owen, who remained beside her, where she was seated at the kitchen table with the laptop in front of her. He was grinning, but as Rainey turned back toward them his expression turned into what passed for an irritated frown.

Rainey closed the refrigerator. She followed up her pills with a long draft of water. "Okay, done," she said. "I'll leave you two to your…research." She grinned again.

Selena wondered if her aide's imagination was as much of a headache cure as the aspirin. "Oh, I think we've finished it," she said. "I'm ready to go back to the meeting house to wait for everyone to return there. How about you, Owen?"

"Yes," he said. "I'm looking forward to getting a report from the shifters. And also about Sal."

Selena nodded. "All the more reason to wait where everyone'll know where to contact us," she said. Then to Rainey, who hurried toward the door ahead of them, she called, "I hope everything on the mountain continues to go well and that your head feels better." Selena hurried to partially close the door until she could attach Lupe's leash to her collar. "We're going for a short walk first, before we go back to the other house," she said to Owen. "Want to join us?"

Owen watched as Lupe tried at first to catch up to Rainey as she headed along one of the paths through the forest that led up the mountain. Selena didn't let her, but tightened her grip on the handle of the leash. "This way, girl," she said to Lupe.

Not for the first time, Owen considered how this wolf-dog looked so much like Selena when she was shifted. He had seen her that way.

But he hadn't seen her get that way.

Nor had he, that day, gotten to see Selena completely undressed even though they had made love.

He wanted to see her naked again—before touching her and having more hot, hard sex with her.

"Are you thinking about how I look shifted?" Selena asked. "And whether I do similar things as Lupe?"

Startled, he looked toward her. Her smile was huge.

"In a way," he admitted. "Mostly, I was thinking about how I wished I'd seen you completely bare today." His turn to smile. "Maybe next time."

"But—"

"I know. There might not be a next time. But I can always hope."

She looked away from him. Her lovely face was pensive, even as she watched Lupe lift her nose and smell the air.

"We've talked a lot about times that I get completely bare," she reminded him. "Would you still feel so... interested if you saw me shift? You've seen the guys change, so you know what the process is. It's cool, but it's not sexy."

He hesitated, but for only an instant. And then he responded, "It's you." Her glance seemed to suggest she was startled. And did he see a ray of hope in her expression?

Heck, letting her know he was attracted to her no matter what her background was fine, but he didn't want to give her any hope that there would be something between them in the future. There couldn't be. They were too different. They had to live in the here and now.

Make love as much as they could…in the here and now.

But to make sure she didn't misunderstand anything on his mind, he grinned at her and said, "And in case you haven't figured it out by now, I'll take any opportunity I can to see you naked, Selena."

Chapter 17

They were back in the meeting house.

Needing something to do while they waited for the return of the shifted CAs—and word on Sal—Owen watched Selena start a pot of coffee for them as he wiped the kitchen counter.

How she could look so lithe and pretty doing such a mundane thing? But he realized why. No matter how inappropriate it was, he was falling for her in more ways than just wanting sex with her anytime, anywhere.

He liked her. A lot. Despite her being a shifter.

Loved her?

He wouldn't go there—even though he had heard that her Alpha Force included a number of couples in which one was a shapeshifter and the other wasn't. How did they get together? How did it work out?

Plus, one of the things he'd gathered was that their

kids would most likely be shifters. How would he feel about that?

It didn't matter. None of it did. They had no future. He would just live in the moment while they had professional reasons to be together.

He'd started out not trusting shifters at all because of his family's experience with the one who'd become a killer. He'd had to start trusting them, at least somewhat, because of his job—but that was all.

A permanent relationship with one—even though that one would be Selena? That couldn't happen.

He sensed Selena step beside him, breaking into his thoughts.

"I know you like it black," she said as she handed him a mug of coffee. He put down the dishcloth he'd been using and accepted the coffee from her.

He smiled at her. "Sounds as if you're getting to know me too well."

She didn't quite hide the look of panic on her face as she quickly turned away.

"I'm getting to know you a bit, too," he persisted. He drew closer to her and, standing right behind her, put his arms around her and pulled her against him. "You like things hard, and sometimes fast, and—"

She pulled away and spun to face him. The expression on her beautiful but pale face seemed taunting somehow, yet sad. "Yes, I guess you're getting to know a part of me, too. But not all." She bent and put her hand on top of Lupe's head. The dog was sitting on the floor, looking up at her. "Right, Lupe?"

"I'll bet she knows the rest," Owen said. *And I'm willing to learn.* But he didn't say that. What good would it really do either of them if he did learn?

Although he hadn't been lying to her. He really did hope he got the chance to watch her shift from human to wolf, at least once.

Maybe it would turn him off completely, shut off any avenue within his mind of wanting to get to know her better.

But he suspected, right now, that it would have the exact opposite effect.

As if she was reading his mind, Selena stood up straight and faced him. "Too bad we need to just wait here for now. Otherwise, I could go downstairs and bring up some of the elixir and one of the magical lights. I could change to look just like Lupe before your very eyes." Talk about taunting him with her gaze—she was a pro at it.

But instead of responding directly, he said, "Maybe we should bring some of that stuff up here, compare the vials to one another to see if we recognize differences. But I think it'll be better to get the results of any testing when Sal comes back with Patrick and Jonas."

"You're assuming he'll come back with them." She crossed her arms and regarded him dubiously.

"Aren't you?"

She relaxed just a little. "Yes, I am, actually. Or maybe that's just hopefulness. I want him to be all right. And I also want there to be a good explanation for his having become ill in the first place."

"Other than tainted elixir?"

She nodded. "You already know how I feel about that. It wouldn't have come from Ft. Lukman that way, but I can't imagine how it was tampered with on the way here or by whom. And—"

Owen's phone rang. Selena stopped talking as he pulled it out of his pocket.

It was Anthony. This wasn't a time scheduled for his superior officer to call. Owen immediately felt his shoulders stiffen, expecting he was not going to like the reason Anthony was contacting him.

He was right.

Selena watched the expression on Owen's face as he leaned his back against the kitchen counter and scowled as he listened to whoever was on the phone. Who was it? Whatever he or she was saying was clearly aggravating Owen.

In a minute, he pulled his phone away from where he had been clutching it against his ear, looked at it and swiped the screen a few times with his forefinger. "Got it. I'll listen and get back to you with any ideas. But I gather that priority number one is to get the CAs off to the target area fast, no later than the day after tomorrow." Owen paused, then said, "Yes, sir." He pressed the button to end the call.

Selena didn't wait. She wanted to know what was going on.

She knew it wasn't anything good.

"Who was that? Anthony?"

"Yeah. He received a message that he needed to pass along to me. Let's go listen to it." He led her into the dining room and sat down on the chair at the head of the table. She grabbed the seat beside him and just waited, while Lupe settled down once more behind her.

He pulled his phone out again and fiddled with it for a few seconds. Then Selena heard a voice crackle out of it.

It was clearly a disguised voice, probably male, much lower than any vocal range she had ever heard, slow and deliberate and understandable. It said, "Greetings, RCMP. You are running out of time to get that ransom paid. Too bad. We are increasing it now by another million dollars and decreasing the deadline by one day. That means we now expect it to appear in the designated foreign bank account no later than Tuesday. And we might change that again if we decide to. We already spoke with Mr. Brodheureux but decided to contact you, too, this time. You need to understand that you Mounties are not in charge here. We are. And if you pretend to do the impossible because you think that will scare us into giving up or allowing you to capture us, you will be making an even bigger mistake. We are much smarter than the RCMP, and you should never forget that. By the way, Mrs. Brodheureux sends her regards. She wants to make sure her husband gets more of his Xanogistics money together fast…or this will also be her goodbye."

That was the end of the call. Selena just looked at Owen, waiting for his reaction.

"I'm not sure what that meant," he said, "besides the obvious. They're tightening the strings, and Mrs. Brodheureux is clearly in even more danger than before. Anthony said he would discuss the additional ransom demand with her husband immediately, but he also made it clear that the CAs had no more time to rehearse. We may not be ready tomorrow, but the day after has to be it. We can't wait any longer."

"Do you think—" Selena began, then stopped. "What about the rest of it? I don't know the details of the prior kidnappings, but there seemed to be a deeper message

in what that man said, don't you think? He was warning the RCMP against doing...what? Something impossible?" She had a sinking feeling she knew what it
meant, although maybe she was jumping to conclusions.

Owen's expression was grim and his eyes stared somewhere beyond Selena. "You want my gut reaction? My
understanding is that most ransom calls are made directly
to the family members. When he said we're pretending
to do the impossible, I think he somehow found out that
we asked Alpha Force for help, and despite its covert nature he's somehow learned about our unit of shapeshifters. The good thing is that he talked about pretense, so
he most likely doesn't know it's true."

"That's what I thought, too." Selena bent her head
to look down at her lap.

"Maybe bringing you Alpha Forcers in was a huge
mistake." Owen's voice was low despite how brutal his
words were.

"No, just the opposite," Selena countered, standing
abruptly. "Don't you see? The kidnappers are worried
about what you Mounties are doing. Maybe they don't
buy in to the idea that you've gotten shapeshifters involved to save their kidnap victim this time, but they
know you're doing something. Something that'll end
their reign of terror once and for all. And they're worried. Damned worried!"

She realized she was glaring angrily at him, even as
Lupe rose and stood beside her, hackles raised as if she
attempted to assess whether she should attack.

Selena felt like kneeling and hugging her wonderful,
empathetic cover dog, but she wasn't about to move or
back down or do anything until Owen recanted what
he had said.

No matter how things did or didn't work out for them, Alpha Force was involved now—and so was his troop of newly recruited shapeshifters.

The possibility of complete surprise against the kidnappers might not be feasible any longer. But shifters could still do one heck of a lot more than regular humans to conduct reconnaissance of the suspected location... and then even to assist in the rescue.

Instead of snapping back or once more attempting to discredit Alpha Force, Owen smiled. It was a dubious smile, but he apparently chose not to continue the argument.

"You're right, of course," he said. "I apologize. But I certainly wasn't expecting to lose the element of surprise when my CAs approached our suspected site. Now they'll need to be extra careful. But they will succeed. They have to. And despite what I said before, they'll have you, and the other members of Alpha Force, to thank for it."

Selena stepped toward him, intending to give him a quick hug to reassure him that his assumption of success would come true. But in moments, she was in a full embrace once more and his lips were on hers.

The kiss reassured her that Owen was upset and concerned, but he wasn't refuting what his unit could do. Nor what hers had taught them.

Even more, it reassured her that, anger and worry be damned, Owen wasn't blaming her...and that he still wanted her.

A noise sounded from the front of the house, and at the same time Lupe stood and ran in that direction.

Selena quickly pulled away from Owen. "Who's here?" she asked him.

* * *

Owen guessed correctly, partly because it was too early for the CAs to return from their reconnaissance exercise. The people who had just entered the meeting house through the front door were Sal and those who had gone along to help him, Patrick and Jonas.

Sal was still pale, but he was walking on his own—a good sign.

"Are you okay?" Selena had hurried past Owen and the others to join Sal in the entryway, her hand on his arm below the short sleeve of his black T-shirt. The strain on his face made him look older.

"I'm fine," he managed to answer, "but I think it'll still be a while before the idea of food sounds good to me. Is Yvanne here yet?"

"No," Owen said, trading glances with Patrick.

"It's okay," the senior Alpha Force officer said. "Sal wasn't in any condition to contact his sister at first, but I promised I would if… Well, he improved very quickly, so I let him be the one to call her."

"She was worried," Sal elaborated, "but I told her when we were on our way back here and said she could come and see me."

"That's fine." Selena sent Owen a look that told him to drop the subject. "Why don't you come here, into the living room?" She held on to Sal's arm, and Jonas took his other one. The aide was also dressed in black, since he was initially supposed to have remained on the mountain as the CAs did their practice recon.

Owen watched them go but stayed back, glad that Patrick did, too. "Is he really okay?"

"He is now." The shapeshifting doctor looked worried, though. His pale brown eyes were narrowed, and

Owen half expected him to growl like the wolf he changed into.

"Any idea yet what happened to him?"

"I want to hear, too." Selena had returned to the entry area. Owen looked at her. Her hands were on her hips, and she appeared ready to argue if either man suggested she didn't need to hear whatever Patrick was about to say.

Owen, for one, wasn't about to tell her to leave. To the contrary, he believed she should know everything that was going on. Analyzing and conveying to others what they, too, needed to know was her job.

"Fine," Patrick said. "Let's go out on the porch. Everyone will need to hear this eventually, but I want to get them together and observe their reactions."

"Why?" Selena's tone had the same edge that Owen figured his would have if he'd asked the same question.

Patrick didn't respond directly. Instead, he turned the latch and opened the front door, then motioned for the two of them to go outside. Selena went first and Owen followed, not wanting her to be out there alone even for a few seconds—not until he knew what was going on and, if necessary, could protect her from it.

Twilight now darkened the sky. The wooden porch was largely in shadow, and so was the open area in front of the two houses, but Owen did not return inside to turn on the light. He'd do it later so the CAs did not need to return in darkness. For right now, though, shadows were just fine.

"Okay, what's going on?" He approached Patrick, who had taken a position in what might be the deepest shadow on the porch near the closed and draped window into the living room. Or maybe he was just listening to what was happening inside. Owen heard voices but could not make them out.

Shapeshifters probably could, even while still looking human.

"Actually, it's too soon to tell." Patrick's expression was ironic and, if Owen read it right, rather frustrated, too.

"Then what do you think?" Selena sounded as impatient as Owen felt.

They all stood there in the growing darkness, which made Owen think of eeriness and midnight and all the stuff kids were taught about things that were supposedly paranormal—like shapeshifters. If he wasn't a trained police officer, he might even feel nervous. Instead, he felt protective. Of Selena.

How weird, under the circumstances, was that?

"Well, we did take Sal to that urgent-care clinic near Tim's former home, where there are clearly shapeshifters living. After a bit of careful discussion on both sides, as well as dropping the names of Tim's family, the doctors there admitted to being shapeshifters, too. We didn't get into details like why we were in the area or what we were doing, but we did ask, and receive, access to the clinic's laboratory. I didn't want them to do any analysis on the elixir since its contents were none of their business, but I wanted a shot at figuring out if anything was actually wrong with that vial."

"And was there?" Owen asked.

"I brought it back with us since we'll need to get a more thorough and trustworthy analysis back at Ft. Lukman," Patrick said, "but our initial thought after a preliminary testing was that it was no wonder Sal had become ill."

"Why?" demanded Selena. "Don't keep us in suspense."

"Have you ever heard of ipecac?" Patrick asked.

"I think so," Owen responded. "Isn't it something that's supposed to make people throw up if they've swallowed poison?"

"Did Sal swallow poison?" Selena demanded. "Did the doctors at that clinic want to give him ipecac?"

"The stuff has been somewhat discredited over the years as being potentially more dangerous than what it's supposed to help cure," Patrick responded. "But our initial thought, Jonas's and mine, was that somehow ipecac had been added to the vial of elixir."

Ipecac? Selena hadn't really known anything about it before, but now she'd learned a little—how it had slightly discolored the blameworthy bottle of elixir with a hint of pink and how it smelled somewhat bitter.

She still wasn't certain how dangerous the stuff was, although she figured that the higher the dosage, the more damage it could do. Fortunately, there hadn't appeared to be much in the elixir.

Selena was particularly glad that Sal apparently would be fine.

She hoped Patrick would keep her informed as he learned more. In fact, it wouldn't hurt to ask now since Owen, too, would need to know. It was his subordinate who had been affected. Besides, he might need some reassurances that the elixir worked fine and was a good thing—nearly all the time.

Selena only hoped that remained true and that nothing like this ever happened again. Not to the CAs and not to Alpha Force.

"When do you think you'll know for sure if it was ipecac?" she asked Patrick, wishing she could see his expression better in the growing darkness. She'd trained with him some back at Ft. Lukman and had always found him to be a kind and courteous man and superior officer. But his tone of voice now had suggested he was holding back a whole lot of anger—unsurprising, of course.

"This isn't something we have facilities to deal with here," he said, "nor will we want to ship it and let it out of our control. We'll keep the vial refrigerated for now and take it back to Ft. Lukman when we head there."

"Have you told Major Connell about it?" Selena was certain that the officer in charge of Alpha Force would want to know all about the tainting of the elixir—especially since he was the one who had been in charge of its development.

"I called him, of course. He's having the rest of the elixir at Ft. Lukman checked to make sure it's all okay and telling all Alpha Force members out on assignment about it, too. But none of us believe we took it from the post that way when we headed here."

"Then how do you think it got tainted?" Owen asked. A sliver of light shone near Owen from between the curtains inside the living room window, allowing Selena to see his face. He, too, looked grim. And so he should. Sal could potentially have died. The kidnapped hostage, too, if the mission failed because of treachery.

Selena fought the urge to hug Owen in sympathy and understanding. It would have been inappropriate with Patrick standing beside them.

"We don't know," Patrick countered, almost as if he felt Owen was accusing him. Or maybe he really was feeling defensive, defending not only the elixir, but also himself—and Alpha Force. "We will find out, though," he said. "You can count on that."

"Right." Owen's tone didn't divulge whether he was genuinely agreeing or full of irony. Not that it mattered.

Selena decided this might be the time to change the subject or suggest they go inside to check on Sal. But before she said anything, lights suddenly appeared along the driveway.

A car was approaching.

Should they head inside and wait to see who it was? That might be the best defensive move. But because neither man moved, she didn't, either.

The car appeared, not one she had seen before. The light-colored sedan parked right in front of them.

In a moment, two familiar women exited the vehicle— Yvanne and Craig's girlfriend, Holly.

Sal had been permitted to call his sister and keep her updated about his condition. But who had contacted Holly?

Even if Yvanne knew that her brother was a CA, and what the CAs were about, Selena didn't think that Holly was supposed to know any more than that her guy was a shapeshifter.

When were the CAs due back here? What form would they be in? Would Holly still be here?

The day had already proved to be interesting. She had a feeling the evening was about to get even more so.

Chapter 18

"Where is Sal? Is he really okay?"

Even in the dim light, Selena could see the panic on Yvanne's face. Her pale brown eyes glowed as they looked from Patrick to Owen to Selena, stopping on her as if the woman sensed that she was an ally.

"He's inside, back from seeing a doctor with...appropriate credentials." Selena glanced toward Holly as she said that. Craig's girlfriend might know that he was a shifter, but none of the CAs was supposed to talk about the new RCMP team or what its characteristics were. Holly might not know that most of the people here were also shifters. Then again, she might. The main thing was that she wasn't supposed to know the reason they were here.

If she only knew her boyfriend was a shifter, though, Selena wasn't going to be the one to broaden her knowledge.

"That's what he said, but is it true?" Without waiting for an answer, Yvanne headed inside, followed by Patrick.

"Is Craig in there?" Holly demanded. "Is he okay?"

Selena took a moment to consider how to answer—clearly "no" to question one and "we hope so" to question two. But Owen took that task away from her.

"He's not here. He had an errand to take care of and isn't back yet. I'm sure he's fine." Owen's tone was clearly intended to soothe Holly, and Selena admired him for his kind attitude.

"When will he get back?" Holly persisted. She looked different when not hanging on to Craig. Her large blue eyes seemed accusatory, despite the concern demonstrated by the way she gnawed her full, lipstick-covered bottom lip.

"Possibly not for another hour or so."

Was it getting that late already, or was Owen just trying to keep Holly calm? As far as Selena knew, the CAs were not supposed to end their dress rehearsal until the sky had been dark for at least a couple of hours.

That was because it wouldn't be clear how long they would need to scope out the genuine target area, so they needed to practice all possibilities now. Especially now, since their exercise today would be repeated as reality the day after tomorrow.

The shifted CAs, believing they had another day or two beyond that, wouldn't yet know of that urgency unless they were in the presence of the aides. Owen might have informed Patrick and the aides, though, about the change of circumstances, triggered by that kidnapper's phone call.

Given a choice, Selena would tell Holly to wait for

Craig at the hotel where they were both staying—most likely in the same room at times, she figured, despite what Owen and others had been told. But she didn't want to spark any bad reaction from Holly. Even so, she didn't feel comfortable inviting her inside.

Once again Owen handled the situation, and Selena appreciated that about him.

That wasn't all she appreciated about him. Even out here in the dimness, she could see his muscular physique silhouetted against the light. She wistfully thought about the last time they had been alone and kissed and made love.

When would they be alone like that again? Not tonight. Maybe not ever.

Selena shrugged aside her sadness, making sure to paste an interested, unemotional expression on her face.

"Why don't you come inside for a while?" Owen said to Holly. "I can't guarantee when Craig will be back, but you can wait with us for now, although you'll need to leave if we decide to go back to town to wait for him."

That wasn't going to happen, but Selena was glad Owen had left the door open to a way to eject Holly from the area.

Selena let Owen lead the way, ushering Holly inside first, and then she followed.

Selena heard voices as they passed the living room, down the hall from the dining room.

Sal sat at the table with his sister beside him. She was asking questions about what had happened, and he seemed to be responding cagily.

Yes, he had drunk something he shouldn't have and had reacted to it badly. Yes, one of the other people he'd been vacationing here with—Tim—was from a nearby town, so they'd figured out where Sal could get appropriate care.

Never mind that Tim had shifted and been unable to speak and give directions when Sal had become ill. Sal didn't get into any details about how things had worked out.

Patrick and Jonas were around the table now, too.

"Let's sit down," Owen said to Holly. He pulled his phone from his pocket, and Selena figured he was looking for messages or checking the time or both. "Anyone hungry?"

They decided on take-out Chinese, and Patrick asked Jonas to go to town to pick it up.

While they waited, everyone sat around the table and talked, mostly in groups of two or three. Selena wound up talking to Holly, which wasn't exactly her choice. She had to be careful what she said but kept the subject neutral, on how much she was enjoying this visit.

"Me, too," Holly said. "Of course, I always enjoy myself when I'm with Craig. He's why I came here." As if Selena didn't know that. "He's so special, you know." Selena knew that, too—but she wasn't sure if Holly was referring to Craig's shapeshifting abilities.

"He's a very nice guy" was all Selena said.

"Are you like him—a shifter, I mean?"

Selena felt her eyes widen. She supposed it wasn't too wild a guess that the people Craig hung out with would share that characteristic. But she didn't want to admit it.

"Not everyone here is like your boyfriend," said Owen from across the table. "Even if we wish we were."

Once more Selena could have hugged him. Her status remained vague, and Owen had told the truth.

Jonas arrived a while later with the take-out boxes of Chinese food. If Selena weren't aware of the tension in the room, she might consider this a pleasant dinner with friendly acquaintances.

But she knew better, especially when, each time she looked at Holly, Craig's girlfriend was glancing at the doorway or checking her cell phone for the time.

Not surprising. In a similar situation, Selena figured she would be doing the same thing.

They were all finishing their meals when Lupe stood and woofed. Selena heard something outside, too.

Were the others back? It was eight o'clock, so it was certainly possible.

Would Andrea, Craig and Tim still be shifted? If so, she needed to get Yvanne and Holly out of there. No matter what they knew or didn't know, the two women did not need to see the others in their shifted forms. That would only add to the questions they probably already had.

Even though Selena wanted to stay here and greet the shifters, no matter what form they happened to be in, she had a responsibility to Alpha Force and, consequently, to the CAs.

"I just thought of something I need to get from my room," she said brightly and stood. "Yvanne and Holly, would you like to come with me? I'd like to show you my room." She'd take them out the back door so they wouldn't pass where the others would be entering.

"No, I'd rather stay here with Sal," Yvanne said, remaining seated.

"And I want to wait and see if whoever's outside there that Lupe's excited about includes Craig," said Holly.

Selena looked toward Patrick to see whether her commanding officer was all right with that or if he had an idea of his own how to get the women out of here at this potentially critical time.

"That's okay," Owen said. "You ladies can stay right here. But I've got something I need to talk over with you, Selena. Would you come with me?"

Ah, she got it. Owen and she could go meet the others and lead them downstairs, where the CAs could shift back, if necessary.

"Oh, please," Holly said in a sarcastic voice that got Selena's attention and seemed to capture the others' as well. The attractive, fashion-conscious woman apparently had a temper. "Yvanne and I know what's going on. Sal and Craig let us in on it. They also let us know the information could go no further than us, and it hasn't, right, Yvanne?"

"Absolutely." The other woman grasped her brother's arm more tightly. Their family resemblance, with their light brown eyes and shining hair, seemed enhanced here despite Sal's continued pallor. "I'd do anything to keep Sal safe—plus, I'm all for what he and the rest of your group of CAs is up to. I wouldn't do anything to jeopardize it."

"Me, either." Holly was standing now. "Let's go welcome them back. I'd love to learn how things went for them." She glanced at each of them. "You don't need to worry about our discretion."

Really? Selena hoped that was true. But Holly and Yvanne hadn't been hanging out with the CAs 24/7.

They'd all already seen Holly flirting with that server at the Yukon Bar—Boyd, was it? Sure, maybe that was just to get Craig jealous, or maybe it was a harmless and meaningless flirtation, but who knew what either of the women had done with the supposedly secret information they'd been given?

Selena looked toward Owen again to see how he was reacting to the two women—and the fact they'd been told more than they should have been by shifters under his command.

Judging by his unreadable expression and the way he failed to meet her eyes, Selena assumed he wasn't happy.

"All right," he finally said in a voice that would have resembled a growl if he'd been a shifter. "Let's go greet them."

Saying nothing more, Owen rose and started toward the front door. He figured the others followed him and in fact heard footsteps as well as whispers he did not try to understand.

Nor did he want to say anything else, not then. He didn't even want to talk to Selena because he figured she would express sympathy or concern, or even anger on his behalf.

As much as he appreciated her empathy, he didn't want it just then or he might wind up venting that anger at her, which would be totally inappropriate.

What he really wanted to do was shake sense into all of his recruits. Or even abort their mission and disband the CAs. But the latter would be self-defeating... and impossible. And against everything inside him as a longtime member of the RCMP.

Yet he had told them all, from the minute they had each been recruited, to keep everything about the CAs and their very sensitive assignment secret. But he'd figured before, and had it confirmed, that Sal would have given at least some information to his shapeshifting sister no matter how much Owen stressed discretion. Even so, that might be okay, given her apparent interest in joining the CAs, too.

He couldn't do anything about the fact that Holly knew the true nature of her boyfriend. But Craig never should have let Holly know that his spontaneous "vacation" here was with other shifters, let alone that they were joining a special police unit. He wouldn't be surprised if Craig had also revealed to Holly the mission they were undertaking after their training here. Sure, it might seem exciting and glamorous to outsiders, something that might even stoke a girlfriend's admiration that could lead to interesting physical contact. But that mission was vital. And dangerous. A woman's life depended on its success. And to be effective, it needed to be kept secret.

But it was too late to boot out Craig for any indiscretion he might have committed or even to punish him for infringement of RCMP rules. Not now. It was also impossible to retract whatever he had told his girlfriend.

No, for now, it would be better to keep Holly in the loop so he could keep an eye on her, as well as on Yvanne.

Patrick was the first of the group to reach the front door. Good. He could assess the situation, see what form the three shifting CAs who'd been out training were in now.

"Hi," he said quickly. "Welcome back. We're just

finishing dinner but left some for you, too. Sal's doing
well, and his sister and Holly are here with us."

Good. He was cautioning the others not to start talking about their hopefully triumphant, but possibly less
successful, training day, at least for the moment.

"Great," Tim said. "It's been quite an experience, and
topping it off with dinner will be awesome." So the trio
was in human form. He was thankful for that, at least.

In short order, they fussed over Sal and said their
hellos. Then they all sat around the dining room table,
where the new arrivals ate dinner. It was like a family gathering, Owen thought—if you ignored the fact
that most of the people here had met each other only
a week ago.

But as friendly as everyone was, Owen felt the underlying frustration of nearly all of them. The group
who'd just returned clearly wanted to talk about their
experiences. The others wanted to listen to them—as
long as the two women were excluded.

Owen struggled for a way to get rid of them, at least
for now, so they could hold a proper debriefing. He was
grateful when Selena stood up and corralled the two
outsiders. "Let's go wash the dishes," she told them. "As
an extra incentive, I've got some information I want to
share with you two about the secret nature of this group
that I know you've got only some knowledge of."

Patrick stood, too. "Now, Selena, we—"

"We've got to be realistic," she interrupted. "You
two with me?" The two women nodded.

Owen wasn't sure whether he wanted to kiss Selena
or strangle her.

But on the whole, he trusted her, and clearly Patrick
and the other members of Alpha Force did, too.

Even so, he definitely wished he could hear what she said to them in the kitchen. Too bad he didn't have those extra shifter senses to help him out.

Chapter 19

Selena started gathering the dirty dishes that remained on the table, although some had already been cleared away. She handed a few to Yvanne and Holly to carry while she collected the rest.

Then she led them into the kitchen.

She wasn't quite sure what she would say to them. But one thing she was certain of was that she would do all she could as an Alpha Force member to help accomplish her special unit's needs. Right now one of those needs was for the group in the dining room to rehash all that had gone on that day.

From that, they would have to determine what exercises should and would be conducted tomorrow, the final opportunity before the mission went live.

She put the dishes into the sink, wishing not for the first time that this house had a dishwasher. It would be easier to let the machine do the work.

On the other hand, maybe this time it would be better to do it all by hand. It'd give the group time to debrief.

"Yvanne," she said, "you scrape the plates, I'll wash, and then, Holly, you dry. Okay?"

"If we must," Holly said with a sigh.

"And if you really talk to us the way you said," added Yvanne.

So what was she going to do? Selena wondered about it, but for only an instant.

She was going to tell them the truth.

But it would be a modified and abbreviated version that might actually gain their cooperation.

Was that still too much? She figured she would be able to explain to her CO and get him to buy in to her plan after the fact.

But Owen? This was really his operation, and he had clearly wanted total secrecy.

Secrecy that had already been breached. Surely he had to realize that. But would what she suddenly planned to reveal violate it even more in his opinion?

Would he despise her for it?

The idea made her place her hands in the hot water as if it would give her relief instead of discomfort. If she had to choose one kind of discomfort over the other, getting mildly scalded sounded better to her than garnering Owen's hatred.

But she believed that, with the proverbial cat out of the bag anyway, she might be able to ease the problem, if just a little.

"Look," she said, keeping her eyes on the plate she held over the sink. "I gather that Sal and Craig have most likely told you more than they were supposed to because they love you. I understand that. But did they also tell you that, not only were they supposed to maintain the secrecy of what they're doing, but that it would also be dangerous for them to reveal it to anyone, including those they love?"

"No," Holly whispered from beside her. "What do you mean?"

"The exercise they were on today—well, you might have gathered that it's preparation for something else."

"That's right," Yvanne said. "Sal did tell me that, and that it's something really exciting and important, but you can be sure he didn't tell me more than that."

It was more than enough, Selena thought, but instead of criticizing Sal she asked, "How about Craig, Holly? Did he tell you more than Yvanne just described?"

"No, but I really wanted him to." She paused. "Why is it dangerous for them if they told us?"

"I can't tell you that without violating the secrecy they're sworn to. Suffice to say that no matter what you actually know, and whether they've told you more than they should, you need to understand that Sal and Craig can be in great trouble—life-threatening danger, even—if word gets out about this. You need to promise that you won't tell anyone what you know or even suspect. Got that?"

She looked first at Yvanne, then at Holly. They both wore solemn expressions, and each nodded at her as if providing the promise she had asked for.

Still, she wanted a verbal agreement. "Say it aloud," she said.

"I promise," Holly responded.

"Me, too," said Yvanne. "But this is all so dratted frustrating." She shoved the plate she held against the side of the garbage can as if breaking it might make her feel better. The plate survived, fortunately, and so, apparently, did Yvanne's temper. "I'm a shifter like my brother. I know he was so excited that he was going to get to use that skill in a really special way, but he didn't tell me how, just teased me that I'd envy him because of the way he'd be able to shift from now on."

"And do you envy him?" Holly asked.

"I don't know enough about what he's talking about to be sure, but just being able to use his shifting ability for something special… Well, yes."

"I envy you both, in a way," Holly said. "I love Craig. A lot. We'll marry someday. But I'll never be able to do all that he does, even though he has told me how it feels to shift and be a wolf creature and all that, and our kids should be like him." She moved toward Selena. "You're a shifter, too, I gather. I envy you, too."

"Thanks," Selena said. "There are good and bad things about shifting. Not everyone believes in our ability and some who do fear it. It's generally important for shifters to keep quiet about it because there are those who fear and hate us and would even kill us if they learned we were real. I'm glad you're not one of them, Holly. It sounds like Craig is a lucky man to have you."

And Owen? Selena couldn't help thinking about him in the context of this conversation. He knew shifters were real. From what he'd told her, he had known it for a long time, but his initial experiences had made him despise them, too—until he had spent this week with a new set of shifters.

Good thing she already knew what a bad idea it would be to really let herself go and care for him for anything but wonderful, hot sex—assuming they ever got to be alone together again, which at this point seemed highly unlikely.

Holly could envy her all she wanted, though, as long as she didn't tell anyone.

"Okay," she finally said. "I think I've said all I can, and we need to dig in and finish the dishes."

Owen appreciated Selena's removing the two women from the dining room so tactfully. He and the others needed a summation of what had really gone on today during his CAs' exercise.

Selena's act was worth even more gratitude when he considered that she, too, would want to know the same information he and her fellow Alpha Force members learned. She would hear it later, of course, either from him or the others. But he had gotten to know her well enough to realize her action really was a sacrifice on her part.

She liked to learn as fast as possible, or at least that was the impression she gave. That way, she could work on how to include any appropriate new knowledge in the instructions she provided about shifting.

He listened as his recruits recounted their experiences.

At first, Andrea had waxed eloquent about how well things had gone from her perspective. "If our target area is anything like this, I'll be able to soar like any other raptors present. And Craig, Tim, Sal and I talked before about how I'll communicate by circling right or left or which wing I dip." Her thin face was one huge smile beneath her prominent nose and caused Owen to grin a little, too.

"That's right," Tim agreed. "Andrea succeeded in

directing us to a particular clearing, where Craig and I headed. No kidnappers there, unsurprisingly, but we did stalk a couple of squirrels. Didn't harm them, though, since there was no need to." The round-faced guy appeared to attempt to look serious, but he clearly was beaming. "It was so cool to be out there and know we were people on a mission, even though it was just an exercise."

"We conducted an exercise today," said Patrick, who sat beside Owen. "There'll be another one tomorrow. But… Owen, please let everyone know about the phone call the RCMP received." Owen complied, and when he was done Patrick continued. "So you now know why we're stepping up the timing. The actual operation begins the day after tomorrow. Were there any particular things you felt needed some work today?"

"My presence," Sal said. "I want to experience what they did today so I'll be of help during our real mission. Okay, guys?" His youth shone through in his eager expression.

"Of course," Craig assured him. "I especially like those mini video cameras that were strapped around our necks. They're small enough not to be too visible, and it was great having our aides not only monitor what we saw, but also be able to talk to us. But what if we're separated and one of us thinks we need to meet up? We can't exactly talk and tell the aides monitoring us what's on our minds when we're shifted."

"What we often do is also plan ahead where to meet and how often," Marshall said, leaning forward at the table. "But with your specific instructions, you may not be able to do that. You should decide ahead of time where we'll be—your aides—so that'll be the place you return to. You should also determine a signal of urgency for Andrea to give you if things start looking bad from her perspective so you can rejoin us. And likewise, there should be some signal any of you can give to her so she'll know she should inform the others that you should leave what you're doing and all meet up with us."

"Sounds good," Tim said.

"To me, too," Andrea added. "We did a little of that today but it wasn't organized enough. Let me think a bit about what I'll be able to see most easily from the air, and we'll practice it some more tomorrow."

"One thing, though—something I asked before." Craig, at Andrea's other side, had one hand up, palm out. "Even though we shifting CAs appreciate all we've learned from you Alpha Force guys, I thought we were going to be an independent, all-Canadian team to take care of a Canadian problem." He looked at Owen, who nodded, but before he could speak Craig continued, "Then why aren't our aides part of the CAs? Or at least from our country? Will they be soon?"

"That's our ultimate plan," Owen responded quickly and firmly. He was glad he had taken a seat at the end of the table. He was in charge, as he had to be. He had a sense, though, that he was facing some kind of small rebellion from Craig without knowing why. If so, it was bad timing, coming on the heels of his lack of protocol in telling Holly about their group. "For right now," he continued, "we needed not only to get some of the elixir and instructions from Alpha Force, but also to get backup assistance—fast. It's crucial that we rescue that hostage immediately without her being harmed any further. Once this operation is complete, we'll have more time to learn more and train others, including aides, for the future." If they were successful, of course, and didn't have to deal with another kidnapping right away.

Craig apparently wasn't satisfied. He looked Owen right in the eyes and belabored his point. "But we have two great potential aides right here with us." He turned to face the others, starting with Sal. "Your sister, for one. She's a perfect aide since she's also a shifter. She might become one of us later, but for now there's no one better to be there as an aide for us. And my Holly would be an asset, too, because she cares. A lot." He looked toward the far side of the table, meeting Rainey's gaze. "I don't mean in any way to offend you, honest. You've done a great job, and you, too, Marshall. And, Jonas, it was great that you stayed to help Sal. But I love the idea of the CAs and what we can do and also what we can become—starting now."

Owen stood up. "I understand your concerns, and we'll certainly address them," he said in a firm tone that brooked no argument. "But not until after the rescue of that hostage."

"But—" Craig stopped and looked down at the table. "I get it."

Owen decided there and then that if he had had more time he would have booted Craig off their team, or at least suspended him.

But he didn't have time. He needed the full complement of these shifters. Craig's insubordination would have to be dealt with later.

"Now it's time for all of us to turn in," Owen said, maintaining the tone of a senior officer in control. "Tomorrow will be another big day. We'll meet here again early so you all, including Sal, can get in as much practice and training as possible."

He was glad to see the whole group, including Craig, rise and begin the routine of saying good-night. Selena reentered the room just then, too, with the two women who would also accompany the CAs back to their hotel. She nodded as he gave her a quick look that he intended to convey his thanks.

This day, as good and as difficult as it had been, was finally drawing to an end. He could only hope that tomorrow would be better. It had to be, he told himself. They were running out of time.

Selena was dying to know what had gone on in the dining room while she'd acted as nursemaid in the kitchen to the two visiting women.

Okay, it really hadn't been that bad. But she was glad to see the entire group of CAs get into their cars and head down the hill toward town for the night.

At least she was glad to see all of them but Owen go.

He said good-night to her before heading to his car. He also said good-night to Patrick, Jonas and the rest. Nothing appeared personal between Selena and him, and that was fine.

At least it should have been. But she was well aware that their days with one another were numbered. In fact, tomorrow would be the last one.

She wasn't sure where Owen would be when the CAs were off conducting their designated operation the day after tomorrow. She assumed she and the other members of Alpha Force would hang out here to await the return of Jonas and Rainey. Or perhaps they'd go somewhere else, where Jonas and Rainey would meet up with them when done with the mission. Either way, she doubted she would be with Owen.

She walked Lupe for her last outing of the night and was glad when Rainey joined her.

"Boy," her aide said in a muted tone, "too bad you weren't with us in the dining room. Your buddy Owen had to assert his power over at least one of his minions—that Craig. He did a good job of it, too. No wonder you find him sexy, with all that testosterone and all."

"What?" Selena exclaimed. She wanted to hear more, but Patrick caught up and started walking with them.

"Did you learn anything from the women?" Patrick asked Selena.

"Like what?" She watched Lupe squat though she would have preferred looking into her CO's face to catch whether his expression was critical.

"Like how much they know besides the fact that the men they're here visiting are shifters."

"I didn't find out much really, although I tried to. I still gather they know more than they were authorized to be told. But whether they know it all—that I can't tell you. I at least tried to impress on them how important it was that they stay quiet about whatever they do happen to know." Selena bent, a plastic bag in hand, to clean what Lupe had done, then rose again.

"Did they tell you they intend to become the aides to the shifting CAs?" Rainey asked.

Selena turned toward her. "They didn't mention it. Is that the plan?" She looked at Patrick.

"It wasn't ours, although it could wind up being the case. But there's no time to train them for it now. Craig suggested the possibility, and I was wondering, too, if the women were already in on the idea."

Selena shook her head. "If so, they didn't tell me. And yeah, it's a really bad idea, at least right now."

"So they were told," Patrick said. "Owen made it very clear it wasn't going to happen."

They all headed toward the house, Lupe included. Selena pondered what the women had told her. But even though Yvanne and Holly made it clear they were there for their shifting men, they hadn't even hinted that they hoped to wind up as aides.

The idea was potentially an okay one for the future, Selena mused. But not now. Definitely not now.

As she led Lupe to their room on the ground floor, the other Alpha Force members, who'd fetched bottles of water from the kitchen, trooped upstairs.

As she started getting ready for bed, her mind was not on the two women and their future use, but on the recruits who'd be facing their last day of training tomorrow.

Yes, tomorrow was going to be an important day.

But what if it started out with the same kind of problems as today?

She might not be able to ensure it didn't…but she had to try.

Selena hadn't been able to sleep. She'd lain in bed and developed a plan that she intended to accomplish very early in the morning, waking before the rest of the household.

But she could do it now instead—although it would undoubtedly require a follow-up, at least for her peace of mind.

The time was approaching midnight, only an hour since she had headed into her room while the others went upstairs. She could still get a reasonable night's sleep—depending on what she found.

"Stay," she whispered to Lupe as she exited their bedroom. She dressed in a dark long-sleeved T-shirt and black jeans and did not turn on any lights. She did, however, carry a small flashlight in case she needed some illumination to get her where she needed to go.

She wished she could shift now so she could make full use of her sense of smell. But even when she was in human form, that sense was still much better than that of most people. She'd noticed that a lot over time, and it had been proved to her on Alpha Force exercises.

She was glad the other Alpha Force shifters hadn't brought their cover dogs. If they had and they'd heard her open the front door, they might have assumed the roles of watchdogs and barked, alerting their humans that someone was on the move. Fortunately, Lupe was good about following commands—including *stay*—and she would know it was her mistress she heard.

Outside, there was very little light on the cement-covered area between the houses, but the moon was building up to being full soon and that illumination was enough for her. She kept her flashlight in her pocket as she approached the other building, then extracted her key card from that same pocket.

Once inside the meeting house she used her flashlight to get to the stairway to the basement.

And stopped at the closed door.

She had thought she wouldn't need to use her acute sense of hearing much that night, but she had nevertheless heard something downstairs. Who was there?

Someone tainting the remainder of the elixir?

Knowing she should run for help, she wanted to know first what she was dealing with. She reached carefully for the door and pulled it open just a little—and saw that a light was on downstairs.

She was about to turn and hurry out to seek assistance when she realized that those same enhanced senses of hers told her who it was. She smelled the light, masculine tangy scent that had become familiar—and delicious—to her.

Owen's scent.

Really? What was he doing here? Or was it someone else who knew how shifters thought and was attempting to smell like him?

She decided to find out rather than run away. But as quietly as she started down the stairs, it was almost as if Owen had enhanced senses, too—or at least his hearing.

"Is that you, Selena?" he called quietly. "I've been expecting you."

Chapter 20

Selena felt her heart rate accelerate. What did Owen mean?

And was anyone with him…or was she going to be alone with him in this unoccupied house?

She straightened her shoulders as she walked down the well-lit stairway in a manner that she intended to look cool and professional.

"What do you mean you were expecting me?" she demanded. "I didn't know I was coming here until a few minutes ago."

He waited at the base of the stairs, dressed, like her, in black. His smile was anything but nonchalant or impersonal. His gaze rolled down her body, making her tingle with desire.

No. That wasn't why she was here. She had a goal to accomplish this night. She couldn't allow herself to be diverted from it.

In moments, his eyes rose again to capture hers, and his smile disappeared. His abruptly serious expression seemed to rob her of the sexual interest that had permeated all of her only seconds before.

Well, it wasn't completely gone. But she realized that no matter what he felt, that wasn't what he was about to discuss.

"As good as it is to see you alone in the middle of the night again, that's not what I'm talking about," he said. "I've gotten to know you a bit in the last few days, Selena. I know how dedicated you are to Alpha Force, and thanks to your devotion you're clearly concerned about the success of my CAs' mission. I figured you'd want to check on the condition of your elixir before anyone else drank it tomorrow—and the best time to do that was the middle of the night."

She found herself laughing. "Yes, it does sound like you know me. Is that why you're here, too?"

He nodded. "I wanted to check out the elixir. I was hoping you'd join me. I even planned to call you in a few minutes after I did my initial assessment. I can look at the stuff and even smell it, but I figure you'd be a lot more skilled, with your senses, in confirming whether there are any problems or not."

"You definitely know me," Selena said. Or at least he understood some of the abilities of shifters, even when they weren't in shifted form.

She remained on the next-to-last stair, with Owen facing her at the bottom. She had an urge to reach out, to pull him close and kiss him...but they both had work to do. Instead, she moved sideways and stepped onto the floor.

She looked around. She hadn't been in the basement

here before, since the only shifting she had watched in this location was Andrea's, upstairs. The male CAs had come down here for their changes.

There appeared to be only one large room with cement walls and several long, upholstered ottomans where the nonshifting aides could observe their charges as the elixir began to work on them.

They were probably sitting there earlier, too, when Sal started to react to the liquid he had drunk. Selena suppressed an angry shudder. "I see a refrigerator over there." She pointed to a tall metal unit against the wall. "I assume that's where the elixir is being stored."

"Yes, that's where Rainey and Jonas and the others have gotten it from."

They both walked quickly along the concrete floor toward the refrigerator. Owen reached it first and opened the door. Inside were a dozen vials in the shape that had become familiar to Selena since she had joined Alpha Force. All the vials contained clear liquid that had to be the special shifting elixir.

"Let's check them out." Selena reached for two on the top glass shelf. They both had metal screw-top caps that were easy enough to open and close. Maybe from now on Alpha Force should package its elixir differently. She held up the vials before her eyes one at a time with the ceiling light in the background. Both appeared still to be clear.

Next, she unscrewed the caps and inhaled. They seemed the usual mild citrus scent she was used to.

No indication of any kind of contamination, let alone ipecac.

"They're okay?" Owen asked.

"They seem to be. Let's check the rest." She put

the two she held back into the refrigerator on one side. Owen removed the rest one at a time and she similarly checked each of them.

All seemed fine.

"Then the one that hurt Sal was a fluke?" Owen asked her.

"Is that what you really believe?"

He pursed his lips. "No, but under the circumstances it's what I hoped."

"We can check them out again tomorrow before any of the shifters drink them, but I know you'll lock the house again now, so it'll probably be fine." Or so Selena said, even though she wished she could be certain.

The house had been locked up before, too, yet a vial had become contaminated. That hadn't happened on its own. Nor did she believe that the supply Patrick and the other Alpha Force members had brought from Ft. Lukman had been tainted there or somewhere on the way.

What was the answer? Did the CAs all have keys to this meeting house? Even if they did, surely none of them would have tainted the elixir—would they?

She wished she knew.

"Too bad your elixir isn't somehow primed to let people know what's happened to it," Owen said, echoing her thoughts.

She laughed nevertheless. "I know you must think of shifters like me as woo-woo kinds of entities, but that idea out-woo-woos everything. A liquid that communicates with people around it? I'll have to relay that idea to our superiors who formulate the tonic and see if they can figure out a way to do it."

"Guess you've opened my mind to possibilities I'd never imagined before."

"Then you've really got an imagination," Selena responded, still smiling. "Got a million dollars? I'll sell you shares in a company that'll make that imaginary elixir."

It was Owen's turn to laugh. "Wish I had that million bucks, but I don't think I'll buy in to your company. Sorry."

He remained standing near her, beside the refrigerator. His expression was lighthearted as he looked down at her. He appeared both boyish and all adult male. All gorgeous, sexy adult male.

Selena knew she had to get out of there. Go to bed, since they'd need to awaken early the next morning for their regularly scheduled breakfast and discussion of what that day would bring—before any shifting took place.

She was tired, and it was the middle of the night.

Yet all she was telling herself was nonsense. What she really wanted was to stay right there with Owen. Throw herself into his arms and take advantage of this completely unanticipated opportunity to make love with him yet again.

She made herself take a step backward. Putting her hand up to her mouth, she feigned a yawn. "Anyhow, it's definitely late. We'd better get to bed."

"My thoughts exactly. How about here?" Owen's tone was low and rough and filled with suggestion that made Selena's insides heat up and churn. She didn't resist when he closed the short distance between them and took her into his arms.

She threw her head back, eagerly awaiting the kiss that came immediately. His lips were hot, his tongue more than suggestive as he pressed his lower body against hers.

She could feel his hardness and could not keep herself from moving her hands from behind him and forward, caressing everything in their path outside his warm clothing—his back, then his buttocks, his hips and, finally, his erection.

His moan made her move even more, one hand finding its way inside the front of his pants until she could grasp his hot stiffness. His readiness made her gasp against his mouth—or was it caused by his hands stroking her similarly, starting with her back and behind, then moving to her breasts?

How did he get her shirt and bra off so quickly without her even realizing what he was doing? Or had her movements assisted him in his efforts?

She had a fleeting thought, as they moved in unison toward the ottomans, that their privacy here might be limited.

But it didn't matter. Not when she easily stripped Owen of all his clothing, too.

Hadn't she believed they would never have this kind of opportunity again?

Was it part of the woo-woo auras around them somehow that they did, just this once more?

Again he had come prepared. In moments, his erection was encased in a condom and she was lying on her back on top of two of the ottomans pushed together against the wall. They were firm and velvety against her bare back, not the best place to make love but certainly adequate.

Selena stroked Owen outside the condom even as he gently pressed his hand against her heated moistness and thrust one finger, then two, inside her.

She wanted to scream out her need. Instead, she once more gasped and said, "Please."

She didn't have to say any more. He adjusted his position and was suddenly inside her, moving and heating her and arousing her even more as she thrust her own body up in a primitive, wonderful rhythm.

She heard him moan her name even as he pounded and pressed harder. "Selena..."

And then she flew over the edge.

Okay, so he had taken advantage of her, here in the silence of the currently unoccupied house.

He had taken advantage of himself, too, Owen thought as he walked behind Selena up the steps to the main floor. As phenomenal as making love with her had been—again—he shouldn't have done it.

The more he made love with Selena, the more he wanted her. But soon they would be in a position of never seeing each other again, even if the CAs' mission was successful. Which it had to be.

When they reached the front door, he reached out for the knob, then stopped. "Okay to open it?"

"You mean you want me to listen and sniff the air to ensure there's nothing or no one out there we don't want to see?" Her tone was wry, but her brilliant amber eyes shone as if she appreciated his acceptance of her. He considered teasing her, lying to her, claiming that wasn't what he'd meant at all. But it had been, at least to some extent. And he did accept her, maybe too much.

Although he still hadn't actually seen her shift...

He had, however, seen her while she was shifted. Watching her in the process would simply give him another reason to see her naked.

Did he really want to see her changing as he had viewed the male CAs actually shifting into their wolf forms?

He well knew the answer was yes, as strange as that seemed even to himself.

"You got it," he told her. "Use all those wolfy senses of yours and make sure we're okay."

He put his arm around her slender, black-clad shoulders as she did, in fact, turn up her nose into the air and inhale. She stood still, and as he watched the concentration on her lovely face, he figured she was listening, too.

In a moment she said, "All seems well, at least as far as I can tell. Time for us to go back to our respective quarters and get some sleep. Tomorrow is going to be filled with one vital exercise."

"That's for sure," he said. But he still didn't open the door. Instead, he pulled her back into his arms and gave her one final, hot, deep kiss for the night, then finally led her outside into the darkness and walked her to the front door of the house where she was staying. There, he gave her another kiss—much quicker and cooler. "See you tomorrow," he whispered.

"No, later today." She stood on tiptoe for a moment and gave him another quick kiss in return, then used her key to enter the house.

Good thing he had parked down the hill so as not to be so obvious about his presence up here. He remained on alert with his human senses as he made his way down the driveway, and the brief walk gave him some additional time to think.

As Selena had not had to remind him, tomorrow was damned important.

Despite not being a shifter, he had special senses, too—more intuition than enhanced bodily senses, though.

His gut told him that they would all have to be particularly careful tomorrow in the last round of exercises.

Would something go wrong?

Not if he could help it.

Despite lying in her bed and hearing Lupe snoring gently on the floor beside her, Selena didn't sleep much that night.

It wasn't entirely because she kept rehashing in her mind her latest round of great sex with Owen. No, she was worried.

She had come here as a member of Alpha Force, and her very special unit had been trusted with a very special assignment.

They had all, every one of them, performed well so far, demonstrating and teaching and advising.

But was it enough?

For it seemed there was something else they had to do, something that hadn't been fully anticipated.

They had to protect their students. Protect them potentially from perhaps the most vital part of what they were contributing to help the CAs—the Alpha Force elixir.

Maybe. Maybe the presence of that ipecac, or another chemical, had been a fluke. An accident. It wasn't present in the remaining vials. Selena was pretty convinced of that.

At least it hadn't been tonight, when Owen and she had been there.

But tomorrow?

Did the Alpha Force team dare to allow the CAs to drink the stuff again, just in case?

Did they dare forbid them from trying it—especially when that could ruin their entire pending mission?

One ugly thought in particular imposed itself in Selena's mind.

What if Owen truly had been waiting for her that night? What if he had fully intended her to be there with him checking out the elixir, to ensure that it was pure and untainted, so she could report that to Patrick Worley and the other Alpha Force members here?

She hadn't actually seen Owen leave this enclave.

What if he had gone back inside the meeting house, down into the basement, and contaminated one or more vials of the elixir that she would, at least theoretically, vouch for tomorrow?

Was that why he had made love with her again—as one hot, major, sexy distraction?

No. Surely not. He couldn't do such a terrible thing… could he?

Or was she convincing herself he wouldn't because, despite all her better judgment, she was falling in love with him?

She wasn't certain. Couldn't be certain.

As a result, she would definitely get up very early in the morning and check out the elixir yet again, before Owen arrived. Or appeared to arrive.

During the rest of the day she would be cautious, too. She loved Alpha Force. She owed it to Alpha Force to do her job right. A life could be riding on the result— that kidnap victim's.

The lives of the shifting CAs, too.

"Oh, Owen," she whispered into the night and heard

Lupe's doggy nails on the wooden floor beside her bed as her cover dog stood at her words. She reached over and petted Lupe's soft, furry head. "It's okay, girl. I'm just talking out loud. We'll be fine. I'll make sure of it."

She hoped. And she definitely hoped she would not have to accuse the man she was starting to love of treason against his country.

Owen received a phone call very early in the morning from his superior, Deputy Commissioner Anthony Creay.

The call didn't wake him, though. He hadn't slept well that night. And he wasn't surprised.

He had a lot on his mind, including Selena Jennay... and her many, diverse, amazing assets.

"What's up, Anthony?" he asked after their initial greetings. He didn't rise from bed but just lay there, waiting.

"Another message from our kidnappers," he said. "This one was another warning—and a recorded message from their hostage begging for help. They're trying to ratchet things up as they play games with us. And before you ask, we've again put some of our most skilled technical people on it to try to track down where the calls are coming from, but these guys are smart. The signals are bounced around the entire solar system, or so it seems. In any event, there's some satellite involvement from what I gather, as well as pinging from several different countries all over the world. But some newer-technology drones we had flying in the vicinity where we believe they're hiding did sense some kind of outside human presence within the woods—before their electronics were hacked into this time. The kidnappers might just have some kind of undercover sentry on duty, though, since there wasn't any indication of anyone going to or leaving the site. All the more reason to send in your shapeshifters, since the drones also conveyed indications of wildlife in the area."

"What was the warning this time?"

"Basically the same kind of thing, reminding the RCMP that poor, frantic, screaming Madame Brodheureux will be killed in days unless her loving husband dips into the coffers of Xanogistics really quickly now and pays them off. Oh, and all games must stop and reality is the key, whatever that means."

"It still sounds to me as if they've heard rumors of something like shapeshifters supposedly coming to save their prisoner, don't you think?"

"Yeah, I think. And I also think that, if so, we have a traitor in our midst—one who has to be outed before your actual operation begins tomorrow. Any ideas?"

"I'm working on it," Owen said, and he was. The problem was that he hadn't yet reached any conclusions. Whoever it was had to have knowledge and somehow have the ability to reach those kidnappers. Or perhaps be one of them in a double-agent role here.

Who? And how?

One of his new team? A member of Alpha Force? Either way could be deadly to the CAs.

"Any further information on that shifting liquid?" Anthony asked, changing the subject somewhat. Or not. The likely scenario was that the same person who was in contact with the kidnappers had also tainted the elixir.

"Not yet, although I worked with one of the Alpha

Force members to confirm that what we still have here appears pure and workable."

"Let's hope so. Now, keep me informed about to-day's exercises as they're undertaken. I'll want to feel sure that tomorrow's a go."

So will I, Owen thought. "Yes, sir," he said. They soon hung up. A good thing.

It was definitely time to start this new day.

Chapter 21

That morning, before they all went to the meeting house for breakfast and to help the CAs prepare for their day, Selena requested a brief session with her fellow Alpha Force members.

Patrick looked at her curiously as they all headed into the sparsely furnished living room—their CO was wearing official camo fatigues. "Something wrong?"

"You mean besides some of our elixirs being tainted yesterday?" Selena had stopped beside the fireplace, Lupe at her side, and stood watching the others. She felt too restless to sit down. Too uneasy, and too eager to accomplish something, anything.

Seeing Patrick's displeased grimace at her sarcasm, she realized she needed to settle down and act like the professional military member she was.

"Sorry," she said. "It's just that I've been concerned

about it, as we've all been. I even wound up visiting the meeting house in the middle of the night and going to the basement to do what I could to check the remaining vials."

"Really? By yourself?" Rainey, sitting on the edge of the sofa, looked hurt, as if she thought she should have been asked to accompany her.

Selena had already gone through several scenarios in her mind and decided to be truthful—to a point. "No, it turned out that Owen was as worried as I was, so we met up there and checked out all the vials. He recognized that I would be better than him in noticing any inappropriate odors, but we both studied the coloration. They all seemed fine. But just so you all know, that's where I'm sneaking off to first thing this morning, too—the basement of the meeting house, and I won't want the CAs to know. I just feel I need to double-check those vials again. Okay?"

What if whoever had contaminated that one vial purposely allowed the rest to remain pure—until this morning? She still hadn't zeroed in on one person she thought was guilty, but that didn't mean whoever it was wouldn't act again surreptitiously despite their keeping closer watch on the elixir. She looked again at Patrick.

"I think that's a good idea," her commanding officer said, "at least for today's final exercises. But you all should be aware I was concerned, too—so much so that I ordered a new supply of fresh elixir to be flown in today. Jonas and I will drive down after breakfast to pick it up at the Vancouver airport. It'll arrive too late to be used today, so your checking out the current supply again is a great idea, Selena. But we need everything to be perfect tomorrow, and if anything goes wrong it won't be because of anything Alpha Force could have prevented."

"Thank you," Selena said as gratefully as if she was the one in charge and would be blamed for any failure. She almost wanted to laugh at herself. But she did feel relieved, not just because she wasn't the only one who was truly worried, but also because there was a probable solution on the way.

She was surprised when Jonas came over, shook her hand and followed it with a hug. And a laugh. "Since when does our newest member consider herself in charge?" he asked.

"Since this new member is a former schoolteacher and learned fast that anything that goes wrong in her classroom is ultimately her responsibility," Selena responded, feeling a lot more lighthearted.

"Okay, let's head on over there," Patrick said, breaking up the emotion-fest, which was fine with Selena. "When we get breakfast going, you can excuse yourself to head for the bathroom or whatever. We'll make sure everyone else remains in view while you run your new assessment, okay?"

"Fine with me." Selena felt immensely relieved, first that Patrick was on her side and, second, that she would in fact get the opportunity to make one more inspection.

She only hoped that Patrick found a way to capture Owen's attention, or at least secure his presence. Not that Selena truly suspected him of anything—or did she? In any case, she'd feel a lot less uneasy if, this time, she remained on her own.

Owen had driven himself back to the enclave alone that morning, parking this time in the area at the top of the hill. He had followed the other CAs, who rode in the rental car driven by Sal. The young man clearly wanted to show that he felt fine this morning.

Was that some kind of indication he had poisoned himself yesterday to remove any suspicion against him about things that might go wrong in the next couple of days?

Highly unlikely. Not that upbeat, enthusiastic kid, right?

Yet at the moment, Owen wasn't ready to dismiss anyone from his list of suspects who could have caused yesterday's incident.

Now he was in the kitchen with his entire group of CAs, who all sat at the table, chatting eagerly about their upcoming day. The two other wolf shifters were priming Sal about what they were likely to see and do in final preparation for undertaking the real thing tomorrow.

"The mountains here are likely a lot different from the ones we'll face tomorrow," Tim was saying. "Less craggy, and maybe even more wooded, is what I've gathered. But we'll rehearse it today as if it was the real thing. Both times, especially tomorrow, the main thing we have to do is remember to act like the wolves we'll be, and prowl, and watch—and help the guys back at our headquarters, who'll be monitoring the video from the cameras we'll be wearing so they can zero in on where the hostage is being held."

Exactly, Owen thought. If only it was that easy.

He wondered when the Alpha Force team intended to join them for breakfast. In the meantime, he and Andrea seemed to be the designated chefs this morning. They were cooking pancakes, easy stuff, quick and filling. That should be enough, along with the caffeine in the coffee he had already brewed, to help stimulate the shifting CAs' energy. Or maybe their adrenaline would be sufficient.

Did shifted werewolves or falcons produce adrenaline?

Heck, he really didn't know much at all about shifters—and here he was, relying on them to lead the way on this highly critical mission.

He nearly pounded the stove with the pan he was holding, the one in which he had just poured pancake batter, but caught himself. His lack of complete knowledge wasn't the only source of his frustration.

He wanted more information about the origin of yesterday's elixir problem. He wanted to feel fully comfortable that tomorrow would be a highly successful day, that the captive would be rescued and the kidnappers caught—or killed.

Speaking of frustration…where was Selena?

As if she had heard him, there she was, along with the rest of the Alpha Force team. They seemed to breeze into the kitchen and take over, as though their confidence in who they were and what they did was secure.

If only he could feel that certain of how things would go.

"Good morning," said Patrick, clearly asserting his position as their leader. He even wore a camouflage uniform this morning, which perhaps was standard for the Alpha Force members on official duty at their own posts. That was fine, as long as he stayed up here and didn't head down the hill to West Columbia, where townsfolk might see him.

Owen assumed he was making a nonverbal statement by his clothes—making sure the CAs remembered who Alpha Force was and what they were doing here.

None of Patrick's subordinates were clad similarly, though. Selena, as usual, managed to make a black T-shirt and jeans look highly sexy. The two aides, Jonas and Rainey, also wore black, but Marshall, though similarly clad, had on deep green clothing.

"Are we all ready for the final exercise today?" Patrick looked around the room at the other CAs, who sipped their coffee and talked softly to each other. Owen wished he had the hearing of a shifter so he could have heard what they'd been discussing. Were they revving each other up for success? Or priming themselves to do what they could, yet potentially fail?

It should certainly help to have the Alpha Force members among them.

"Pancakes? Yum." That was Selena, who joined him at the stove.

"Care to help me cook them?" he asked.

"Sorry. I need to take a potty break, and hopefully you'll be finished cooking by the time I get back here."

Really? Potty break, when she had just arrived from right next door? She didn't look ill or uncomfortable. That seemed like too much information anyway.

Owen had a thought, that what she'd said was intended for everyone to hear. He also had an idea where she was really going when she left the kitchen. Would she go downstairs to the basement alone to give the elixir a final check for the day? He hoped so.

On the other hand, what if she was the person who'd contaminated it? He didn't think so, didn't want to think so, but...

She had been gone a little more than a minute when

he decided he wanted to join her if his assumption of where she had gone was correct. He could then observe to make sure she didn't do anything she shouldn't with the elixir. Despite believing his suspicion had no merit, he couldn't be positive.

He sidled up to Andrea, who was whipping up some additional batter in a bowl on the counter. "How about watching this for me? I need to take a short break, too."

"Sure," she said and took his place at the stove.

But before Owen got to the kitchen door, Patrick joined him. "We need to talk," he said. The guy spoke with command, and Owen had a feeling that if he said no, Patrick would find a way to ensure that got changed to a yes, but he decided to try anyway.

"About today's exercise? Sounds like a good idea. Soon as I get back."

"No, now."

"Like I said, I need a break." Owen kept his expression calm but put an edge into his voice.

"You want to do an exercise today, then let's talk now."

That convinced Owen all the more that not only was Selena checking out the elixir again, but her commanding officer was also well aware of it—and didn't want anyone else there.

Did that prove Selena was trustworthy…or that Patrick and the other Alpha Force members were not?

No matter. Owen's superiors had entered into the arrangement with Alpha Force trusting them fully. What reason would they have for turning it upside down? Because they were somehow affiliated with the kidnappers? Because the US wanted to sabotage what the RCMP needed to accomplish and allow the hostage to be murdered for some international purpose he couldn't fathom?

It was possible, but highly unlikely. And if Owen decided to dig in his heels, maybe his CAs would get no more access to the vital elixir.

"Okay," he finally said, holding up his hands in what he hoped appeared like surrender. "Let's talk."

But surrender wasn't really in Owen's vocabulary. He had every intention of finding out where Selena had gone and why.

Selena came into the dining room a short while later, practically panting from being out of breath.

She'd done what she needed to and had hurried as she had checked out each of the dozen vials of elixir one more time.

All had still seemed fine. Even so, she would quietly advise the two shifting aides, Jonas and Rainey, to do a final check of each bottle they had their charges drink.

She trusted them. Both had been members of Alpha Force for a while, both in the role of aides to shifters. They hadn't been responsible for yesterday's problem.

And if it turned out there was a problem today? She second-guessed herself. Well, if so, it might be one of them despite her trust.

Taking a deep breath to calm herself, she smiled as she walked toward the end of the large table, where Patrick sat beside Owen. There was an empty chair across from them. "Sorry for the delay," she said without elaborating. She sat down, and soon pancakes and a bottle of syrup were passed to her.

"Are you feeling okay?" Owen asked her. She looked into his face and found that his strong, dark eyebrows were raised over his intense blue eyes. He looked more amused than concerned, and she had a feeling he knew exactly what she had been up to.

"Oh, yes. I wound up checking something on my phone and time got away from me." She smiled brightly, knowing she wasn't fooling him.

But neither did he look worried. If he was guilty of something, his handsome face would surely be blank if he didn't appear uneasy. That was a good thing.

Just because she hadn't found any problems, though, she couldn't categorically dismiss him from her suspicions.

"Mmm," she soon said. "These pancakes are great. You made them?" She raised her own brows questioningly as she looked at him.

"Yes," he said, "mostly, although Andrea helped."

"Guess you're a man of many talents." Selena took another bite of pancake, knowing she was both teasing and goading him.

Today was likely the last day they would get to see each other. She hoped that all went perfectly with the CAs' last exercise, and she certainly intended to do all she could to guarantee it. But she also planned to enjoy as much as she could her last interplay with Owen. Especially knowing that getting close to him in any manner from now on would be impossible.

Owen hurried from the basement behind Jonas, who, in turn, was behind the three male wolves loping up the stairs ahead of them.

He had just watched them shift. Once again, he could only marvel at their transformation.

Sal, the last of this line of wolves, had seemed fine

this time, fortunately. Because Selena had made sure all the elixir remained untainted? Owen was sure that hadn't hurt. He hadn't yet confirmed his assumption about what she had done this morning, but he felt fairly certain of it.

Was that because he had begun to be able to sense things about her? Maybe, or maybe that was just his wish.

He quickly reached the main floor, where Patrick and Marshall waited in the hallway. Their heads were turned to observe the wolves who'd passed them, heading toward the front door. When they turned back Owen saw the smiles on their faces.

"Andrea's already outside," Patrick said. "Selena and Rainey, too, watching our falcon soar above this place. Marshall and I are just hanging around to see our wolves head out for the exercise, but we've got something we need to do, so we'll be leaving in a few minutes."

"Fine," Owen said, then realized, with Jonas and Rainey again heading into the woods to remain at a designated clearing in case they were needed, that would leave him alone here with Selena.

Thoughts of what they could do alone together made his body start to react, but he tamped down those errant ideas. There was too much they still needed to do, no time to make those thoughts become reality.

It was too bad, but he told himself it was better that way. They'd already said that kind of goodbye to one another.

He was the last to go outside, but he was still able to see the wolves run through the paved area toward the woods, followed by Jonas and Rainey. Selena already stood near the path the wolves took, and she turned to watch as they disappeared among the trees.

Above soared the falcon who was Andrea.

The exercise had begun.

He watched as Selena talked briefly with Patrick and Marshall. Then the two men crossed the paved area and got into their car.

As they drove off, Owen thought once more about how he was now, once again, here alone with Selena. But instead of considering how best to seduce her, he waited until she joined him near the front door of the meeting house and told her, "Looks like it's just us to finish cleaning up after breakfast."

If anything was a turnoff, it had to be that. But Selena's expression as she regarded him with a warm smile somehow still seemed to convey interest in him.

All she said, though, was "Lucky us. Let's get it over with."

As they walked inside, Selena asked once more what he'd thought about watching the men become wolves.

"I doubt I'll ever become blasé about it," he said. "It seems incredible every time I watch, even though I know it's real."

She was ahead of him and turned back, as if wanting to see his expression, to try to read his mind about what he really thought about it. "It's definitely real," she said. She preceded him past the living room door and into the kitchen.

The morning's plates and flatware had been stacked in the sink. He moved past her. "I'll wash, you put them into the drainer, okay?"

"Fine."

They seemed to coordinate well with no effort. He

remained highly aware of Selena's curvaceous form beside him, taking the soapy objects from him, rinsing them, then sticking them into the dish rack in a very organized manner. He wasn't surprised about that. Selena seemed organized, logical, in all she did.

Was she that way while shifted, too?

He'd seen her as a wolf a couple of times, but only briefly. He would likely never see her again that way or learn more about her in her canine form.

Too bad, especially now, when he really had become interested in shifters. His earlier distrust of them had been replaced by at least somewhat of an admiration. He was glad he was the officer in charge of the CAs— and he hoped he would continue to be after tomorrow.

Would they succeed in their operation?

Would they—

His phone rang. He smiled as Selena handed him a towel and he dried his hands.

When he pulled his phone from his pocket, he noticed immediately that it was Anthony Creay calling. "Hello, sir," he said. "I was going to call you a little later. Our exercise of the day has begun, and—"

"There's been yet another message from the kidnappers," Anthony interrupted. "It didn't make much sense, but this is what it said—'Grab on to today since things will go wrong and tomorrow will be worse.'"

Selena realized that Owen did not intend for her to hear his conversation with his boss, but with her enhanced hearing she couldn't help it.

Not that she tried to avoid eavesdropping.

But what did that message mean?

Was something off about what the shifters were planning today as practice for what would actually occur tomorrow?

Would whatever it was lead to failure the next day?

She had to do something to ensure all went well, no matter what that cryptic message meant.

She knew how the mission at least had to begin, and so when Owen ended his conversation and hung up, his expression distant and grim, she said, "I know what I have to do, Owen, at least for now. And you need to help me."

Chapter 22

Was she overreacting? Or was she using this new twist as a reason to do what she'd wanted to do for days, to learn Owen's true feelings about shifters, about her?

Maybe both. Or neither.

"What are you up to?" Owen's expression was both quizzical and amused.

She feared the latter part would undoubtedly change quickly once he knew what was on her mind.

"I want to learn what's really going on," she told him. "Do my own kind of observation today so we can feel comfortable everything will be as good as possible tomorrow. But as I said, I will need your help."

"Sure," he said, sounding anything but sure. "What exactly do you want me to do?"

"Act as my aide. I'm going to shift."

She watched his expression even more carefully, as

if her human sense of vision was effective not only for viewing what was happening around her, but also for delving into someone's mind. Owen's mind. Too bad that wasn't really true.

He said nothing for a few seconds, and his expression was unreadable. Did he hate the idea? Would he find an excuse to say no or just come right out and object? She could conceivably handle a shift on her own—but the test part of this equation was important to her, too.

"Good idea," he said finally, half surprising her. "But you're going to have to let me act as your aide not only for shifting, but also for helping to watch out for you during this exercise."

His reaction was interesting. Sure, she knew he was protective, a worthy member of the RCMP, but this went beyond his duty. She didn't ask how he intended to watch out for her. In reality, if she didn't want his help beyond her initial shifting, she would be able to outrun him and ensure he couldn't catch up or be anywhere near her.

She would have to determine what was the best course of action later.

While she was shifted.

At last. He was finally going to get to watch this lovely, human woman go through the clearly uncomfortable— and incredible—process of shapeshifting.

His wish—one of them, at least—was apparently about to come true.

Be careful what you wish for. The old cautionary expression suddenly invaded his mind.

He shooed it out just as quickly.

It turned out that Selena had been particularly smart.

Not that he was surprised, since he'd already been impressed by this woman and her knowledge and teaching capabilities and intellect.

Not to mention her physical assets.

But she had also been wise enough to camouflage what was the final vial of elixir that Rainey and she had had with them when they had first joined Anthony and him, before he had taken the women here to join his CAs.

It was in the refrigerator in the basement of the house in which the Alpha Force members were staying, hidden in what appeared to be a brand-new carton of orange juice.

He found that out after she told him to follow her back to the other home. There, after unlocking the door, she first knelt and gave Lupe, who had been with them, a big hug, then secured her in the bedroom. Afterward they trekked down to the basement fridge for the precious vial.

Now, in the kitchen, he watched as she peeled the cardboard of the orange-juice container away from the glass vial inside. She stood leaning against the counter near the sink, studying the liquid it contained.

"It looks clear, no contamination." She unscrewed the cap and held it to her nose. "No indication of anything but the usual citrusy scent, nothing like ipecac. Of course, I doubt anyone but Rainey and me knew this was here. But even so, there's no guarantee no one else got into this place to do some damage."

"You still think that's what happened with the contaminated bottle Sal drank." He made it a statement, not a question, because that was his belief, too.

"What else could it be?"

He didn't want to get into the other possibilities again, like some kind of problem at the source or en route. No, it was better to assume the trouble originated here and remain cautious.

Like Patrick was doing by retrieving the new supply of elixir that had been shipped here. The stuff that would be used tomorrow. It was a good idea, and Selena had just informed him that was what Patrick and Marshall were up to.

"Okay," she said. "Time to go back to the other house. I want to shift there, in the basement." She opened up a cabinet and withdrew a plastic shopping bag. "This will be strictly an observational detail on my part, and nothing else should be necessary today. I just figure that by watching who's doing what, I'll be able to give some advice to your CAs about how to act tomorrow during the real rescue operation."

That was probably true, but only in part. He knew that her need to do this had been precipitated by his phone call from Anthony Creay and the additional threat it seemed to contain.

He hoped that the techie team set on tracking down the call's source was successful this time. But since it hadn't been before, he remained dubious.

Having someone who knew what she was doing—Selena—provide the kind of advice she was clearly intending to give could be essential to the success of the CAs tomorrow.

They definitely had to be successful on this first attempt. It might very well be their last.

He watched her seal the bottle again and place it in the yellow plastic bag with a supermarket logo on it. If anyone happened to notice her carrying it, she would simply seem to be moving food from one of the houses to the other.

Another smart move on her part, he thought. But when had she done anything other than act smart?

On their way back to the other house, he wished he had some of her enhanced senses. Would he hear anything beyond the normal breeze in the treetops, an occasional car engine from below the driveway, additional chirps from local birds? Would he smell anything more than the slightly sweet aroma of the surrounding fir trees?

They didn't talk. He had a lot of questions about what she would be looking for…and what her shift really would feel like. But he assumed she was using those enhanced senses of hers to ensure their safety on their hurried walk and did not want to interrupt her.

Once they'd reentered the other house and locked its doors again behind them, Owen followed Selena down the steps to the basement.

He knew the drill. He'd seen it several times now when Jonas had acted as aide to the wolf-shifting CAs. Without Selena having to say anything, he crossed the large, concrete-encased room to the refrigerator. Beside it, on the floor, sat a wooden crate. It contained the special battery-operated lantern that created the light resembling that of the full moon.

That would now be his responsibility: aiming it on Selena's naked body to cause her to shift once she had drunk the elixir.

Did he want this to happen? Yes. Maybe. Would he think differently about her once he actually saw her shift?

No. Maybe. But he was more than aware that she was a shifter. Had seen her already shifted.

And between then and now, he had also had the real pleasure of seeing her naked.

"Okay," she finally said, her tone bright and her face beaming. She was clearly looking forward to this.

Was he? He wasn't sure, but he hoped to make her think so.

"This is great," he said, pumping enthusiasm into his voice. "I'll finally get to see you shift." He held the light but did not turn it on yet. No need until she was ready—meaning naked.

He was sorry to see her expression falter, but for only a moment. "Yep," she said. "So you know, once I'm in wolf form my intention is to follow the same path as the wolfen CAs did. I'm sure I'll be able to use my senses to figure out where they went, and if I have any difficulties I'm sure I'll see Andrea flying above them. At this point, I only intend to observe them, make sure all's okay despite what that call Anthony described to you said. I'll also make mental notes about any suggestions I have for tomorrow. This is simply a way of assuring myself, my fellow Alpha Forcers and you that whatever was claimed in that call was a bunch of horse pucky." She grinned. But then she added, "And in case it's not, I'll do what I can to fix it. That may mean my showing up where Rainey and Jonas are, so it wouldn't hurt for you to head there, too, if you can determine where it is. That would be a good way for you to follow up on your intent to not just observe my shift, but to keep an eye on what's going on."

"I'm sure I'll find them," Owen said. In fact, he was certain, since they'd described their rendezvous location to his CAs yesterday and repeated the information earlier that day. The clearing they described was part-way up the mountain, along their initial path—the one Selena would follow.

"Okay," she said again. "Here goes." She stood near him as she removed the clear glass vial from the plastic bag. She placed both on the floor.

She started to strip. First, she pulled her black shirt over her head, mussing her silvery-brown hair, but she did not attempt to smooth it out. She next kicked off her athletic shoes, pulled off her socks and then stepped out of her jeans. She stood there in her underwear for just a moment, looking at him. Smiling softly at him, as if teasing…and tempting.

In moments, she had removed her bra and panties. Without getting near him or waiting to see if he got closer to her, she knelt, picked up the vial of liquid and drank it all quickly.

"Now," she said, "let's get that light going."

And he did.

Ignoring his initial surge of lust at seeing her naked, he watched as if mesmerized as, in moments, her change began. Her limbs grew thinner, changed shape, even as her lovely, smooth skin started to grow hair. Her eyes, still looking at him, remained the same for a long moment, but the rest of her head began quickly morphing into the shape of a wolf's.

He didn't say anything. Couldn't say anything. Was he completely turned off by what was happening?

Yes—and no. He was as fascinated as he had been when the men changed into wolves, even though this was Selena, the woman to whom he was so attracted. With whom he had made love.

He wasn't sure how long he had been watching, but soon there she was—a sleek, fur-covered, attentive wolf.

She stared up at him with her newly modified eyes, her muzzle in the air, watching him stare back at her.

What had he thought of her change? What was he thinking now?

She couldn't ask. Did not want to ask.

She needed to start moving. She had something to accomplish.

She loped to the stairway and up its steps. At the top she had to wait since she could not open the door. She felt Owen's legs against her side as he reached around her and pushed the door so she could get out.

She again had to wait until he opened the front door, and there he maneuvered around so he was the first to go through.

Ever the gentleman, the cautious police officer, he glanced around before allowing her to exit, looking, she imagined, for interlopers.

She waited just in case, not wanting to intrude on what he was doing, yet even in waiting she was not idle. She moved her ears to listen, again lifted her nose to scent the air.

She sensed nothing of any concern.

When Owen stopped walking she sprinted past him, enjoying her freedom to run unimpeded on four legs, swiftly, to the pathway beneath the trees and into the forest.

She did not wait to see if he followed. They had discussed what he would do before, when they could both speak and negotiate and each comprehend what the other was saying.

He called, "Selena, wait," but she did not obey. She was not a trained pet canine. She was an Alpha Force wolf with work to do.

She ran and ran as pine needles scratched at the base of her paws, sometimes feeling only soft dirt instead. Around her were the aromas and sounds of those trees and, sometimes, their occupants—squirrels, birds of many types, wildlife even she did not recognize since this was not her usual habitat.

Finding a small clearing soon that was void of tree branches in the center, she tilted her head back and looked upward. No falcon soaring there.

She picked up only stale aromas, from when the other shifters had trudged through here, yet she slowed her pace when she started off again because she had sensed a different clearing, the one where the aides waited.

What would Rainey do if she knew her shifting charge was so close and in wolfen form? Selena did not know and did not want to find out.

Another clearing appeared, and this time, when she looked up, Selena did see the falcon soaring in circles.

She stalked more slowly this time, not wanting to startle her shifted counterparts into attacking her as if she was truly a wild wolf, a foe of theirs.

She made small woofing noises to alert them, in a pattern humans might recognize as Morse code even if unfamiliar with what the pattern stood for. In this instance she used dash-dot-dash-dot, then dot-dash.

This was one form of communication she had informed these CAs about, should they need to let an-

other one of their kind know of their presence. It was the pattern for C-A.

She approached, scenting all three wolfen forms near her. They were similar yet different in appearance and in scent, and she knew who was who.

Craig was the closest when she entered their clearing at the top of a mountain, along its far side. They each watched her warily as if anticipating she might not be one of their kind.

She simply sat and watched them, nodding her head. They soon appeared to accept her, and she observed them start to ignore her and resume the exercise they had been conducting before she'd joined them.

One at a time, they lowered their bodies closer to the ground and slunk to the edge of the clearing. Then they each raised their heads and looked out from among the trees over the nearby valley to the mountain slope just beyond. They scented the air as their ears moved to capture sounds.

As if they were in fact in a similar area, searching similar mountains for signs of life. Human life. Kidnappers and victims.

She found no indication of any problems, any danger, despite the message received by Anthony Creay. Even so, she waited and watched, curious, cautious... and concerned.

Owen had just joined Rainey and Jonas at the clearing, where they waited as backup for the shifted CAs. It had been challenging to locate it, but he had finally succeeded.

The area was small, with several boulders in the center, where they sat and waited and chatted.

They looked up, no doubt to watch for a falcon circling overhead. Owen had seen the soaring bird that was Andrea several times on his way up here when there had been other breaks in the trees, and he couldn't help but marvel. Despite her falcon form, she was actually another person…most of the time.

As was Selena.

Now, joining the aides, he told them he was here to observe, went through the motions of acting normal, as if he hadn't just seen the most incredible situation in his life—watching Selena shift into wolf form.

Yes, he had anticipated everything that had happened during her shift. Hadn't he already viewed the men changing from human to wolf form several times? He'd known what to expect.

But this time, it was Selena. Gorgeous, nude Selena.

"Why are you here?" Rainey asked as she walked over to where he stood by the path. She cast a look over her shoulder at Jonas, who was surveilling the woods. Her dark hair seemed even more a nest of curls than usual, maybe because of the breeze here. "Where is Selena?"

"She's—"

"She shifted, didn't she?" An amused and too-smug smile appeared on the aide's face. Did she know that Owen had made love with the shifter she'd been assigned to assist? He had a sinking feeling she did.

Well, so what? It was over now. *They* were over now, except for working together on this difficult assignment for the organizations they worked for.

"Is she up on this mountain, too?" Rainey asked next when he didn't directly respond to her other question. At least that one he had no issue about answering.

"Yes, she's joining the CAs for now."

"But why?" That was Jonas, who had hurriedly strode over to join Owen. He, too, wore casual dark clothing.

Talking to them forced Owen to focus on what they were saying instead of the vision of Selena and her shift that still occupied his mind.

"My superior officer called about yet another communication from the kidnappers. They made vague references that suggested that they knew we were about to take action against them. They didn't mention shapeshifters but indicated something was going to go wrong with whatever was planned. So Selena decided to shift and come up here to check on the CA shifters. Have you heard anything from them?"

"No," Rainey said, "and that probably means all's well."

"Maybe," Owen said slowly. "But…you know, maybe I should just have called to let you know Selena is here on the mountain, too, so you can watch out for her as well as the others. But right now I think I need to get back to our headquarters and wait for everyone there."

It had just occurred to Owen that it was a vital location that was currently unguarded by either CAs or Alpha Force members. It was probably fine, but he couldn't shake the unease. The kidnappers' threats continued to ring through his mind.

With the shifters up here on the mountain rehearsing what they would do tomorrow, these aides here to be their backup and Patrick and Marshall away from the headquarters picking up new elixir, the enclave was left particularly vulnerable—if the kidnappers had learned of its existence and it was the target of whatever they'd threatened to do.

Someone needed to be there to make sure it stayed secure.

That someone, Owen decided, had to be him.

With some help, perhaps. He would move Lupe to the main meeting house. She could bark if anyone appeared who shouldn't be there—and could act as Selena's cover if she happened to show up.

He headed to the Alpha Force house to get her.

Chapter 23

*E*nough. *Selena had been there, with the other shifters, for a while. In this form she had the same sense of time as she did in human form, and it felt like an hour. More than an hour. Too long, especially since all seemed fine in their exercise. Nothing appeared amiss in their rehearsal of how they would best fulfill their assignment tomorrow to observe, to learn, to save a life.*

She would not be there with them. Would not need to be. And as it had turned out, she did not need to be with them now to confirm all was going well despite her concerns.

Only, had she not come, she would not be certain of that, especially not this soon.

Now Sal sat with her in the clearing while Craig and Tim prowled nearby, continuing to assess this mock situation. She stood and edged toward Sal, then nudged

*his side with her muzzle to ensure he knew she intended
to communicate with him. When he looked at her and
made a noise deep in his throat, she nodded sideways
toward the path down the hill.*

*Then, without waiting for him to acknowledge what
she had conveyed, she began walking in that direction.*

Toward that other clearing, where the aides waited.

Where Owen waited.

*Only, when she arrived there, just Rainey and Jonas
were present. She stood at the edge of that clearing for
a while, observing, expecting to see Owen emerge from
the trees on one side or another, but he did not.*

*Rainey spotted her, though. That was part of her job
as an aide, being available as assistance for the shifted
CAs—remaining aware of all around her and prepared
to act as cover or backup or protection or whatever a
shifter might need.*

*Now Selena needed to know where Owen was. She
could not ask that question and in fact preferred that
the aides, Rainey in particular, did not even recognize
her desire to know.*

But Rainey was ever aware. "Selena? Everything
okay?" *She rushed toward her.*

*Selena nodded her head. There were times when
she was in wolf form that she wanted more than anything the ability to truly communicate with humans.
Times like now.*

*But with Rainey, she did not necessarily need to
speak. Her aide knew her well. Perhaps too well.*

"I figure you checked on the CAs, right?" *Rainey
asked her now.* "That's what Owen said. Are you looking for him? He headed back to the meeting house to
wait."

Now Selena was glad she could not speak. She did not need to acknowledge she was seeking Owen. She merely turned and began loping along the path toward the enclave.

As she neared it, apprehension and concern seemed to speed her up, as if turning her legs to limbs that were even more fleet than a normal, swift wolf's.

Where did the concern come from? She did not know. She only knew it was there.

As soon as Owen exited the path from the trees he saw an unfamiliar car on the pavement at the top of the hill along with the known rentals. He froze and immediately reached for his service weapon—which he did not have with him.

As a police officer on regular duty he was often armed. But his latest assignment was far from regular duty.

He would have to be cautious checking out who was there, but just because someone had come to the enclave did not mean there was a problem.

Looking around from the edge of the path, where he could duck behind the trees and call for backup if necessary, he observed movement. A person stood at the front door of the meeting house.

He recognized the man who was holding what appeared to be pizza boxes. He was one of the servers from the Yukon Bar. What was his name?

Oh, yeah… Boyd.

He didn't look threatening, especially not if he had brought dinner. But who had ordered it? No one had mentioned it to Owen.

In case it was some kind of ploy, he would continue to be vigilant.

"Hey," he called out as he strode from the trees, "what's going on?"

"Pizza." The guy raised the boxes in his hand. His light brown hair was blowing in the breeze, revealing how his ears stuck out. As Owen drew closer, he noticed that Boyd was frowning, but he wasn't acting at all threatening.

"I don't think anyone here ordered pizza." Owen figured that acting negative would get Boyd to reveal his mental state faster than simply okaying and paying for the pies.

"Yeah. It was called in some time ago. Whoever called said to deliver it now—around three o'clock." Boyd repositioned the boxes so he could balance them on one arm, then reached for his pocket. Owen froze, waiting for a weapon to appear, but instead the guy pulled out a phone and looked at it, probably checking the time.

"Do you know who made the call?" And who, therefore, had neglected to reveal it to Owen and possibly anyone else.

"Craig, I think. He's one of the guys I met at the Yukon. But this stuff was ordered from the pizza shop next door where I work during the day. I don't know if he's staying here, but I was told he hangs out here."

Craig. Why would he have ordered food when he was out for training, especially without telling anyone?

"And did Craig pay for it?" Owen asked.

"No, he didn't." Boyd's voice was suddenly chilly and he stared straight at Owen in the fading daylight. "Is he here? Let me talk to him."

"I'm not sure where he is." That wasn't a lie. Owen had a general idea of where the shifter might be, but he wasn't sure of his exact location. "I'll pay you for it."

"Okay." Boyd seemed to relax. Maybe this was legitimate. But Owen didn't like it.

He'd have to have a talk with Craig later about being responsible, particularly on days when an exercise was scheduled, especially a shifting exercise.

Owen reached into his trousers, pulled out his wallet and drew several bills from it. "Keep the change," he said, then exchanged the money for the boxes.

He didn't go into the house but stood there watching as the guy got into his car and drove off.

Only then, shaking his head, did Owen enter the Alpha Force house.

No! Something was terribly wrong. Selena had had an inkling of it before, but now she was certain of it as she watched the exchange between Owen and the server—Boyd—from the edge of the woods.

She smelled the spicy scent of the food Owen now carried into the house.

If that had been all she smelled, she would not feel so worried.

But the scent of ipecac assaulted her nostrils. Not as strong as the tomato, onions, oregano, garlic and a whole lot of red peppers. Much more subtle, but it hung in the air and nearly made her feel ill.

Or was that her concern, her fear for Owen?

Was the ipecac in the pizza? But the odor did not seem to entirely disappear into the house with Owen.

Then Boyd had some on his body? Maybe. But with his departure, shouldn't the scent have left, too?

*Would it help for Selena to go into the house and find
a way to warn Owen that all might not be well? That
he should not eat that pizza? That he should perhaps
call for backup, get her Alpha Force aides back down
the hill and into action here, to protect their location...
and Owen, too?*

*She had heard a dog woof when Owen went in. It
sounded like Lupe. Owen must have moved her into this
house after Selena had run off in wolf form. That familiar woof was her normal reaction to a person entering
someplace where she was located, but she was trained
well enough not to react as a watchdog unless confused
or specifically given an order to react that way.*

But now, suddenly, Lupe barked loudly but briefly.

What was happening? Selena had to find out.

*And she had to reassure herself that Owen was un-
harmed...or so she hoped.*

Odd, Owen thought. Maybe it was nothing, but it
just didn't feel right. He went straight to the kitchen, not
only to put down the food, but also to let Lupe loose.

He was quite surprised to see Yvanne there, kneeling on the floor and petting the now-quiet wolflike dog.
She was rather dressed up, in a silvery scarf over her
charcoal-colored shirt that matched her slacks and low-
topped boots, and seemed to be getting along famously
with Lupe—two wolves communicating? Yvanne was
a shifter, of course.

Despite being in human form, she did not look prepared to communicate with Owen. In fact, she appeared
a bit startled to see him. She stood up immediately and
faced him.

What was going on?

"Hi," Owen said, assuming as casual a demeanor as he could despite being on high alert. "What brings you here?"

"A late lunch," she said. "I was told the exercise being held today would be over but only those who'd shifted would be around." Which meant she knew too much, but he was already aware of that. "Where's Sal?"

"He's not back yet," Owen said. "Did you order the pizza?"

"No, I heard Craig did."

Something definitely seemed off here. Why would Yvanne think only the shifters would be around now? Or was this some kind of ploy on her part? Had she ordered the pizza and decided on this pretense of innocence for reasons of her own?

"You know," he said, "I was just up on the mountain with our aides. Why don't you and I go back there and see if they know what's going on?" He didn't want to leave this woman here alone. He didn't especially want her with him, either, but at least this way he would know where she was and what she was doing, even if she had some kind of nefarious plan in mind. He needed some backup, and the aides could help to watch her while Owen determined what he needed to do next.

"I don't know," she said. "I was told to wait here."

"By whom?" Owen demanded.

"Would you like a piece of pizza while we're waiting for everyone?"

What he would like was some answers. Yvanne was clearly avoiding answering anything directly.

Which made Owen feel certain he wouldn't like the truth.

"Come on," he said. "We're going up to the aides'

station. Now." He wasn't certain that was the best solution, but for the moment it was the best he could think
of. "We'll come back and have pizza when the rest of
the crowd's ready." He hoped that would take some of
the onus off his giving her an order.

"Well…" She looked nervous, concerned. Which
made Owen all the more certain about their leaving.

He grabbed her arm firmly, but not strongly enough
to hurt her. "Let's go."

*She had forced herself to stay hidden as she watched
Boyd's car drive off.*

*She saw then that the front door of the meeting house
was closed, but she nevertheless heard Owen talking
with someone else. There were no other cars up here
except for the rentals that belonged to the group. Who
was there?*

She needed to go inside. Now.

*Slowly, stalking along the ground, she drew nearer.
Below the strong odor of the ipecac wafted the softer
scent of another human beside Owen. That scent soon
joined with another. Identifiable. Human.*

She knew then who was inside.

She wasn't certain but believed she knew why.

And just in case, she had to find a way to help Owen.

Owen didn't want to drag Yvanne or do anything
physical beyond what he had already done to garner
her cooperation. He wasn't acting as a police officer in
charge here, and even if he'd had his weapon, this wasn't
the kind of circumstance in which he would use it.

He was glad, then, that although Yvanne resisted his

initial touch, she shrugged off his hand and started moving slowly toward the kitchen door and into the hallway.

And stopped.

"Oh, there you are, Holly." Yvanne sounded relieved.

Holly Alverton stood there, and despite her small stature she blocked the way Owen had intended to go. A disproportionately large purse was slung over her shoulder. What was she doing there?

What were both women doing here?

"I know this is supposed to be a surprise," Yvanne continued, "and I didn't say anything, but I think maybe you need to let Owen in on it."

"What kind of surprise?" He kept his tone cool even though he wanted to demand an answer. Was this some kind of game? A joke?

This was not the time for either. And the women should not have been here.

"A celebration." Holly aimed her large blue eyes down at the floor. "We know today's just practice for something that will be real tomorrow. Yvanne and I love our shifters and we wanted to do something both to thank them and to wish them luck. We just figured having a pizza party here when they got back would show them that. I ordered the pizzas for Craig. It won't be a long party, though, since we know they'll need their rest." She looked around Owen and into the kitchen. "I see Lupe there, but is everyone else up on the mountain?"

That seemed too nosy a question. She didn't need to know where any of the CAs or Alpha Force members were. He'd already mentioned to Yvanne that the aides were up on the mountain and she could probably guess where the others were, too. But Owen didn't choose to answer Holly.

"I appreciate the thought," he lied, "but since you know things might get a bit more intense tomorrow, you should understand that we really need some privacy here to finish our plans."

"We can't party, then?" Holly looked up at him, a mournful expression on her pretty young face. But Owen had no desire to placate her.

"Sorry, no. In fact, it's time for you to go." Then, to ease things just a little to encourage them to leave, he said, "If all goes well in our actual job, we'll all celebrate afterward, including you." Maybe.

"Well...okay. I want to take the pizza with us, though. Okay with you, Yvanne?" Holly looked toward the other woman, her expression still hurt.

"I guess."

Holly maneuvered around Owen into the kitchen, Yvanne following. Lupe came up to them, too.

Holly patted the dog, then moved sideways, not toward the table.

In moments, Owen saw that she had taken a hypodermic needle from her purse and, with no fanfare, stuck it into Yvanne.

"Hey," the other woman said, looking confused.

"What the—" Owen began, then stopped.

He found himself looking down the barrel of what appeared to be a Smith & Wesson pistol similar to one of the kinds available to RCMP officers.

Holly no longer looked sorrowful. Determination and glee now framed her face as she raised the gun to his head.

Chapter 24

*S*he heard.

From the back of the house, Selena had been able to listen to some of the conversation that must have been occurring in the hallway.

Holly and Yvanne had planned something that did not sound right, some kind of party.

She heard much more when they all reassembled in the kitchen, and it made her fur stand on end.

"What the hell did you do to her?" Owen demanded. "What was in that needle?"

"Something temporary until I decide on the best way to kill her—more drugs or a gunshot wound like you'll die from soon. I know exactly how to use this gun." That was Holly's voice. Had she drugged Yvanne? "I have to figure out how to make it look like you took one another out."

"Why? What's this all about?"

Owen's voice sounded furious. If only she was in human form and could enter the house at will. But shifting back would take time she didn't want to expend.

More important, her being shifted like this was better. Holly might not expect it.

Yet she might, with so many shifters around.

And she apparently had a gun.

If only Selena could tell Owen she was here. Could have him arrange for Lupe and her to change places.

"This is about your interference in my life. Our lives. You and your damned CAs." Holly spit her words out loudly enough that Selena needn't have been in wolfen form to hear them.

But she was. She also had her human mind. Now she needed to employ both. Quickly. To save Owen as well as the mission of Alpha Force and the CAs.

Staying low to the ground, she growled softly, loud enough for Lupe to hear, but not a human.

Lupe responded right away, giving one short bark. It did not, fortunately, sound like a bark of alarm that would tell Holly of anyone else's presence—human or wolf. Or so Selena hoped.

"I haven't had her out since I've been back here," Owen said. Did he suspect Selena was there? Or was he just looking for an excuse to get to the door?

"Fine. I'll let her outside."

"She needs to be leashed."

"She'll survive—or not." Clearly, the nonshifting woman was a bitch of a different kind.

There was shuffling inside. Selena guessed from the noise that Holly was making Owen accompany Lupe and her to the door. She slunk around the side of the house toward the front.

In moments the back door opened and Lupe ran out. Fortunately, the door closed again before her cover dog reached her side.

Two canines together. Selena was pleased. She wished she could confine Lupe where she would be safe. Alternatively, she wished that she could communicate with her and order her to the clearing where the aides waited. Just her presence there would alert them to the trouble.

But commanding her cover dog to go there was not possible, not while she was shifted.

She needed time. And help.

One thing she knew she could accomplish in wolfen form was to run. Fast. And so, making sure Lupe followed, she began dashing as rapidly as she could toward the clearing where the aides waited—two silvery fleet and cunning canines with a mission.

Would Owen be alive when she returned?

The question made her rev up her speed even more.

"So what are you going to do now?" Owen asked.

"Stop talking," Holly demanded. "Now."

Owen had attempted to appear scared and obedient in the face of a weapon. He currently sat on a chair in the kitchen. Yvanne lay on the floor near him, and Holly stood against the wall, facing both of them, her gun pointed straight at Owen's chest.

If he was honest with himself, he would accept that he was, in fact, a bit scared of this deranged woman. But his determination to do his job, and ensure everyone else was able to do theirs, outweighed any fear within him.

He would succeed…or die trying.

He had hoped that by letting Lupe out, he would buy some time, and maybe the dog would dash off to find her Alpha Force trainers and get help.

But Lupe was just a dog, not a shifted human. Not really Selena, despite being her cover dog.

He wished he could at least have one more conversation with Selena. See her again one more time.

Kiss her again.

But that was the least likely scenario of all.

He just hoped she was off assisting his CAs so that, no matter what happened to him now, they would follow their orders, save the hostage and help to bring down the kidnappers.

The kidnappers.

Was this disturbed woman affiliated with them? His mind raced for a connection.

Either way, she'd indicated she was working on a plan to kill Yvanne and him. Would she start shooting the instant she zeroed in on what to do?

One way or another, *he* had a plan. He would disarm her, perhaps emotionally at first. But definitely physically. Somehow.

He took his time about saying anything, then began another attempt at distraction. "That guy Boyd," he said. "When I first saw him here with the pizza boxes, I wondered what he was really up to. You and he seemed to have something going on before, and—"

"I was just using him," Holly spat. "I wanted someone else in town to look interested in all of us visitors, mostly you CAs and the people from the States you were working with. I flirted with him partly to make Craig jealous, but also so the rest of you wouldn't think too much about Craig and me."

"That worked," Owen said, then changed the subject to something of more concern. "I'd still like to know what you drugged Yvanne with. I assume you didn't use ipecac on her or she'd be awake and throwing up. You were the one to taint the elixir with ipecac yesterday, weren't you?"

"Of course." She looked proud about it, if for only an instant. "I intended to do more today, even brought some more ipecac along." She gestured toward her purse, which she had put down on the floor. "But the stuff that's already here should be enough to deal with what's planned for tomorrow. I'll add more ipecac in a few minutes." She waved the gun at him menacingly. "And you won't be in condition to do anything about it."

He didn't dare focus on how deranged she seemed to be. He needed to focus on distracting her, no matter what her mental condition was. "We're having fresh, untainted elixir shipped here, but I guess you didn't know that. Patrick requested it. Did you know he's supposed to return any minute after picking the new shipment up? That's what they'll use tomorrow, and once they're here and on guard, you're the one who'll not be able to do anything about it."

It was actually an hour or more before Owen expected Patrick and Marshall to return, but he wasn't about to reveal that to Holly.

"Damn." Her blue eyes that had appeared so sweet and innocent before today now looked crazed. She left her post near the wall and began walking toward him. Owen braced himself, preparing to use any kind of offensive action or self-defense move to disarm her, but she didn't get near him. Instead, she approached Yvanne and gave her a light kick.

The other woman didn't move, although she did appear to still be breathing.

"So what did you drug her with?" he repeated again. "Will she survive it?"

"She'd better," the woman spluttered. "She was only supposed to be knocked out for a minute or two, and it's been nearly twenty minutes now, damn her. Okay, I've decided. When she wakes up, she'll shoot you, then be so upset about it that she'll shoot herself in the head. I'll just be walking in and see the end of it." The expression she next leveled on him looked horrified and mournful. The witch was a good actress.

Not to mention a psycho.

He needed to keep her talking, sidetrack her—and, if possible, learn what all this was really about.

"What will Craig think of all that?" he asked.

"He'll be upset. So upset that he'll leave your horrible CAs, or what's left of them, and come home with me so we can get married the way we planned before you and your miserable Mounties interfered."

Now she was facing him again, her gun aimed at his forehead, but she had taken a few steps back once more and was too far away for him to disarm her.

He still needed to keep her talking. "Then you like shapeshifters?"

"I love them. I love Craig, at least. We're going to be married and I'm going to have his children, and they should all be shifters like him. That's why I had to stop this stupid CAs mission and—" She glared at him and ceased talking.

She had to stop the mission? She had made one CA ill with ipecac, but that wouldn't necessarily have prevented the rest of them from proceeding with their assignment.

Owen wondered again if she had something to do with the kidnappers, even indirectly.

Anthony Creay and he had suspected some kind of mole riling the kidnappers even further, driving them to taunt the police and act faster.

Could it have been Holly? If so, how?

He wasn't going to ask her that. Not now, at least.

"You know," he said quietly, "you and I have something in common."

He paused, waiting for her reaction.

"What? Are you mad about what your stupid team is doing, too?" Her tone was scornful.

"No, I believe in the CAs and how they will help our country. But I only realized recently that it was possible for nonshifters to truly care about shapeshifters, and not just be amazed at who they are and what they do."

That seemed to startle Holly, who lowered the gun a bit and stared at him for several long seconds. "You and that Selena? I kind of wondered about the two of you."

"Yes," he said. He knew he wasn't lying now. He'd already admitted to himself that he cared about Selena despite what she was. Or maybe her ability to shift only added to her appeal to him. Could he use this truth to shut this woman down? "I love her. I want to be with her. I think she cares for me, too." He stuck a pleading expression on his face. "She and I need to be together, like Craig and you do. You obviously understand about love with a shifter. If you kill me, what do you think that will do to Selena? Imagine how you'd feel if something really bad happened to Craig."

Oops. He could tell from the change on her face—from confusion and interest to fury—that he'd gone too far. "I do imagine it. I'm sure it'll happen if he stays with your damn CAs. That's why I didn't want him to join at all. I just thought you'd all give up if the kidnappers knew more and told your damned RCMP handlers about it. I didn't think they'd speed things up this way, but—"

"You contacted the kidnappers?" Now Owen was the one to feel fury. He only partially attempted to keep it to himself. "And you thought that would somehow protect your Craig? Did you tell them what the CAs were all about? Are they going to be ready to attack the CAs who come to observe them and bring them down?"

Was that actually a look of contrition on Holly's face? She once more stood with her back against the kitchen wall, but now she seemed to be trembling, from her shoulders to her hands holding the gun. "I…" She swallowed hard and seemed to try to still her hands, but failed. "Did Craig tell you I'm a tech consultant for a cutting-edge Canadian software company?" She didn't wait for his reply before she continued. "I figured out how to send information back, in reverse of how I gathered from news reports that the kidnappers contacted our national police with their demands. I didn't tell them Craig or the others were shapeshifters, honest." As Owen continued to glare at her, she said, "I just hinted that they weren't ordinary people and that, just like I might be using sci-fi-like connections to reach them, the people tracking them down had some offbeat stuff behind them, too. I laughed to confuse them when I hinted even more about the kind of offbeat stuff I was referring to."

Okay. Owen realized he was accomplishing what he'd hoped to at first—distracting this crazy, yet apparently very smart, woman. Maybe even making her feel a little guilty.

But she was still the one who was armed. And now he had even more reason to leave here alive, and fast, to pass this information along to his superiors.

"I—I really do understand why you'd care so much for your Selena," Holly continued softly. "I assume she cares about you, too. I'm really sorry that I have to kill you, but—"

A noise sounded from somewhere in the house.

"No!" Holly screamed, but before she could pull the gun back to aim it at Owen, a silver streak of fur, snarling and barking, leaped into the room and onto her, knocking her over.

"Thanks, Lupe," Owen said, dashing forward to retrieve the gun from Holly's grip.

But then he looked into those brilliant, flashing amber eyes glaring at him as the canine stood on Holly, holding her down.

"Thanks, Selena," he corrected himself with a huge and warm smile.

Chapter 25

It was the day after Selena had used her skills and wiles as a shifter, as well as her strength enhanced by wolfen adrenaline, to help save Owen and bring down Holly.

While Selena had stood guard over the prone, defeated woman, Owen had gotten in touch with his superior with this latest development. Soon, someone even higher up in the RCMP had apparently contacted the nearest police detachment and given them orders, and Selena, changed back into human form, had watched from a back room as Owen had helped them take Holly into custody. Holly now awaited transfer to the national police headquarters in Ottawa, where she would eventually be prosecuted for interfering with an official RCMP operation and more.

And now that critical op the CAs had been training for had begun.

It was midafternoon. Selena waited at the meeting house with the others not directly involved in today's mission. That included Owen; despite his being the officer in charge, he would not be assisting in the field. Alpha Force members Patrick and Marshall were with them, too. And Lupe, as always, remained close to Selena.

Yvanne, recuperating from the mild but potent sedative Holly had injected her with, was also with them. The car she had ridden in with Holly had been parked at the bottom of the hill, and she hadn't yet been ready to drive it, so she had stayed at the headquarters compound. She seemed fascinated, involved and definitely willing to become an aide when the CAs moved forward without the direct assistance of Alpha Force.

Not Holly, of course.

Craig had been astounded—and crushed—to learn the truth about her. When the four shifted CAs had returned from their exercise yesterday and changed back to human form, he had been informed what had happened and the many ways Holly had tried to thwart the mission, including somehow getting in touch with the kidnappers.

"I'd wanted to marry her, too," he'd said sadly, "but I'd no idea she resented it when I agreed to join the CAs. She seemed to like the idea." But clearly the opposite had been true.

Despite what had happened, Craig had pleaded to not only remain a CA, but also participate in their operation the next day, promising that the others could watch his every move and rip out his throat if he did anything wrong. He said he wanted them to feel certain he was one of them and not the traitor Holly had wanted him to be.

His attitude had sounded genuine to Selena and apparently to the others, too, for he was now in the middle of the operation.

The aides who had accompanied the CAs part of the way and assisted them in shifting had again been Jonas and Rainey. Now those who stayed behind were grouped around the dining room table. Patrick sat in front of the laptop computer he had brought and the others huddled around him.

He had been able to log on to the covert website where the images from the cameras attached to the CAs were being transmitted—the same site being observed by the special RCMP team waiting in the field to thwart and capture the kidnappers. They were apparently intending to simply observe that day, acquire the needed information and most likely move in the next day to complete the rescue. They were stationed as nearby as possible, though, so they were prepared to move in at a moment's notice, if necessary.

Everyone was silent in the room now, intently watching what the cameras picked up.

Selena had chosen a seat next to Owen. She was very aware of his presence, his tension from worrying about how things would go down that day, whether the new team he headed would be successful—or even whether they would survive.

If she had been able to, she would have gripped his hand and held on for the comfort of both of them, for she worried, too.

Instead, she took reassurance from their occasional shared glances of mutual support—and a bittersweet sense that, no matter how things went down today, they might never see each other again.

So far, the mission was going according to plan. Whatever Holly may have been able to convey to the kidnappers, they apparently had no concern about wildlife in the targeted area. Aircraft, including drones, had intentionally been kept away—initially at least. But birds, including one very special falcon, flew overhead.

Three wolves sneaked through the forest and up to the mountainside. To shift, they had used the new doses of elixir that had been shipped to Canada and picked up by Patrick and Marshall yesterday. The older bottles still at this enclave would be taken back to Ft. Lukman and analyzed, but would then be dumped rather than used. Maybe something could be learned from them, or maybe not. In any event, no one wanted to take a chance on possibly tainted tonic.

She watched the video transmission. The Mounties suspected there were security cameras near where the shifted wolves now prowled, since satellite views and drone flyovers had failed because of electronic jamming, but fortunately no one came around now to check out—or harm—any roaming wolves. They soon located the openings to several caves, and with their acute senses of smell and hearing they had determined which one to enter.

Although they could not verbally communicate where they were to those who observed them, they knew to turn their heads slowly and allow the cameras around their necks to pan the area, marking the location. The cameras also had GPS tracking attached, so determining where they were was no problem.

Those cameras had begun showing the walls, floor

and ceiling of rock-lined passageways, presumably in mountain tunnels that were not completely dark, implying that someone—the kidnappers?—had installed some kind of lighting. The leader of the wolfen group appeared to be Sal, with Craig in the middle and Tim bringing up the rear.

Selena's head was near Owen's shoulder as she managed to watch the slowly unfolding drama on Patrick's computer.

There! A cavern appeared in front of them, and the sound of human voices was evident. Only one camera appeared to move forward, and in moments a group of people appeared, men in dark sweaters and pants seated on the floor in a circle, talking, and a woman bound and apparently unconscious on the ground against the far wall. She couldn't see her face, but she knew it was Mrs. Brodheureux.

The men appeared angry, nervous, and the talk being recorded suggested panic from being unable to reach their contact after being warned something would occur against them today. The situation appeared critical, the hostage's life in imminent danger.

The camera shots quickly retreated the way the shifters had come, backward at first and then, apparently where the wolves could turn, hurrying forward out of the passageways.

When the wolves were outside and looked up through the trees, the falcon flew overhead, apparently confirming the location.

Twenty minutes later the wolves' cameras showed the arrival on foot of police snipers dressed in protective gear and carrying major weapons. Wherever they'd been deployed from, it couldn't have been far away.

The CAs had succeeded in their part of the operation. The actual rescue and capture had begun.

A week later, Owen returned to the headquarters in Ottawa, where he recapped the successful mission in detail to Deputy Commissioner Anthony Creay. He described where he and the Alpha Force members, other than the aides, had been and how they'd been able to observe what was happening from the shifters' perspective.

When the location had in fact been established and the sniper team rolled in, things became more dicey, but the kidnappers had been subdued—a couple shot, the others surrendering—and, fortunately, the kidnapping victim had been rescued. Mrs. Brodheureux had been rushed to a hospital for examination and treatment and was expected to make a complete recovery.

"Good job," Anthony said, looking over his vast, uncluttered desk. He appeared right at home there, the top button on his standard white shirt undone despite the loose blue necktie overtop and a look of satisfaction on his steely face. "If your CAs weren't so covert a unit, we'd give them a public commendation. As it is, you'll get a private one."

Owen, back on official duty at their headquarters, was also in his usual daily uniform, but his buttons were all buttoned and his tie tight. He relished the praise but felt he had to be honest, both with himself and his commanding officer. "We owe a lot to Alpha Force," he said. "They really helped us get our CAs ready in almost no time, and their special elixir was what made the entire operation possible."

"It makes the entire CA force possible," Anthony

said. "So does a continuing relationship with that special US military unit. Are you prepared to work in conjunction with them?"

Was he? Owen wasn't sure.

That would mean seeing Selena again. Or maybe not. She might not be around when he went to their Ft. Lukman for meetings or additional training.

What he really wanted was to work with her. To be with her. But they worked for important agencies within their respective, though adjoining, countries. They might as well have lived a world apart, not across the border from each other.

Not that that could matter. He was a police officer. He did not allow his emotions to rule him.

He regarded his commanding officer and responded. "Of course I'll work with them," he said.

"That's good, since I've set up a meeting. Let's go into our conference room." Anthony rose and headed for the door to exit his office.

Owen followed, feeling his heartbeat increase. What meeting was this? It didn't matter. It wouldn't bring Selena any closer to him in the long run, even if she happened to be there. Which she wouldn't be.

Oh, they'd hugged each other after receiving word that the operation had been resolved so quickly and so favorably. Once Selena had left the area the next day with her fellow Alpha Force members, they had traded a few friendly text messages. They had even spoken a couple of times on the phone, mostly congratulating themselves and each other and their respective organizations. Their farewells had been soft, and Owen had thought he had heard regret in Selena's tone. Maybe he had been imagining it, hoping that she felt even a fraction of the regret that he did about their being so far apart and possibly never seeing each other again. He had later fought the urge to get on a plane and join Selena on the US East Coast to say hi—and to touch her once more, preferably all over.

But the CAs, including Owen, had remained head-quartered in the enclave in West Columbia after that, and the shifters had immediately taken over the rooms the Alpha Force members had vacated upon their return to Ft. Lukman, Maryland. To locals, word had been spread that these tourists had fallen in love with the area, and fortunately their respective technically oriented careers as advisers to some companies that did business with the government allowed them all to telecommute to perform their jobs. A sham company was even being set up to act as their future employer.

Discussions were under way about getting the CAs cover animals—three wolf-dogs and a falcon. Plus, they required aides. Jonas and Rainey had promised to return to train them. It appeared that Yvanne Emarra would join her brother, Sal, and the rest of the group as possibly a shifter, an aide or maybe both.

As far as Owen knew, he would remain their officer in charge. It would be worthwhile for him to stay in touch with Alpha Force, since his unit would continue to obtain advice and to purchase the shifting elixir from them, and perhaps engage in joint exercises, or even joint missions, if appropriate.

Was that what this pending meeting was about? A new mission?

He felt his mouth roll up into a huge smile as he walked in and saw Selena sitting at the conference table along with the other Alpha Force members who had been in West Columbia with them. "Hi," he said, intending his greeting to include the entire group. The others also said hello, but he heard only Selena's.

Anthony took his place at the head of the oval table. Owen sat beside him across the table from Selena so he could watch her. Was she glad to be here? Why hadn't she let him know she was coming? Maybe talking to him, seeing him again, was the last thing she wanted.

If so, he would deal with it. At least he would have this chance to say a final goodbye.

The meeting was fairly short. Anthony made it clear that the RCMP appreciated all that Alpha Force had done, as well as its offer to continue to work with the CAs.

Then he dropped the bomb that Owen had not anticipated.

"Sergeant Major Dewirter," he said to Owen, "we know you'll be the primary liaison between our CAs and Alpha Force. There's been some discussion about who from Alpha Force will play a similar role, and the decision has been made, pending your approval, that it be Lieutenant Selena Jennay. Is that acceptable to you?"

Owen felt his eyes widen but managed to keep his grin small and, hopefully, professional. "That's fine with me if Lieutenant Jennay is all right with it."

"Fine with me," she said. "But you should know that part of the discussion has been that I'll need to stay in West Columbia at your facilities the majority of the time so I can work with your group, ensure they learn how to work with cover animals and train nonshifting aides, that kind of thing."

Owen strove to keep his expression neutral as he asked, "Is that acceptable to you?" He would have done anything to jump up, run over to her and give her a huge kiss in the hope that it would make her say yes. On the other hand, it might be the kind of thing to repel her, make her say no instead. Maybe it was a good thing this was a professional meeting. He sat still awaiting her response.

"Fine with me," she said. "In fact—" her eyes glinted with humor "—I'm looking forward to it."

The meeting that confirmed some major changes in Selena's life dragged on for a while. Deputy Commissioner Anthony Creay departed soon after she had agreed to move officially to West Columbia. That left Patrick and Owen in charge, as they'd been on the recent training mission.

Selena had forced herself to listen and participate in the conversation in which a lot of logistical concerns were discussed. Everything seemed cordial, and all of them, including the aides in attendance, continued to congratulate each other on how well the actual mission had gone down.

It appeared that all the kidnappers had been apprehended. Mrs. Berte Brodheureux was deemed recuperated after several days in the hospital. Her husband, Rene, the CEO of Xanogistics, had thanked the RCMP profusely and offered a lot of money to its retirement fund, or to charities it supported if that was not appropriate.

Once the meeting finally ended, the group decided to meet for dinner one final time, as they had previously when working together.

As they walked out of the room, Selena held back. So did Owen. Once the others had left, she looked up at him. His blue eyes were gleaming as he smiled down at her. "You're really okay with this?"

"I am," she said with a smile of her own. She looked ahead of them. The other Alpha Force members had stopped and Patrick was looking back at her. "Sorry, gotta run," she told Owen. "But I'll see you later at dinner."

It was much later that night. Dinner at a small steak house near the RCMP offices had been fine but relatively quick, and Selena and her fellow Alpha Forcers were in their hotel rooms near the Ottawa airport. They were grabbing a plane in the morning to go back to Maryland. There, she would pack all her belongings, put what she wouldn't need in Canada into storage, then move the rest to West Columbia.

Rainey would join her for now, although she would return to Ft. Lukman once the CAs had suitable aides in place. She'd been thrilled to be able to work with the Mounties for at least a little longer.

But had Selena made a big mistake? Had she said okay too fast because of her dream of getting to know Owen better? He had seemed happy enough about it, but was he just being polite?

Damn. She really wanted to know—since, even though it might not be wise, she had really fallen for him. They would have to remain professional as they worked together, but could they nevertheless develop a real relationship? Or was that something only she wanted?

Before she took any major steps, she needed to talk with Owen. Sitting at the desk in her room—a private one, fortunately, since she didn't want anyone to hear this conversation—she reached for her cell phone.

But before she could press in his number, it rang—
and it showed that Owen was calling.

"Hi, Selena," he said when she answered. "I'm downstairs. Can I come up—and are you alone? We need
to talk."

"How did you know where I was?" she demanded
first.

"I'm a police officer," he replied. "We have our
ways." She heard the joking of his tone even though
what he said was accurate.

"Yes, you can come up, and yes, I'm alone." And,
fortunately, her room was on a different floor from the
rest of the Alpha Force members, not by design but now
she was glad of it.

She heard a knock on her door only a few minutes
later. She looked out the peephole, then opened the door
to let Owen in.

He shut the door behind him, and in moments she
was in his arms.

His kiss was hot and demanding, his hands holding
her tightly to him—and she recalled even more vividly
their lovemaking as she felt his hardness against her.

But he pulled back nearly at once. His blue eyes regarded her with even more intensity and desire than she
thought he ever had. "Selena, are you okay with this?
Moving to Canada and working directly with me and
the rest of the CAs, I mean."

"I thought you were asking if I was okay with making love with you while we planned to continue working together." Though she tried to sound teasing, her
voice was breathless.

"That, too."

She looked up at him, smiled, then reached to pull his

head down to meet hers again. This kiss was even hotter than the last, and she immediately started undressing him, even as he touched her breasts, then lower.

"We'll need to be discreet," she whispered against his mouth. "And remain professional. And not let anyone... Oh—"

He was touching her intimately now, removing her clothes, and she swayed against him.

"And you should remember," she continued unevenly, "I'm different from most women. I'll be shifting some to help your CAs. And—"

"Shut up," he said softly, still smiling as he finished removing her clothes. And as he pulled down the cover and they both climbed onto the bed he said, "I've come to think of shapeshifters as damned special, one in particular. And I want to get to know her a lot better." He paused, his eyes fixed directly on hers. "I love you, Selena."

She drew in her breath. All her concerns about how Owen really felt about her and who and what she was evaporated in that instant.

Her smile broadened even more. "I love you, too, Owen. And I think I'm going to really enjoy living in Canada."

* * * * *

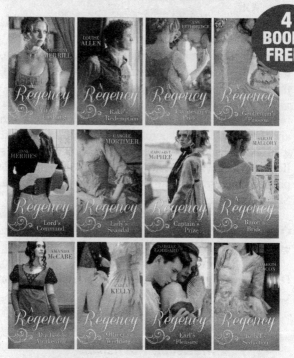

315_ST17

MILLS & BOON®

Want to get more from Mills & Boon?

Here's what's available to you if you join the exclusive **Mills & Boon eBook Club** today:

✦ *Convenience – choose your books each month*
✦ *Exclusive – receive your books a month before anywhere else*
✦ *Flexibility – change your subscription at any time*
✦ *Variety – gain access to eBook-only series*
✦ *Value – subscriptions from just £3.99 a month*

So visit **www.millsandboon.co.uk/esubs** today to be a part of this exclusive eBook Club!